Warwickshire County Council

NOL 3|17
3 APR 2019
6 NOV 2021
4
5 NOV 2022

This item is to be returned or renewed before the latest date above. It may be borrowed for a further period if not in demand. **To renew your books:**

- **Phone the 24/7 Renewal Line 01926 499273 or**
- **Visit www.warwickshire.gov.uk/libraries**

Discover ● Imagine● Learn ● *with libraries*

Warwickshire County Council

Working for Warwickshire

Author Note

Whilst I am interested in most periods of British history, I find the overlapping of the early Celtic, Viking and Anglo-Saxon eras particularly fascinating. It is not the violence, battles and bloodshed that intrigue me most, but the position of women in those societies. They were obliged to balance their own desires and needs against those of husbands, fathers, the decrees of society, the King and religion. The constraints must have been enormous, and yet we know there were women who managed to make things work in their favour.

This is why I like to make my heroines women who rise above the difficulties in which they find themselves, become stronger as a result, and find love in the most unlikely circumstances. After all, to most British women there can be few more unlikely circumstances than being caught up in a series of conflicts as world-changing as those between the tenth-century Anglo-Saxons and the Vikings of Denmark.

My story may be a work of fiction, but I believe there must have been situations not unlike this one which did not claim the attention of the chroniclers. I like to think that in this small way I am redressing the balance.

CAPTIVE
OF THE VIKING

Juliet Landon

MILLS
BOON

Published in Great Britain 2017
by Mills & Boon, an imprint of HarperCollins*Publishers*
1 London Bridge Street, London, SE1 9GF

© 2017 Juliet Landon

ISBN: 978-0-263-92573-9

Printed and bound in Spain
by CPI, Barcelona

Juliet Landon has a keen interest in art and history—both of which she used to teach. She particularly enjoys researching the early medieval, Tudor and Regency periods, and the problems encountered by women in a man's world. Born in North Yorkshire, she now lives in a Hampshire village close to her family. Her first books, which were on embroidery and design, were published under her own name of Jan Messent.

Books by Juliet Landon

Mills & Boon Historical Romance

At the Tudor Court

Betrayed, Betrothed and Bedded
Taming the Tempestuous Tudor

Stand-Alone Novels

The Widow's Bargain
The Bought Bride
His Duty, Her Destiny
The Warlord's Mistress
A Scandalous Mistress
Dishonour and Desire
The Rake's Unconventional Mistress
Marrying the Mistress
Slave Princess
Mistress Masquerade
Captive of the Viking

Collaboration with the National Trust

Scandalous Innocent

Visit the Author Profile page
at millsandboon.co.uk for more titles.

Chapter One

The year 993—Jorvik, now known as York

Even at that early hour of the day, a dense pall of smoke lay over the thatched rooftops of Jorvik like a grey blanket filtering upwards into the haze of dawn. The furnace was already roaring from the blacksmith's workshop, from the glassmakers and potters, the bakers and the moneyer, whose task was no less exacting than the swordsmith's. The Lady Fearn and her young maid, Haesel, kept to the path on the outer edge of the city and soon came to the river from where, for safety, the merchants' ships had been moored upriver well away from the main wharves and the warehouses. They rocked gently on the brown water as the ferryman pulled his boat into the bank just as the two women reached it.

'Morning, lady,' he called. 'You not taking the bridge, then?'

The bridge over the River Ouse was close by the wharves, now deserted in readiness for a fleet of Viking longships that had been reported entering the Humber Estuary two days ago. The merchant ships would be an obvious target. Fearn chose not to answer him. 'Can you take us across, Gaut?' she said. 'We're bound for Clementhorpe.'

Last evening, she and Haesel had put the last few stitches into a pile of linen smocks for the invalids at the little nunnery where frail and elderly townsfolk were nursed through their illnesses by twelve devoted Benedictine nuns. As the foster daughter of Earl Thored of Northumbria, Fearn did not intend an imminent Viking raid to prevent her acts of charity.

The nunnery at Clementhorpe was little more than a cluster of thatched huts, animal sheds, a larger infirmary and a church with a shingled roof situated on the very edge of Jorvik. The dense woodland sheltered pigs beyond the plots where two cows and their calves grazed, where an orchard, herb garden and neat rows of vegetables were tended by soft-spoken women in serviceable long kirtles of undyed wool. Their noble birth counted for very little here, all of them being known as 'sister' except Mother Bridget, the founder of the nunnery.

'Welcome, my dears,' she said, taking the bundles from them. 'This is so kind of you. I hope, my lady, the Earl doesn't mind your coming here so often.' Her voice held an Irish lilt that set all her words to music.

Fearn smiled at her concern. Earl Thored had been baptised as a Christian, but found it difficult to shake off the advantages offered by his former paganism, believing that to call on the services of several well-tried-and-tested gods was of great help in times of emergency. The priest had done what he could to explain the meaning of sin, but so far without an unqualified success. 'He doesn't mind at all, Mother,' Fearn said, following the nun into the warm interior of one of the larger houses. A fire glowed in a central hearth and two nuns stood over by one wall, working at a large upright loom taut with white woollen threads, their hands working in unison, lifting, beating, passing the shuttle. 'He has other things on his mind,' she added. 'Messengers are reporting to him day and night since the Danes were sighted.'

'He's sure they're Danes, then? Not Norse?' She indicated cushioned stools and went to a bench from where she poured buttermilk into three earthenware beakers. Handing one to Fearn, she could not help but look directly at Fearn's beautiful features: the thick black curls escaping from the white veil and gold circlet, at the black eyelashes and brows that framed her most unusual feature, her eyes, one of which was a deep mossy green, the other as blue as a bluebell. She would have been uncommonly lovely even without this strangeness, but with it, her beauty was like a magnet that held the gaze of anyone who looked on her.

Mother Bridget had hoped she would come this morning, having spent the night in prayer for her safety. One look at the woman would put her in mortal danger, for the Vikings, Danes *and* Norse, were renowned for their unbridled ferocity towards women. Fearn and Haesel would stand no chance against them.

'Sure to be Danish,' Fearn said after a sip of the cool liquid. 'Swein Forkbeard's men. Coming for another pay-off. He'll not damage Jorvik again when more than half the city is made up of his own people, will he? I doubt they'll be doing much raiding this time, Mother.'

The Reverend Mother put her beaker to one side, only her years of discipline preventing her from showing her fear. She had, after all, lived close to fear for most of her life. 'Fearn,' she said, as emphatically as her musical voice would allow. 'Listen to me.'

'I always do, Mother.'

'Yes, but this is especially important, my dear. Whatever these men are coming for, we women are in some danger and you more than any of us. You must know what I mean. It's taken our little community years to recover after the last time, but I refuse to run away, for then what would happen to those we care for? But if you're right about them coming only for payment to cease their raiding, then I still believe the safest place for you and Haesel would be out there in the woods, hiding until they've gone. Once you show your faces in the Earl's hall, they will want you as well as money. Stay here out of the way, I beg you.'

It was difficult for Fearn not to be moved by Mother Bridget's concern. Such fear for her welfare was rarely shown these days, particularly not by Fearn's husband, Barda, one of her foster father's chosen warriors. A boastful, swaggering bully of a man, he had adopted the new Christian religion only in order to marry her, not for any other reason. Yet Fearn used his name now in the hope of persuading her blessed hostess of a better protection, knowing how he would put up a fight to protect anything that was his. Even his horse. 'I am grateful to you, Mother. Truly I am. But I will not hide like a fugitive when there are so many of the Earl's men to protect me. And Barda. He would not allow them to take me. Whatever else he is capable of, he would prefer not to lose me. Please stop worrying.'

Even as she said his name, all three women's minds turned to what else he was capable of. Violence towards his wife, for one thing. Mother Bridget had seen the weals on Fearn's body when she'd come here for treatment. Love was not something Fearn had ever felt for a man and Barda did not know the meaning of the word.

A reluctant sigh left Mother Bridget's wrinkled lips along with a shake of her head. 'Well,' she said, softly, 'I didn't really expect you to agree, my dear. Is there nothing I could say that might persuade you?'

'I could leave Haesel with you, being so young.'

'Thank you, but, no!' Haesel said, suffering two surprised stares. 'I'm sorry, mistress, but I shall not leave you. The Reverend Mother must know that.'

'Of course I do, child. Lady Fearn knows it, too. Let's just hope her possessive husband is as loyal as you are. Does he know you've come here? Last time, you were in some trouble, I remember.'

Fearn smiled, ruefully. 'The Earl sent him off with two others to find out what they could. They'll be following the river up towards the coast. They may even have returned by now with some news.'

'In which case, love, you had better drink up and head back to the hall. And think again about what I've said. You'll get no better advice.' Especially, she thought, from that obnoxious pair, Fearn's mother-in-law and her foster mother, neither of whom had displayed any motherly traits towards Fearn, whose entry into their lives was a constant source of jealousy. 'I'll come with you as far as the river,' she said, taking their empty beakers.

The River Ouse flowed deep and wide past the end of the nunnery's orchard on its way to the Humber Estuary and the North Sea. Usually so clamorous with men's shouts, dogs barking, the clang of hammers and children's squealing, the river path opposite the workshops seemed eerily quiet as if the city were holding its breath. Haesel had stopped on the track and was facing in the wrong direction, towards the sun, now well risen but hazy, her body rigid with apprehension. 'What is it?' Fearn called. 'You see something?'

'Smell,' Haesel said without turning round. 'Can you smell it?'

Fearn and Mother Bridget lifted their heads to sniff. 'Smoke,' they whispered. 'That's not Jorvik smoke.' Their eyes strained into the distance where lay several small villages along the banks of the river where plumes of white and dark grey smoke rose almost vertically into the sky pierced by sharp spears of flame. 'It's them!' Fearn said. 'Oh, may God have mercy on us. They *are* raiding. They'll be here in no time at all. We must run. Warn Earl Thored. Quick! Run! Mother Bridget....go back! Go!'

The elderly nun balked, fearful not for herself but for the two lovely women who now seemed closer than ever to her worst predictions. 'Fearn, please come back with me...don't go...be one of us...hide in the woods...it's safer...' The two, old and young, clung together, parted and clung again.

'No, Mother. They'll not ravage the city again. Now, go quickly. I'll send a message when they've gone. Hurry!' she called, already running with Haesel towards the ferry. 'May God protect you.'

But Mother Bridget did not run and, as Fearn looked back to see, she was standing on the path with both hands holding her head. The masts of

the boats would soon be seen rounding the bend
of the river—that was certain.

Expecting Gaut to be manning the ferry, as
before, they were horrified to see that he had
deserted it, though fortunately the boat was on
their side of the river. They took an oar each,
fumbling and rattling them in the rowlocks to
bring them into some kind of unison which, in
more normal circumstances, would have made
them double up with helpless laughter. But not
this time, for the current was strong enough to
push the boat further down the bank than the
jetty, making it impossible for them to clamber
out without wading up to their knees in muddy
water. Their walk along the path up to that corner of the city known as Earlsbrough, where the
great Hall of the Earls was situated, was by no
means as dignified as their exit had been one
hour earlier. And to make matters worse, their
arrival through a small opening in the enclosure
was seen and intercepted by her two most critical
relatives, horrified to see the two muddy young
women with wet gowns clinging to their legs.
Catla, her mother-in-law, and Hilda, her foster
mother, wife of Earl Thored.

Having been advised more than once by the
priest that a little subservience in her manner
towards these two would not come amiss, on

occasion, Fearn decided that now was not the time, with a Viking raid imminent. 'Yes…yes, I know,' she said to Catla, 'but never mind the mess. Where is Earl Thored? There are raiders coming up the river and they're not far away. Is he in the hall?'

'If you mean the Danes,' Catla said, icily, 'your foster father has already been informed, so there was no need for you to act the heroine and be the first to tell him so. The situation is well under control.' Her lined face registered a cold dislike of her daughter-in-law.

'He knows?' Fearn said. 'Then Barda has returned?'

'No, he has not, yet. But when he does, he'd better not see you looking like *that*, had he? Now I suggest you go inside and get that maid of yours to earn her keep and tend you, instead of playing silly water games. I have a mind to have her whipped.'

'You'll do no such thing, Catla. She probably saved me from drowning.'

With looks of deep disapproval, Catla and Hilda turned away, but not before making sure that Fearn heard Catla's parting shot. 'Pity,' she muttered.

Fearn had never been under any illusions about the woman's hostility towards her, but this undisguised malice stung, especially when women were expected to support and comfort each other in times of crisis. All the same, she could hardly subdue a leap of guilty relief at the news of Barda's continued absence. The longer he took to do his scouting, the easier she would feel, but she refused to imagine what might be the reason, for that was a dangerous path to tread.

Waiting until the two older women were out of sight, Fearn went directly to the great hall where Earl Thored would give her the latest news. Her skirts still clung to her legs and her bootees squelched on the wooden floor as she approached, though her efforts not to attract attention to herself were rarely successful. For one thing, few women were allowed to take part in any discussion unless they had a role to play and, for another thing, so many of the Earl's men desired her that it was asking too much of them not to be affected by her presence, dripping wet or not.

The great hall was by far the largest hall in Jorvik, even larger than the wooden church of St. Peter nearby. Massive wooden pillars held up the roof beams carved with grotesque faces and interlace patterns, the walls almost entirely covered with colourful embroidered hangings, with

weapons, shields and polished helmets, decora-
tive but functional, too. Earl Thored half-sat on
the edge of a trestle table surrounded by some
of his personal *thegns*, men of property, influence and loyalty, well dressed and well-armed.
Their deep voices overlapped, but Thored's was
the one they listened to, authoritative and compelling. 'I tell you,' he was saying as Fearn approached, 'they'll not raid Jorvik this time. It's
wealth they're after, not our land or property.'

'But, my lord,' one of the men protested,
'they're burning already. Why would they do
that to the villages and not here?'

'To show us what we'll get if we don't pay
them off,' Thored said as if he'd already made
that point. 'Scaring tactics. They'll be looking
for provisions, too. But I shall not bargain with
them like a common merchant on the wharf.
They must come up here if they want payment.
They can carry it down to the ships themselves.
Is Arlen the Moneyer here?'

'Here, my lord,' said Arlen from the back of
the group.

'Good. Start filling sacks with coin, then have
it brought here.'

'How many…how much?'

'In Thor's name, man!' Thored shouted. 'How
do I know? Just prepare for the worst. These dev-

ils won't go away without fleecing us for every last penny—that much I *do* know. Get that young lad of yours to help. He'll have to learn the new way of fighting, though I'm ashamed to see them off in this fashion. I'd rather do it with a sword in my hand, but we don't have their numbers and that son-in-law of mine hasn't yet made up his mind how to deal with the problem.' There were murmurs of agreement and dissatisfaction, too, but no open criticism of King Ethelred's wavering policies, apart from that of his father-in-law. Then Thored caught sight of Fearn standing beside one of the oak pillars. 'Ah, Lady Fearn, you'll be wanting to hear news of your man. I'm as puzzled as you are. It doesn't usually take three men two days to glean some news of the enemy. Well, we don't need them now when we can see for ourselves where they are and what they're doing. He'll be back. Don't worry.'

'Thank you, my lord. I shall stay well out of sight until then,' she said, turning to go.

'No, I want you here. You can add some colour to the discussions, eh? Ye gods, woman! Where have you been?' he bellowed, catching sight of her lower half as the group parted.

'The ferry, my lord. Gaut was not there to row us. My maid and I—' She got no further with her explanation before her voice was drowned by politely sympathetic laughter tinged with a masculine superiority in matters of river craft.

Pushing a fist beneath his moustache to stifle his laughter, Thored's blue eyes creased into the weathered wrinkles of his skin. 'Then you'd better go and change into something more worthy of a noblewoman, my lady. The Danes will not have anything as good to show us, I'll swear. Go by the kitchens and tell them to prepare mead, *beor* and ale for us and our guests. The least we can do is to drink them legless.' Unconsciously, his large hand stole upwards to grasp the solid-silver Thor's-hammer pendant that hung from a leather thong around his neck. 'Now, I need three of you to go down to the wharf and wait, then escort their leaders up here. And where's the harpist? And the scribe? Let's show the ruffians some culture while we're about it.'

Passing the kitchen building, Fearn relayed the Earl's orders, knowing that on her next entry into the hall, an army of servants would have attended to every detail, relying on his word that the Danes would be there to bargain, not to wreck. Inside the confines of her own thatched dwelling, she found that Haesel had anticipated her needs, laying out an indigo-dyed woollen kirtle to be worn over a fine linen shift that showed at the neckline,

wrists and hem. Fearn had worked gold thread
embroidery along all the edges that glittered dis-
creetly as she moved, picking up the deeper solid
gold and amethyst of the circular pin that held the
neckline together. Her circlet of patterned gold
and garnets was one of several she owned, but
when she asked Haesel to pass her jewel casket,
she discovered that it had been packed, along
with extra clothes and shoes in a lined leather
bag, the kind used for travelling. 'What's this
about?' she asked her maid.

Haesel sat down on the fur-covered bed and
looked pensively at her mistress, obviously finding it difficult to give a convincing explanation.

'Haesel? Have you been seeing things again?'
Fearn said. 'Tell me.'

'It's not easy to know what I see and what I
think I see, lady. I don't know what it means,
but we were travelling, and there was a strong
wind…blowing…you needed your cloak, but you
were wearing the one you made for your husband. So I packed…well…everything I thought
you'd need…and…'

'Wait a moment! You say I'm wearing Barda's
new cloak? But he's taken it with him.'

'Yes, lady. That's what I don't understand.
Unless he allows you to wear it.'

Fearn looked at her maid in silence. As a mere

sixteen-year-old, she had served Fearn for the last four years when her family's house caught fire. Her father had been a potter on Coppergate, but the kiln had exploded and Haesel had been the only one to survive, albeit with severe burns to one arm and the side of her throat. Her mass of fair curls had now grown back and the sweet prettiness of her features more than compensated for the wrinkled red skin that she usually managed to hide under the white veil swathed around her neck. Fearn had soon discovered that Haesel possessed a strange talent for seeing into the future, though it was often rather difficult to make out how the information related to events, as it did now when Barda's cloak was not in Fearn's possession. By now, however, Fearn had learnt to take the predictions seriously, although they were both enigmatic and quite rare. 'So what have you packed, and where shall we be going?' she said.

'Your jewels, clothes, shoes, your recipe book of cures. I couldn't get your harp in. I know nothing about where we'll be going, lady. Just the wind blowing.'

'Then we shall just have to see what happens. Was my husband there?'

Haesel shook her head. 'No, lady. He was not with you.' It happened occasionally that she

withheld information she thought either too un-
reliable or not in her mistress's best interests to
know in advance. There had been many men
there in her sighting, but Barda had not been
amongst them.

The Dane known as Aric the Ruthless had
hardly expected that the four longships in his
command would be able to slip into Jorvik un-
seen, even so early in the morning with the sun
obscured by clouds of smoke rising up from the
riverside villages. His men had needed to take
provisions on board after rowing against the current all the way from the river estuary, and since
it took too long to ask politely for foodstuffs,
they had taken it without asking. Coming to the
last navigable bend of the Ouse, Aric noticed
that the trading wharves and jetties were devoid
of merchant ships and the stacks of produce that
usually littered the area. The only sign of life
was a small group of armed men waiting, grim-
faced, to meet them. So, the Earl of Northumbria
had come with his elite corps to conduct him,
personally, to the place known as Earlsbrough.

Their greeting was civil, though hardly warm.
One warrior drew his sword from his scabbard,
catching the light on its menacing blade. But as
Aric stepped off the gangplank, he called to him

to put it away. 'We have come here to talk,' he called. 'Which of you is the Earl?'

'The Earl of Northumbria awaits you in his hall,' the leader said. 'He prefers not to trade with you for Jorvik's safety here on the wharf like a merchant. Be pleased to come with us.'

'What, and be surrounded by Englishmen?' Aric said.

'Bring as many men as you wish, Jarl.'

The walk took a little time, though they soon discovered that their Danish words so much resembled the Anglo-Danish spoken in Jorvik that there were very few misunderstandings. Adjusting the beaver-skin cloak on his broad shoulders, Aric walked with his hosts and a group of his own chosen men through the deserted dirty streets of Jorvik to the mournful cry of seagulls and the yapping of dogs chasing an escaped pig. The air was tense with uncertainty, for the rank odour of smoke still clung to the invaders' clothes. None of them were under any illusions that the show of politeness would last, for at the nod of a head or the click of a finger, they could all slaughter one another without a qualm.

Earl Thored stood waiting outside the stout wooden doors of the great hall, unmistakable to Jarl Aric by his imposing figure, tall, broad-shouldered, with a shock of thick white hair echoed in the luxurious drooping moustache, an exceptionally handsome man of some fifty years, and experienced. He greeted Aric with a brief nod, noting the Dane's appreciative look at the fine carvings on the doors and crossed gables. 'Not so different in Denmark, I don't suppose,' he said, leading them into the hall.

'The same in most respects, my Lord Thored. Our requirements are the same as yours.'

'Our requirements, Jarl, are for peace above anything.'

'Then we have that in common,' said Aric, determined not to be wrong-footed by the older statesman. 'I see no reason why we cannot agree on that. Eventually.'

Thored's look held an element of scepticism for the Dane who had just led a series of raiding parties along the East Anglian coast. The 'eventually' was something that would demand hard bargaining, with no guarantee that the Danes would not return for more next year, as soon as the days lengthened. But his look was also laced with an unwilling admiration, not only for this man's youth compared with his own, but for his undeniable good looks, which Thored was sure would have the women enthralled. More used to looking down upon his men, Thored found that their heads were level and that the Dane's keen grey eyes had already swept the hall in one observant stare, as if to assess the wealth contained there.

In the yellowish light from lamps and candles, Aric's hair shone sleek and pale, pulled tightly back from his face and gathered at the back into a short plait. A narrow gold band was set over his forehead, his sun-bleached brows and short neat beard emphasising the square jaw and determined set of his mouth, which Thored took as an indication that he would be no pushover. A chill crept along Thored's arms and neck. Thirty years ago, he, too, had had this man's arrogant stance, legs like tree trunks encased in leather breeches and a slender waist belted low down on slim hips. He, too, had made women blush like girls.

Aric's thoughts on Earl Thored ran along similar lines with admiration for his elegant deep red tunic and the massive gold buckle at his belt, a sign of authority. Negotiations with this old fox, he thought, would have to proceed with care, for although the Danes' demands would have to be met, one way or another, he had heard that Earl Thored was a man with more than one strategy up his sleeve. Other things he had heard about the Earl were less complimentary, things which would have to be addressed today while there was a chance. His king, Swein Forkbeard, had given him the task of taking four of the ninety-four longships up the coast to Jorvik to treat with Earl Thored on his behalf. Swein was also aware of Aric's other mission which, although secondary to the business of Danegeld, was of great importance to his family's honour. Aric himself might have only twenty-seven winters under his belt, but he was one of King Swein's most trusted *jarls*, a military leader of numerous missions across the North Sea. He would make sure his name was remembered as a man who got what he came for.

Tipping his head towards his hovering wife, Thored beckoned her forward to begin her duties, showing the guests to their seats in order of precedence with no more to go on than their clothing and the number and size of gold armbands, pendants and cloak pins. Standing further back down the hall, Fearn held a flagon of red wine, waiting for the signal to begin pouring it. But her attention was instantly kindled as the Danish leader moved into the direct light of a lamp hanging from a low beam, casting its glow over the smooth back of his flaxen hair with its stubby plait resting on the beaver fur of his cloak. Clutching the flagon close to her body, she

strained her eyes to search for the darker streak
on the fur she knew so well, then for the band of
red and green tablet-weaving in a zigzag pattern
that bordered the hem. As he turned in her direction, she saw how the bands continued up the
two front edges, and she knew without a shadow
of doubt that he was wearing the beaver-fur cloak
she had gifted to her husband only weeks ago
on his feast day. Casually, he threw one side of
the cloak over his shoulder to reveal the brown
woollen lining that she had spun from the na-
tive sheep and woven on her loom after weeks of
work. Barda had worn it, to her dismay, to go on
this latest scouting expedition for the Earl only
because the nights could still be cold this early in
the year and because the beaver fur was brown,
easily hidden in the woodland, waterproof and
hard-wearing. Fearn knew that neither Catla nor
Hilda would notice, but the revelation buffeted
her like an icy blast of the north wind, rippling
the surface of the wine in the flagon. Her body
shook and she was unable to tear her eyes away
from the evidence that must surely mean Barda
had been taken or killed, for no man would willingly give his cloak to the enemy.

Yet even as she stared, frozen with shock, the
powerful Dane stared back at her as if she were
the only woman in the hall. The distance was

too great for details; only the compelling force of his dynamism released in her direction from two unpitying eyes seemed instinctively to understand the reason for her wide-eyed expression of outrage that he was daring to wear the garment she had made for another man.

Screams, accusations and frenzied shows of anguish would have been most women's reaction, at that point, forcing some kind of explanation ahead of the Earl's diplomacy. Yet it was not the Dane's arrogant stare that kept Fearn silent, but the certain knowledge that it would not serve Earl Thored's purpose to embarrass either their Danish guests or him, and certainly not to have Barda's mother screaming and wailing and, naturally, Hilda, too, at such a critical moment in the proceedings. She must keep her secret knowledge quiet. She *must*. Against all her impulses to challenge the man, she must wait until the right moment. Or perhaps not at all. Perhaps the knowledge would emerge in some other way, when the Danes had gone.

Aware of a discomfort against her ribs, she realised she was pressing the flagon tightly against herself, almost to the breaking point, and that of all the emotions chasing through her numbed mind just then, incredulity and relief were the only ones she recognised. The Dane was still staring at her while Earl Thored told him who she was. Trembling, Fearn turned away, thankful that it would not be her to pour his mead, but Hilda.

The rest of that momentous discussion passed like a strange dream in which the information she held struggled in her grasp, waiting for the moment of release that did not come as she moved like a shadow through the hall. Usually, she was aware of men's eyes upon her but, this time, she was aware of only one man's, though she tried to evade them. But by the time she was obliged to respond to his request for wine instead of mead, he had shed the cloak to reveal a fine tunic of honey-coloured wool, which she knew would have been dyed with onion skins, its braided edging round the neck and sleeves glistening with gold thread, the delicate circular pin at his neck surely of Irish origin. For the first time, she came close enough for him to see into her eyes when, in spite of herself, she saw how his own narrowed eyes widened fractionally as if responding to a trick of the light. She saw the tiny crease between his brows come and go as he spoke in the mixture of English and Danish everyone in Jorvik understood. 'Lady Fearn,' he said, holding out his drinking horn to her, 'I understand you are the daughter of the previous Earl.'

Earl Thored, seated opposite, interrupted. 'The *exiled* previous Earl.'

Aric continued, ignoring the correction. 'Do you miss him still?'

The rich red liquid wobbled as it poured, though Fearn tried to keep her voice from doing the same. There was hardly a day when she did not think of her parents. 'I miss *all* those who are taken from me suddenly,' she replied, purposely filling the horn up to the brim so that it would spill when he moved it away. Movement and speech were suspended as the drinking horn was held motionless, as two pairs of eyes locked in combat, hers challenging him to an admission of murder, his countering her challenge with his own brand of indifference. By this time, several men had noticed what was happening, laying silent wagers on the outcome. Aric the Ruthless would not be beaten by a woman, especially not by Thored's foster daughter, though Fearn's only aim was for him to tremble and spill the blood-red wine on the table as a sign of his guilt. He would surely understand her message.

Slowly, and without a tremor, the drinking horn was taken smoothly to Aric's lips and tipped, not a drop escaping, its curved point en-

cased in a silver cone pointing upwards. A ripple
of applause accompanied the laughter, but with
a look of contempt, Fearn turned away, sure that
the Earl would have something to say about her
behaviour towards his guest at a serious meeting. But for her, the meeting was an ordeal from
which she was not allowed to excuse herself, even
though she was now sure of the reason for her
husband's disappearance. This she was obliged to
keep to herself for the time being, though Catla
had expressed concern. 'I don't know where he
is,' Fearn told her, truthfully. She, too, would
have liked to know whether he lay dead in the
woodland or tied up in one of the longships.

Distancing herself from Catla and Hilda,
Fearn went over to sit with Arlen the Moneyer
and his wife Kamma. Obeying instructions,
Arlen had filled sacks with coins and some
hack silver—chopped-up disused pieces to be
melted down for newer coinage—helped in the
task by his young son, Kean, a good-looking lad
of some ten years. He smiled as she sat beside
him, clearly honoured by her presence.

'Do you understand what's happening, Kean?'
she whispered.

'Oh, yes, my lady. The Danes are demanding
a great deal of my lord Earl.'

'You think there'll be enough there?' she said, nodding towards the sacks.

'Hope so. Those sacks are heavy.'

The bargaining seemed to go on for ever, going through all the motions of trading peace for wealth, as if in their minds it had not already been settled down to the last silver penny. Roars of outrage, thumping on the tables, accusing fingers and sometimes the quieter voices of compromise and concession rose and fell as, for two or more hours, Thored faced down the enemy and tried to fob them off with less, even as he knew the price of peace was rising. To some extent, it was a performance that only prolonged the moment when agreement, if one could call it that, was reached in time to give the Danes a period of daylight to carry away the heavy sacks of treasure and depart.

Setting her heart against the arrogant Dane and his absurd demand for ten thousand pounds' worth of silver, Fearn had no option but to watch the Danish warriors enter, wearing swords and shining round helmets with nose guards half-hiding their satisfied smiles, pick up the heavy sacks between them and carry them out across to the gates of the enclosure. No words accompanied this disgraceful looting, only a heavy silence, glowering faces and the almost unnoticed gathering of armed Danes around their leader.

The Danish demands appeared to have been met, but Aric's demands were not yet over. Turning, he pointed towards Kean, the young Moneyer's son, beckoning him to his side. Thinking that the Dane had some words of wisdom for him, Kean went to him willingly, not flinching as the man's hand rested on his shoulder. Thored's hand went to his sword hilt while, next to Fearn, Arlen and Kamma leapt to their feet with yelps of protest.

'No!' Thored bellowed. 'Oh, no, not the lad!'

Kamma's hands flew to her mouth to stifle the wail, though it leaked through her fingers. 'Tell me,' said Aric to Kamma, 'how old the lad is.'

She ran towards him, her face contorted with fright. 'He is ten years, my lord. He's too young to be taken as a slave...please...he's our only child.'

'*Your* child, is he?' Aric said. 'Did you *bear* him? You? Yourself?'

Earl Thored knew where this was leading. Angrily, he kicked over the table before him with one mighty shove of his foot, sending drinking horns and beakers flying and bouncing across the floor. He strode over the edge of it towards Kean who now looked anxiously from one adult to another, wondering what this was all about. But as Thored moved towards Aric, the helmeted Danes closed in around their leader and the boy in a semi-circular defence. 'So *this* is why you wanted them here,' Thored growled. 'So that you could insult the parents and steal their child. And is this how you repay my hospitality, Dane? Is this the price of peace, after all?'

'We have bargained for peace, Earl,' Aric said, with an icy calm, 'but this is not a part of that and I believe you know it. Cast your mind back twelve years to that time when several young Danish couples sailed into Jorvik asking to settle here. You had been Earl five years then. Remember?'

Impatiently, Thored shrugged. 'Vaguely,' he said.

'Not so vaguely, I think, my lord Earl. You will recall one of the young couples, newly joined, very comely they were. Especially the woman.'

There was a muffled cry of distress from Hilda to whom this situation was all too familiar. Thored took no notice of her. 'So?' he said. 'What are you implying, Jarl? Let's hear it. You're probably quite mistaken.'

'No, I think not. There are enough Danes here in Jorvik to tell their relatives in Denmark what happens here, especially to young husbands who stand in the way of their Earl's needs.'

'Relatives? Which relatives, exactly?'

'Me. Brother to the young woman who sought a life here with her goldsmith husband of one year. Prey to your lust, Thored.'

Lady Hilda's sobbing could now be heard by everyone in the hall, yet Thored would not glance in her direction. 'Your...*sister*?' he whispered, frowning in disbelief. 'You lie. She never mentioned...'

'She wouldn't, would she? I was a mere lad of fifteen then, not a king's *jarl*. But I was not too young to swear revenge on the man who arranged my brother-in-law's death and then took my sister for himself and fathered a child on her. Yes, this lad here. My nephew. *Your son!*'

Furiously, Kean shook himself free of Aric's hand, whirling round to face him. 'No!' he yelled, pointing at his parents. 'No! There is my mother and there is my father. I have never known any others, I swear it.'

'Well said, lad,' Aric said. 'But the truth is, like it or not, that your mother was my sister Tove and your father is a man as weak as water when it comes to women. I took an oath on Odin's name to return you to your own family and my chance has come, as I knew it would.'

Hilda, with her head on Catla's shoulder, was racked with sobbing and of no help at all to her husband, whose unfaithfulness was nothing new to her. She had borne him no live children and had now stopped trying, though the pain of Thored's easily found comfort was like a wound that was not allowed to heal. He had foisted the five-year-old Fearn on her, not as an act of kindness, but because it suited him for her banished parents to know that he had their child's life in his hands. The appearance of the young Danish woman called Tove in their household had lasted only a year. Fearn remembered Tove as a beautiful young woman whose child had been born a year after her husband's violent death in a street fight and had always understood that both Tove and her child had died, although she could recall no burial rites from that time. Now, it appeared that young Kean was Thored's own son and Tove's.

Kamma, the woman Kean had been calling mother for ten years, fell in a heap at Aric's feet, begging to keep her son. 'Lord…my lord…do not do this. We are innocent of any crime. We have cared for him…loved him…please,' she wailed.

'Yes, lady. I know that, too. Your husband was made a moneyer to the Earl for his compliance.

Not a bad reward for your silence. But the facts are there for all to see. Look at his colouring, for one thing. Can you doubt he is of my family?'

It was hard not to see the similarity, Kean's flaxen hair against the foster parents' darkness, his ice-blue eyes like Thored's. 'His home is here, lord,' said Arlen, catching Thored's nod of permission to speak. 'We have nothing if you take him from us. He is our only son. He will be a moneyer, too.'

Thored found his voice again after the shaming revelation that he had taken the life of the husband who stood in his way. 'Revenge,' he said, loudly. 'A blood feud, no less. You intend to tear up the lad's roots and ruin the lives of these two good people, for what? For your gratification? And will he fill the void your sister made, when she left your family of her own free will? She gave herself to me willingly. I did not force her.'

'You took the life of her husband, Earl,' Aric yelled at him. 'Deny it!'

'I do deny it. Tove's man was killed in a street fight. I took her in and cared for her, and—'

'And made her pregnant and killed her in the process.'

'It happens like that, sometimes. The mother is forfeit. Or the babe.'

'As you well know, Thored,' said Aric, making clear his meaning while the Earl's wife howled in anguish. It had happened like that to her too many times and the losses were still as raw as they had been at the time. 'But this child lived, didn't he?' Aric continued. 'And he was a *son*. The only son you've ever had. A bastard, but a son, nevertheless. My sister's son. My nephew. And my family demands his return in exchange for my sister's life.'

'Your sister had already left Denmark, Jarl,' Thored bellowed. 'And the lad belongs here in England with his foster parents and all that he's known since birth. It makes no sense to uproot him from that. He'll be a fine moneyer, like Arlen here. Accept your losses. You've taken enough from us already this day. Tell your family the lad is happy here. Well cared for. Will be wealthy, too. Tell them that and let their revenge lie with the gods. Let *them* deal with it.'

Within the tight cage of her ribs, Fearn's heart beat like a war drum at the sight of these two men facing each other like bulls stopping just short of physical violence, Thored red-faced, angry and discredited by his own lechery, Aric standing proud and fearless on the moral high ground. She could not see Thored ever yielding to the Dane over this, Kean being to him more valuable than she had understood, though now she saw how Hilda must have suffered as much as she herself did at her husband's constant unfaithfulness. To pagans, this was an accepted part of a husband's behaviour, but not to Christians. Thored wanted it both ways: the lax morals of the old religion with the respectability of the new.

Beside her, the boy's foster father was trembling with emotion, unable to interfere in this terrible dilemma, sick at heart at the threat of losing Kean, the lad he loved like a natural son. For ten years, he and Kamma had kept their secret, having every reason to be grateful to Earl Thored for supplying them with a child they could not produce themselves and for the reward that attended the lucrative position of Moneyer, coin-maker to the King. Fearn felt the man's longing to speak breaking through his reluctance to join in the argument without permission. Finally, he could contain himself no longer. Stepping forward, he spoke the first and most obvious words on his mind with little regard for their implications. 'Better still,' he said, looking from the Dane to Earl Thored and back again, 'take an alternative. Is there not someone of more years you could choose, who would be of more use to you?' Flinching under the Earl's furious glare, Arlen stepped back again, too late to undo the damage.

Aric's approval overlapped Thored's blustering protest. 'He speaks well, your Moneyer,' Aric said. Taking everyone by surprise, he swung round to point a finger, like a spear, at Fearn. 'There! That one! The woman. *Your* foster daughter for *their* foster son. How will that do, Earl? I'd call that a fair enough bargain, eh? I'll take her for one year, then return her to you and take the boy. He'll have another winter under his belt by that time and she might well have something interesting under *her* belt. Now that's what I call an alternative. See, Thored? I've backed down for you.'

The collective gasp of shock was audible to everyone in the hall. Even Thored was taken aback by the insulting audacity of the Dane's suggestion. Fearn was the first to find her tongue, released by the outrageous innuendo. 'Then back down further, Dane,' she shouted, taking a step forward until only the upturned table was between them. 'This business is between you and Earl Thored. Count me out of it and don't play word games with my virtue, for I'll have none of it.'

Facing each other like alley cats, glaring eyes locked together, they made the air between them vibrate with open hostility, causing the company to catch its breath at the ferocity of Fearn's defiance. Any woman would have had the same feelings of shock, but few would dare to say so in such terms, especially to an enemy in the hall of one's guardian. Aric's eyes narrowed in admiration. 'You have no say in the matter, woman. Neither you nor your foster parents are in a position to argue.'

Indeed, the Lady Hilda had stopped moaning and was far from arguing against the Dane's latest demand. But Fearn would not be silenced so easily. 'Wrong, Dane. Both the Earl and myself *are* in a position to argue. I've listened to your pathetic story of your sister, but now *you* should admit to the killing of the Earl's brave warrior, my husband, the man whose cloak you've had the audacity to wear around your shoulders. Here, in the hall of his lord. *You* deny *that*, if you can.'

'What?' Earl Thored roared. 'Barda's cloak? Are you sure, Fearn?'

'It's the one I gave him on his last feast day, my lord. Of course I'm sure.'

Aric stood motionless, neither denying nor admitting the murder, though his eyes did not leave Fearn's face, not even when Earl Thored addressed him directly. 'Well, Dane? Does my foster daughter speak the truth? Where did you find that cloak?'

Speaking to Fearn rather than Thored, Aric replied. 'It was handed to me by my men,' he said. 'Searching the woodland along the river's edge, they found the Earl's three men. There was a skirmish. The wolves will have found them by now.' His last words were drowned by a scream from Catla, who would have flown at Aric if the wall of the table-top had not prevented it. Tempers flared as both men and the four women hurled abuse at the Danish group who stood firm and resolute against the insults, being prevented from drawing their swords by their leader's forbidding hand. Cries of 'Murderers!' mingled with hoots of derision until Thored's thundering voice reminded them that the Danish leader and his men were still guests in his hall, though no one was impressed by that. The Danes still had the advantage and, even now, were in a position to demand more Danegeld.

Catla's howls were immediately taken up by others, mingling cries of 'My son…my own beloved son…' with calls for the wrath of the gods to come down on their cowardly heads and for Barda to be found and buried with honour.

'Cease your howling!' Thored yelled at them. 'What's done is done. Those men died protecting their city. They knew the risks. We are proud of them. But this puts a different light on things, Dane,' he said, turning to Aric. 'You came here on a peace-seeking mission and killed three of my best men. You cannot now claim my son Kean and you certainly cannot take my foster daughter from me, now you have made a widow of her. Besides which, she is already hostage against her parents' good behaviour. It would be best for you to go now and take what you've got.'

Having accepted the possibility that she was already widowed, it still came as a thunderbolt to strike Fearn with the reality of her situation, knowing intuitively that she would never be allowed this short-lived freedom from a husband. She had disliked Barda more with each passing day, his disloyalty to her, his crass insensitivity and his disturbing contempt for the new religion he had flippantly agreed to adopt at Thored's insistence, in order to marry her. Now she was sure that Thored would not allow her to keep her freedom. In spite of a Christian woman's entitlement to choose her own husband, Thored would insist on his choice of another of his personal warriors in order to direct her life, as he had directed the lives of the Dane's sister and her husband, his young son and the couple who had reared him. That revelation had come as a shock to her, although she had suspected for some time that that could have been one of the reasons behind Hilda's deep unhappiness.

Possible escapes from the impending danger whirled through her mind as the leaders' arguments continued, as Thored tried every loophole to get out of his predicament. The escape that appealed to her most had already begun to take shape in her mind while her future was discussed as if she were so much merchandise, all her attempts to assert herself ignored and talked over. Kean was, apparently, far too valuable to lose because he was a boy, Thored's natural son, and useful, whereas Fearn's role was as peace-weaver between two factions, the traditional function she had thought would never apply to her.

'I came for my nephew,' Aric said, yet again. 'My family demands it.'

'And my family demands that he stays here in Jorvik, with his own kin.'

'Then I'll take the woman. Since it was her man we killed, it is her duty to weave peace between us and she can best do that in Denmark.'

'I'll be damned if I will, Dane,' Fearn said, making heads turn in her direction at last. 'You had no need to kill my brave man for he was no threat to you. It is you who have played Earl

Thored false in this and *he* who has done the same to you.'

'Brave man?' Aric scoffed, turning on her with a coldness that made her quail. 'It always surprises me to hear a newly made widow sing the praises of her lost husband when she knows them to be lies. You are no exception, it seems.'

'Say what you mean, Dane, but don't dare malign my man when he's not here to give you the thrashing you deserve. He *was* a brave warrior. Ask any of his brothers.'

'Very touching,' said Aric. 'So perhaps you and his *brothers* should know how my men came across him and his two companions. Not being overly brave, you'll agree.'

Fearn felt the thud of her heart betraying her loyalty. 'What?' she whispered.

'Do you really want to know how they were raping a woman in the woodland where she was hiding? Yes, one of the villagers. An English woman. One of your own.'

'You lie!' Thored roared.

'No, Earl. I do not lie. Your man had thrown his cloak and sword aside. Two men held the woman while he….'

'No…no! My Barda would not…' It was Catla who screamed while Fearn covered her mouth with both hands, feeling the familiar churning of her stomach.

'I speak the truth,' Aric shouted above the din. 'Why would I lie? My men dragged them off her and killed your three *brave men*. Go and find them for yourselves. Give them the honours they deserve, what's left of them, but don't whine to me, woman—' he glared at Fearn '—about what you've lost. What makes a healthy man act like an animal when he does not have the bloodlust upon him, with a wife like you at home?' His voice dropped so that she saw rather than heard his words. 'Perhaps I should find out.'

But Fearn's mind had been fed more information than it could deal with in one day and now she stared at the Dane's pitiless expression over her hands while an icy coldness stole like a frost along her arms.

Chapter Two

The hubbub died down, broken only by Catla's loud lamenting that her son had not only been killed but slandered, too, quite unjustly. He would never...*never* do anything so base. Fearn knew that he would. Earl Thored was bound to say it was a lie. 'The Lady Fearn's destiny is in my hands now,' he insisted, 'and I say that she shall remarry. Sitric...here...come, man...you shall have her.' Eagerly, a young man stepped forward, but was stopped by Fearn's strident protest.

'He shall *not*, my lord. I am newly widowed and I demand a year of mourning. You know full well that I may now choose my own destiny. I shall go to live with the nuns at Clementhorpe. I have decided.'

'Then you can *un*decide, woman. You're coming with me,' Aric said, flatly.

But they had bargained without Catla and

Hilda, her resentful foster mother, who saw a way of paying back all those years of humiliation at Thored's hands and for having to bring up a child whose strange beauty had threatened her own self-confidence for so many years. Catla's wailing seemed to give Hilda courage, for now she found a voice. 'Take her, Dane. Yes, take her away…far away. She does not belong here. Never has.'

Catla joined in before anyone could stop her. 'Take her, for she will ever remind me of the son I have lost this day. She is widowed and of no use to anyone, not even to you, Dane, so if you think to bear sons on her, forget it. She bore no grandson for me and I doubt she'll do any better for you. Those witch's eyes turn men's heads. *Take* her.' She strode over to Fearn and, with a disgusting contortion of her face, spat at her.

Being quite unprepared for this, Fearn had not dodged the spittle that ran down her chin, but now her endurance came to an end in an explosion of blazing anger and, without a thought of anything other than this appalling insult, she aimed an open blow at Catla's tear-stained face with all the force of a young woman's deep unhappiness behind it. The power of it sent a painful shock down her arm, but Catla went down like a skittle, tangling her legs in her voluminous kirtle. Hands reached down to help her. Fearn's only impulse was to escape while so much of the attention was being diverted away from her.

Backing away from the crowd, she caught the brief warning from Arlen's lips that told her to look behind. Swinging round and drawing her knife from its sheath at the same time, she levelled it at Aric's throat, her crouching stance practised over years of child's play that sometimes resulted in unintentional wounds. This time, her expression of steely intent told Aric that he had better take this seriously. Nevertheless, Fearn was not in training, she was emotionally upset, her right arm was still tingling from the stunning blow to Catla's head and her reflexes were nowhere near as sharp as her opponent's, nor her strength as great. All it took was one quick lunge from her to send the shining knife flying through the air and to have her hands caught in both of his so tightly that she gasped with the pain of it. His arms were like two iron bands round her body as he pulled her in with her back against him, but just too late to prevent her from taking a savage bite at his hand, sinking her teeth in to touch the bone at the base of his thumb.

Wrenching away, he grunted with pain, but did not relax his grip. 'A nunnery?' he growled into her veil. 'Whoever gave you that idea? Now, let's see if I can change your mind.'

'My lord... Lord Thored!' Fearn yelled. 'You cannot allow this. *Help* me!'

But it was clear to all who watched the undignified tussle that Earl Thored was not going to intervene, that the hand on Kean's shoulder indicated his choice. He would not set his men to fight the Danes in his own hall over a foster daughter who, he hoped, would be returned to him in one year. Though it grieved him to lose the young woman he was so fond of, it was a chance he had to take. Thrusting his son behind him, he watched dispassionately as his wife and the bruised Catla stumbled from the hall before approaching Fearn, who was still trying to escape from Aric's arm across her waist. 'Lady Fearn!' he barked. 'You must stop this unseemly behaviour and remember who you are. Stand still and listen to me.'

'Unseemly?' she cried. 'Stand still? With this ruffian's hands upon me? My lord, you need to remind *him* who I am, not me.' A heavy pall of dread hung over her as she compared this manhandling to that of Barda when he was drunk on mead, when blows would follow as a matter of course. She had always found it hard to believe that her foster father was entirely unaware

of Barda's violence, yet not once had he intervened in what was, after all, a domestic matter.
Now, he was standing passively by yet again,
telling her to remember who she was, which indeed was the only thing that had supported her
through those terrifying incidents. She was an
earl's daughter and he was telling her to use dignity as her weapon.

Over her head, Aric spoke. 'I do not need reminding, lady,' he said. 'I know who you are
and I know your value, too. I think you may be
worth the effort.' As he spoke the insolent words,
his arms loosened their grip across her body.
Stung by his arrogance, Fearn twisted round like
a coiled spring, her eyes blazing, warning him
of her lightning-fast move. Meant to wreak the
same damage as to Catla, her hand was caught
before it made contact and, along with the other,
was held wide apart by the wrists, helplessly out
of range. With Barda as the victor, she would
have received an immediate blow to her head, so
now her instinct was to flinch with eyes tightly
closed. But her reflex action was wasted, for
although Aric recognised the fear as her eyes
opened, he merely lowered her arms and stepped
back, as if to tell her that he understood about
the husband she had loyally called brave.

Trembling, and very close to tears of anger

and helplessness, Fearn straightened the gold circlet over her brow and pulled the veil back into place, rubbing her wrists against the pressure of his hands, giving herself time to blink away the first signs of weakness. Her voice was hoarse with suppressed emotion as she looked bravely into Aric's eyes of cold steel. 'I am worth more effort than you will ever be able to find, Dane. I see now that my foster father means to sacrifice me to your whim, for that is all it is. A whim. You came here for your nephew and you take me instead. A poor bargain, in my opinion. You could mould young Kean to your ways, but you will never do the same with me. You will regret your choice and you will be glad to bring me back here in a year, if not sooner. I'll make sure of that.'

His eyes smiled back at her as he accepted the challenge, though his mouth retained its uncompromising grimness. 'We'll see,' he said. 'I don't have time to argue the point.'

'Lady Fearn,' said Earl Thored, lowering his voice. 'I hope you will find it in your heart not to hold this against me. As you see, the choice is not easy.'

'Forgive you, you mean?' Fearn said. 'No, my lord, I shall not. Nor shall I ever forgive you for banishing my parents and keeping me here, for you seem intent on parting me from everything I know. A pity it is that our beloved Archbishop Oswold died last year and that so far you have not bothered to appoint another in his place, or I might have sought better advice on forgiveness than our lily-livered priest can offer these days. But when I return, I shall not enter this hall again, but go to those who appreciate my worth, and I shall claim my late husband's estate and use it for their good.'

By the time she had finished this rebuke, Earl Thored's eyes were lowered to the floor, his head gently shaking from side to side as if there were things he might have said to account for his seemingly weak decisions. 'Is there anything…?' he began.

Purposely misunderstanding him, Fearn cut him off. 'Yes,' she said. 'I shall need my maid, Haesel. That's all I ask. Could someone go for her?'

'I'll go,' said Kamma. 'I know where she'll be.'

'And a horse for the lady to ride down to the river,' Aric said. 'I'll not have her walk all that way like a slave.' As one of the Earl's men left the hall to attend to the request, Aric took the cloak of beaver fur from one of his men and held it for Fearn to wear.

She put up a hand, frowning in disgust. 'No,

I'll not have it near me with the stink of blood upon it. Take it. Burn it.'

'Lady,' said Aric, reasonably, 'if it had the stink of blood on it, I would not have worn it either. But it was not near him. It stinks only of a Danish *jarl* who would protect you from the winds of the northern sea. Wear it. It would be a pity to die of cold before we reach home.' He held it out again at shoulder height. 'Turn round. Come on.'

As she obeyed him, she saw Haesel enter the hall with Kamma and remembered what the maid had foreseen, earlier that day. Cold, strong winds. And she, Fearn, wearing the cloak she had made for her husband, feeling the warm comfort of the wool lining, the weight of the pelt and two large hands beneath her chin, turning her, pinning his Irish ring pin to hold it in place. She caught the recognition in Haesel's eyes of their mutual conspiracy and saw that she carried the leather bag packed ready for the journey that neither of them had planned. Haesel wore her plain cloak of thick felted wool of the kind that the English exported to those who could afford them. In Kamma's arms was another bag containing Fearn's harp. 'You cannot go without this, lady,' she whispered, handing it to her.

At any other time, Fearn would have knelt to

ask Earl Thored's blessing on her travels and for a token in the form of a ring or an armband. But now, when he beckoned her to come before him, she refused. 'No,' she said. 'I do not want your blessing. You have betrayed me.'

Aric appeared to condone her intransigence with a nod and a slow blink. Blessings were irrelevant and he had got what he came for. Well, almost, for young Kean still remained, standing beside Arlen. 'Be ready for me in one year, young man,' he said. 'Do you have a message for your Danish family?'

Arlen nudged the boy's shoulder and Kean's reedy voice piped up. 'Give them my respects, lord. And please take care of the lady. She has ever been kind to me and courteous.'

'Then you have seen a better side of her than I, Kean, but I will do my best. Who knows what a year will do?' The tip of his head towards his men was all the signal they needed to stay close as they walked to the large doorway, passing Earl Thored with no more than a nod to remind him that he would not have seen the last of them. Fearn treated herself to one last look round the great hall lined with hangings on which she had worked, glowing colours she had helped to dye, threads of gold she had helped to make and couch down with fine stitches of silk bought from the merchants. Aric motioned her to walk before him into the bright light of the late afternoon where horses awaited them, provided with pillion pads for her and Haesel. She would not be allowed to ride on her own.

Kamma, torn between relief that Kean would be hers for at least another year and guilt that, as a result, the Lady Fearn had lost what little freedom had been hers, accompanied the women outside. Recognising Haesel's bewilderment, she whispered words of comfort to her, reminding her to look out for her lady's welfare, above all else. She would have spoken similar words to Fearn, too, but such was the lady's calm dignity that she felt words might have been unnecessary, though she could not have guessed that the show of self-possession was taking every ounce of Fearn's concentration.

Without appearing to look, Fearn saw him giving orders to his men, well in control of the volatile situation in which at any moment they might be ambushed and slaughtered, his longships set on fire. He had emerged from this debacle, Fearn thought, if not with honour then at least with success and certainly without the disgrace brought down upon Thored's head. He was taking away with him the Danegeld he'd come for and her, too, to show the mighty Earl of Northumbria how his strength should not be underestimated. She was now sure that, despite his insults, his only motive for taking her was revenge, for it was not in her gift to appease his relatives, but Kean's, Thored's son. Her fears now concerned the Dane's intentions towards her, for pillaging Vikings were not best known for their honourable treatment of captive women and she need not expect any special concessions for being an earl's daughter. She had not been mollified by his concern for her warmth in an open longship: he needed her alive, not dead. As for riding instead of walking, any attack before they reached the boats would be easier to repulse from a horse.

Her ribs still ached from the steely strength of his arms as he'd countered her struggles with ease. He had been fearless in his dealings with Thored, too. But as a pagan, would he treat her as Barda had done, with little respect for her person, her wishes, or her beliefs? Had she, in the space of one day, been released from one man's tyranny only to fall into another man's? The questions found no reassuring answer as she watched him accept his helmet from one of his men, a terrifying iron construction similar to those the Earl's men wore, fitting low over the face with spaces for the eyes and a long guard over the nose. On top of Aric's helmet stood a huge rampant silver boar, the age-old symbol of man's courage and virility. His eyes appeared to challenge her through the shaped openings, taking on the aspect of a warlord demanding obedience. The hair on her scalp prickled as she lifted her chin in defiance with a show of confidence she was very far from feeling.

He came towards her and took hold of the fur-lined sheath at her belt, slipping her knife into it and adjusting its leather-bound hilt. She felt the warmth of his knuckles through the woollen kirtle. 'Don't ever draw it on me or my men again,' he warned, 'or you'll be eating your meals without it.'

'You have given your word,' she said, 'to return me to Jorvik after one year. Go back on your word, Dane, and I shall do whatever I can to kill you.'

He stepped even closer so that she could see in detail the gold embroidery on the band round the neck of his tunic. 'I have said I will come back here to reclaim my nephew. If I tire of you before then, I shall send you back sooner, on your own, without my protection. Yes, woman, I can do that. The subject is now closed. I have more important matters to think of.'

His words washed over her like a cold deluge,

giving her nothing to cling to and everything to beware of. Had it not been for the unexpected appearance of Mother Bridget standing just beyond the Danish warriors, she might have lost her self-control in a flood of tears. The two of them fell into an embrace that muffled their cries and stilled each other's trembling. 'I have never left Jorvik before,' Fearn said into the nun's homely gown. 'Is it a long way to Denmark? I do not know any of these people, Mother.'

'Yes, you do,' Mother Bridget said, holding Fearn by the shoulders. 'Jorvik is full of them. They're not so different from us. This will be an adventure, my dear. We shall pray for you night and day. Make yourself useful to whoever you live with. You have many skills, remember. Now, come along, the Dane awaits you.' With a tender kiss to both cheeks, the gentle nun gave Fearn a smile and a push towards the horse and rider. Fearn knew what she must do. Hitching up her skirt, she grasped Aric's wrist and placed her foot on top of his as it rested in the stirrup, felt his strong pull and was hoisted up on to the pillion pad behind him, landing with a thump on the horse's back. Aric spoke to her over his shoulder. 'Put your arm round my waist,' he commanded.

Though it was the last thing she wanted to

do, she obeyed, knowing that she was in danger of falling off without him to hold on to. But now she was close against his broad back, feeling his warmth, breathing in his male scent, moving as he moved and clinging to him as she had never wanted to cling to any man, particularly not this one. She grasped his silver belt buckle, her other hand clasping the harp in its bag, making it impossible to wave to the two kindly women whose concerns meant so much to her. Taking a last look at the great hall as they passed through the gates, she saw that Earl Thored had appeared just inside the doorway, his face crumpled as if to avoid the low glare of the sun. Except that the sun was setting the sky aflame behind them like a portent of more burning villages in the future.

Several times on the ride through Jorvik's empty streets, Fearn looked behind her towards Haesel, but could see only one arm of her holding the rider's waist. She recalled Haesel's foretelling and now knew it to mean that there was no way of escaping her destiny, even if they had known it would be decided by Danish Vikings.

There were, however, some details Haesel had not been shown—for instance, the sheer size and scale of the four Viking longships tied up against the wharf at Jorvik. Neither she nor

Fearn had seen anything like them, the merchants' vessels being about half their length and ugly by comparison. These long, sleek craft were like predatory sea monsters with fierce dragons' heads carved on prow and stern, and with more men on one ship than they had ever thought possible. No wonder, Fearn thought, that the Earl did not want to engage the Danes in battle when his own trained warriors would be so outnumbered.

A small crowd of Jorvik men, many of them of Danish ancestry, had gathered to watch the ships being loaded with sacks of silver, to see how quickly the men took their oars and settled into their respective positions once the mighty oars were in place. Some of the crowd were brave enough to shout their disapproval of Fearn's presence there, but Aric made sure she was given no chance to exchange words with them by lifting her down off the horse, making his ownership quite obvious by keeping her close to him and demanding the promise of good behaviour he had not yet been given. 'It's up to you, lady,' he said. 'Either I have your word, or I have you trussed up like a chicken. It's not a comfortable way to travel.'

'If you mean, shall I throw myself overboard or try to seduce your men, you have my word I shall do neither. But don't expect me to look as if I'm enjoying this, Dane,' she said, haughtily. 'I have no liking for your company.'

'It was not for your company I've taken you from the Earl,' he replied. 'Your likes and dislikes don't concern me. Come. This one is my ship. Walk on up the plank. We need to get moving.'

Looking back on this, as she did many times, it was more like a dream than reality to step down into the wide belly of this monster and to feel the instant rocking motion as men moved about, many of whom would take over the oars as the first rowers tired. The deck thudded and vibrated beneath their feet as she and Haesel were hustled past them to a slightly raised platform in the vee-shaped prow where they would be out of the way. A kind of shelter had been erected for them from a heavy double-thickness wool smeared with tar and foul-smelling fat to resist the water, stretched across the space. Open at the front, this gave them a view of the rowers' backs, though the men were denied the luxury afforded to the two passengers of a pile of furs to sit on. So far, they could not grumble about the comfort, but the strong winds of Haesel's vision were not very far from their minds as they sat cross-legged and subdued, aware of the utter helpless-

ness of their predicament. Fearn placed her arms
around her maid, who was visibly shaking and
close to tears. It was a new experience for her,
too, as were the stares of men who had not seen
their wives for two years. 'Where are they taking us?' she whispered, clinging like a limpet.

'To Denmark, eventually,' said Fearn, 'but
first they'll have to row down the river to reach
the sea. Don't ask me how far, how long. I have
no idea. They'll want to keep us alive, though,
or we're no use to them.'

'What use?' whispered Haesel.

Fearn merely sighed. They wriggled into the
furs and watched the wharf move away, taking
the crowd of Jorvik men off into the distance
along with the thatched rooftops, the outline of
St. Peter's church and the few territorial dogs
that yapped at the longships with dipping oars
like the legs of a centipede. They felt the powerful rhythmic lurch as the oarsmen pulled in
unison and heard through the oak timbers the
rush of water. They noticed the change of smell
as they moved through the smoky fug of the city,
then the appearance of alder and willow along
the banks, the affronted squawk of ducks protecting their new downy progeny.

The oar master shouted a command and immediately the oars were suspended over the

water as the acrid smell of smouldering thatch and mud walls reached their nostrils, just before the devastation came into view. A blackened ruined village sent clouds of grey ash into the evening sky, slowly passing them by, peopled only by a few miserable owners who rooted about for possessions or burnt remains of food. In a moment, Fearn was at the side of the ship leaning out to see if there was anyone she recognised, shading her eyes against the glare of the water, but unable to offer them the slightest comfort.

'Sit down!' The unmistakable sound of Aric's deep voice was not to be argued with.

She turned to him, her face reflecting her anguish. 'I know those people,' she said. 'You've destroyed their houses and taken their food. How will they live?'

'That's their problem,' he said, callously. 'My problem was to feed my men. I solved it. So will they—one way or another. Now sit down. We shall be stopping as soon as the light goes, then we'll eat and move on again at dawn.'

She would like to have told him to keep his food, stolen property, but realised that she had not eaten since morning. Much as she rebelled at the thought of eating the villagers' food, she hoped they would forgive her for it, for Haesel's sight had not suggested that they, too, were in

danger of starving. She also knew that there was
some truth in Aric's uncaring words that, one
way or another, they would find something to
eat from the hedgerows or in Jorvik itself, where
kindly people would help them to rebuild.

Watching him walk through his men to the
other end of the ship, she could not help another
comparison of the Jarl to the wretch who had
been her husband, who had shamefully betrayed
her foster father's trust by abusing a woman who
was fleeing from the very danger he was meant
to be assessing. By association, she felt tainted
by his baseness. People would point to her as the
wife of a rapist who, to all women, was the lowest
of the low. Perhaps it was as well, she thought,
that she would be out of sight for a year, especially of the Lady Hilda and Catla who would
never believe the worst of her son. But what
would that year be like in the company of this
man who appeared to get whatever he wanted?

The same question, by coincidence, was oc-
cupying the mind of the man himself as he
joined his two most trusted companions. Oskar,
a year older than Aric and as experienced in
warfare, was from Lindholm where his young
wife and infant son waited for his return. As
he smiled at the wound on Aric's thumb, his

comment was typically unsympathetic. 'Fought
you, did she? Lovely set of tooth-marks, though.
Quite a trophy.'

Aric looked at it, huffing with annoyance that
he was the only man to have been injured and
then by a woman. 'Still bleeding like a stuck
pig,' he muttered. 'I must have lost my wits,
Oskar. I was supposed to have brought the lad
away. I can imagine what they'll have to say
when I get home with that one in tow.'

Oskar's grin widened. 'Probably send you
back to get him. Come over here. I'll bind it up
for you before we stop for the night. We don't
want your blood on the bread.' No ship ever set
off on this kind of expedition without being prepared for wounds of some sort, so now linen
strips were torn and wrapped round the honey-
smeared wound over which had been laid a pad
of moss, while Aric was treated to the banter
of Oskar and the other companion, Hrolf, who
was curious to know what he proposed to do
with the captive woman and her maid. 'We could
have used the lad,' he said, reasonably, 'and you
know how some of the men feel about having
women on board.'

'I don't know what I'm going to do with them
yet,' Aric said, irritably, 'but I don't need your
suggestions, either. We have to join forces with

Swein in Lundenburh before we set off for home, so we'll see what he has to say.'

'And if he forbids it, we throw them overboard, yes?' said Hrolf.

'Fool,' said Aric. 'Let's concentrate on finding somewhere to stop.'

Oskar winked at Hrolf. 'So where will the next bite-marks appear, I wonder?'

In other circumstances, Aric would have welcomed the suggestions of his companions about how they might deal with a problem. But not this time. He had acted on some powerful impulse when he had adopted the Moneyer's proposition of an alternative to taking his nephew. The woman had filled his mind since his first sight of her that day, not only for her stunning beauty but her courage, too, for she had suspected her husband's death well before it had been spoken of. It had taken some guts for her to challenge him so cleverly while filling his drinking horn, hoping he would spill it like a pool of blood on the table, then to keep the knowledge to herself until the right moment. Without a doubt she was certainly a cut above the other two whose shrieking had filled the hall, but from whose line did she derive her strange eye colour? And how much of her fierceness was the by-product of being abandoned by her parents and brought up by women who wanted none of her? She had naturally expected the Earl to put up a fight to keep her with him and so had he, but Thored had seen greater value in the boy, caring little for her distress. He, Aric, had acknowledged Kean's plea to look after her, but in truth he did not know how he would do this when revenge was his motivation for the life of the sister he had lost to the Earl. And as chance would have it, it was the Lady Fearn's husband who had been killed that day, albeit in quite different circumstances. So now he would keep her in thrall to him for the year of her mourning. A just revenge for the death of his sister.

Now, he himself must strive not to be spellbound by her looks, as he was in danger of being, unless he armed himself against her. Still, she would not be in a hurry to let a man near her after her experience of marriage, for it was obvious that she had been in fear of the man she had lost. The recent memory of holding her close to him, struggling and screaming, was both sweet and bitter, for if he thought to damage her by this thraldom, he must recognise that she was already suffering from the Earl's handling of her life, so far.

On a wide stretch of the river, the four longships were anchored and lashed together side by

side so that the men could come and go across
them, share the food and ale, and keep a look-
out for danger. The marshland on both sides
made this unlikely. The morning raids on the
villages had provided them with a plentiful supply of bread and sides of cured bacon, cheeses,
eggs eaten raw, honey and apples, oatcakes and
a churn half-filled with newly made butter. Since
they had eaten very little for the last two days but
dried fish and stale bread, the meal lasted well
into the night, most of the ale being taken, so
the men laughingly told them, from the houses
of the priests.

Privacy was not easy to come by for the two
passengers, but nor had it ever been, even at
home. So when food was brought to them as
night fell and lanterns were lit, Haesel hung an
extra piece of oiled wool across the opening to
give at least the appearance of seclusion while
they drank buttermilk with their food and listened to the noisy eating of the Vikings whose
table manners, it had to be said, were little different from those of the Jorvik men. Later, as
they lay between the furs, neither of them feared
much for their safety while Jarl Aric and his two
companions were just beyond the makeshift curtain, but Fearn thought it more than a little odd
that their captor had spoken no word to her, not

even to ask after her welfare. Perhaps, as he'd said, her likes did not concern him.

Escape being out of the question with so many bodies around and icy water on all sides, they listened to the rush of the river on the other side of the oak hull and felt the gentle movement of the ships as they bent and creaked together. Before Fearn's eyes closed, she watched the glow of lanterns through gaps in the wool curtain and the movement of men adjusting ropes and stowing baggage beneath the slatted deck. Then, as an owl hooted to its mate across the river, she whispered a prayer of thanks for her safety and for a night of freedom from harassment. For how long this freedom would last she did not dare to speculate, for she believed she might have gained it at a very high price.

Naturally, an element of guilt crept into her prayers, for wives did not usually express relief at their husbands' deaths. She tried to alleviate the dark thoughts by searching her mind for Barda's merits, but found nothing to recommend him. Earl Thored had insisted on their marriage and, in the end, her objections had been overruled. Now the situation had worsened, if that were possible, since the arrogant Dane had referred, not too obliquely, to her probable fate.

After which, she would no doubt be obliged to redirect her life yet again.

As she had searched her mind, so she did with the Dane and found, to her interest, that his concern for her comfort had, in one day, exceeded Barda's of two whole years. He had returned her knife to her and the beaver cloak, ordered a horse for her to ride and furs for her to sit on. She fell asleep while thinking of the gold embroidery around the neck of his tunic, wondering whose hands had worked it.

She woke as Haesel parted the curtain, holding a wooden bucket of river water in which to wash. From the deck came sounds of shouts and yelps, then the lurch of the ship as men leapt over the side or hauled themselves back in, slopping the water in the bucket. Haesel's cheeks were pink with embarrassment. 'They're jumping into the river,' she said, 'naked as the day they were born. There's wet everywhere.'

'Swimming, you mean?'

'Washing. It must be freezing.'

The water in the bucket certainly was, but Fearn managed well enough to wash and tidy herself, combing her hair with her antler comb, one of the many and varied contents of the leather bag that Haesel had packed in advance.

The Moneyer's wife had also added things, like Fearn's golden crucifix given to her by the priest when she was baptised. He had taught her to read and write in Latin, too. She found her sewing tools, as well as the tablet-weaving she'd been working on, carefully rolled to keep it from tangling. Her wax-tablet book and stylus was also in there, a detail that Fearn found touching. Now she would be able to make notes.

With her hair plaited and braided with green wool, she broke her fast on cold porridge with buttermilk and honey. The kindly quartermaster had sent two pears for them, so rather than ask where they'd come from, Fearn ate hers with gratitude before venturing out to see what was happening. Standing with his glistening bare back to her was Aric, his wet pigtail dripping between his shoulderblades, his dark linen loincloth sticking to him like a second skin over slender hips, with droplets of sparkling water dripping into a pool around his bare feet. His calves and thighs were as taut and hard as polished oak.

He turned as she emerged and stood upright, waiting as she usually did for a person to decide which eye to speak to. His mouth opened and closed, and then, to give himself time, he hitched up the wet cloth and tightened it. 'Ah,

Lady Fearn,' he said, holding out his bandaged hand. 'Perhaps you could rebind this for me?'

She looked at it with distaste. 'I suppose so,' she said, calmly, 'since it was of my doing. Do we have dry linen?'

Holding his hand in the air, he called to the far end of the ship, 'Oskar! Bandage!'

Her eyes wandered over the shipload of half-naked men slithering about in various stages of undress, laughing and tousled, some of them combing wet hair and beards. Yet her gaze was held, rather against her wishes, by the man before her whose sun-bronzed skin rippled over bulging muscle and sinew, over powerful shoulders and a chest like those men singled out for their wrestling skills for Jorvik's entertainment. He saw where her eyes went before they locked with his. 'Well?' he said, quietly.

She blinked. 'Hold your hand out,' she retorted. 'I need to take this one off.'

Bantering shouts diverted his attention as she began to unwind the soggy linen. 'Are you coming in to bathe with us, lady?' they called. 'We've warmed the water for you.'

Aric grinned. 'Enough!' he called. 'We man the oars at a count of two hundred.'

'Hah!' said Oskar, holding out the linen strips. 'Which of them can count to two hundred?'

Fearn took them from him, flicking a haughty eyebrow. 'Twenty counts of ten?' she murmured. 'Yes, it's healing. I don't need the moss, just the honey. Hold still. It won't hurt.'

The two men exchanged grins, appreciating their beautiful captive's attempt to patronise them in retaliation for her plight, taking the advantage the bandaging offered to watch her hands skilfully tending the row of punctures on his skin. They noted her graceful figure braced against the rocking of the ship and took time to admire the smooth honeyed complexion and the long sweep of black eyelashes on her cheeks. They had time to see the swell of her perfect breasts beneath the linen and wool, and the neat waist tied with a narrow leather girdle. A leather purse hung from this beside the knife in its fur-lined sheath and a rope of beads hung from her neck at the centre of which was a large chunk of cloudy amber, nestling into the valley of her breasts. Just for a moment, the two men would both like to have been that piece of amber.

'There,' she said. 'Try not to wet it. It will heal faster if it's kept dry.'

Aric turned his hand over and over, then nodded his thanks. But Fearn had already turned away to help Haesel fold the skins and furs, pretending not to have seen. She did not hear Oskar's flippant question asking if Aric thought she might bite him some time, but Aric was not as amused as his friend had expected. 'It was not done in play,' he said, pressing the wound. 'Far from it. If she'd done this to her lout of a husband, he'd have knocked her down.'

'Well, so do many men when their women step out of line,' Oskar said.

'Do you?'

'Hit Ailsa? No. Never had to.'

'No man *has* to, Oskar. There are better ways than that to deal with women.' There was a tone in Aric's voice that his friend had not heard before, that made him wonder if Aric was telling the whole truth when yesterday he'd said that he didn't yet know what he was going to do with her. Was revenge his only motive? Oskar thought not.

Chapter Three

The Earl had been right when he'd said how the Vikings' ships moved fast, for now there was a sense of urgency as the rowers took turns to man the oars, thirty-two at a time, speeding through the water with the current to help them. Time and again they passed burnt-out villages, still smouldering, some no more than heaps of charred wood and ash, earning no more than a brief comment from the men who watched impassively. Fearn and Haesel felt the despair and anger of the villagers who saw the ships pass by, who dared not call out for fear they would stop again. At any other time, in happier circumstances, the two women would have enjoyed the sight of swans and their cygnets, the wide stretches of flat countryside in its new greens, the great expanse of sky, the green-brown water rushing past the oars. Now, they sat close to-

gether in silence, always aware of the men's bare
backs straining with the effort, their grunts of
exertion, the hostile situation of being stolen
by Danish Vikings who were under no obligation to be on their best behaviour. The women
were no strangers to the crude expressions men
used, their oaths and unrestrained humour, but
as the Earl's foster daughter, lack of respect had
never been an issue. Here, as comments flew
backwards and forwards between the Danes,
usually followed by a laugh of sorts, Fearn suspected that their vernacular phrases alluded to
women and particularly to them. The fact that
this stopped when Aric the Ruthless passed by
seemed to confirm her suspicions and, although
it should not have concerned her too much, it
did nothing to alleviate her sense of total helplessness.

Apart from access to ale whenever they
wanted it, there was no stopping for food until
the sun almost touched the horizon. Then, as the
river widened considerably between sand dunes
and scrubby woodland, they came to an island
where oars were lifted out of the water and men
leapt over the sides to haul the ships halfway up
on to the sand. Assuming that the deck would
remain at the same angle as it was before, Fearn
and Haesel were quite unprepared for it to tip to

one side, tumbling them out in a sudden lurch on to their fronts, half in and half out on to tufts of coarse grass and clumps of prickly sea holly. Unhurt, but by no means as amused as the men, Fearn controlled the temptation to make a fuss. Gathering herself together, she reached out for her golden circlet lying in the sand just beyond her reach, but not before it was snatched up by one laughing young man who set it upon his own brow, challenging Fearn to retrieve it.

Remembering Aric's threat to deprive her of her knife if she should draw it on one of his men, she deliberately rested her hand on its hilt. 'Give that back,' she said. Without it, her veil had slipped down around her neck, revealing the shining black hair and the thick plait hanging over her breast, and she saw that the young man was making the most of her threat by responding to the men's jeers, hoping she would be goaded into action. He came closer, grinning, yet he was obviously unsettled by seeing for the first time that her eyes were not of the same colour.

Fearn saw his eyes shift, as men's often did, then she deliberately let her gaze flicker over his shoulder as if she had seen Aric approach. In that moment, as the man's attention was distracted, she darted forward to snatch her circlet off his head, whipping out her knife as she did so to warn him not to retaliate.

Hearing the hoots of derision and seeing the crowd of men shirking their duties, Aric barged his way through them to seize the offender by his hair, pull him backwards, and to kick into the back of his knee. The man landed with a thud, but just as quickly sprang to his feet, none the worse and bearing no grudge.

Aric snarled at him. 'Fool!' he said, pointing to Fearn. 'Don't underestimate our passenger.' Holding his bandaged hand under the man's nose, he waited for the realisation to dawn in his eyes, before the man nodded. 'Get to work, all of you, or it'll be dark before we eat,' Aric barked.

Fearn and Haesel dusted the sand and sea holly off their gowns, righting their veils and, in Fearn's case, sheathing her knife. She held a protective hand over it, half-expecting confiscation. 'Self-defence,' she said.

'Stay by the ship,' he said. 'Bring your rugs and furs out here. We shall be making camp on the island.'

'My maid and I need to go…' She pointed to the low gorse bushes and stunted trees making a dense thicket behind them. 'In there. We need privacy.'

'No,' he said. 'Make a shelter and do what you have to do here.'

'With those louts gawping at us?'

'Get on with it, woman. There are ships between you and them. I'll have your food sent as soon as it's ready.'

With little option but to do as they'd been told, they made the best of the situation, erecting a makeshift hide between the prow of the ship and a young willow that gave them some shelter from the salt-tasting sea breeze. They need not have been concerned about the men's interest, for now all hands were needed to light fires and to prepare food, cooked on spits and in pots with enough noise to make whispering unnecessary. 'Haesel,' Fearn said, 'I'm going to creep up alongside the ship and take a look at where we are. I believe the other channel between the island and the shore is much narrower than this side. It'll be shallower, too.'

'You should wait, lady,' Haesel said. 'If you mean for us to escape, we should wait until we've been fed. Then they'll settle down and darkness will hide us.'

'You're right. Look, here comes our food, at last.'

The young man who approached using an upturned shield as a tray carried a lantern, bread, baked fish, a stew of chicken and barley, a jug of wine and an apple each. As he was the same man who had teased Fearn, his manner had now changed to something between respectful and apologetic. This woman had actually managed to injure his leader. Asking if there was anything else the lady required while avoiding her eyes with his, he made a hesitant bow and left, while Fearn and Haesel tried hard to contain their laughter at the sudden change in his attitude. That unexpected lightness of heart and the possibility of an escape into the night gave them an appetite for everything set before them, even the wine. The custom of Danes to drink milk with fish was, unsurprisingly, not being observed, and although Haesel had never tasted more than a mouthful of wine and Fearn only rarely, the last of the jug's contents was used to soak up the last crusts of bread.

Haesel yawned, loudly. 'Should be getting… er…packing ready,' she said.

'What?'

'Packing. Put your knife away…no…*wipe* it first! Are we going soon?'

'Yes, s'pose so.' Fearn stood up, wobbled and took a step forward, then sat down again rather heavily. 'Yes, course we are. What can we carry?' She caught Haesel's yawn as she spoke.

Not too successfully, Haesel was trying to clear away all signs of the meal, paying no attention to the young man when he returned to remove the few vessels from her hands and silently depart. Rolling up a woollen rug, she tossed it over to Fearn who, instead of catching it, keeled over sideways to lay her head upon it, her eyes already closed. The wine had done more to Haesel than send her to sleep, for in the next moment, she was stumbling over to the water's edge to rid her stomach of its contents. Then, staggering back to the untidy pile of furs, she collapsed on the edge, groaned, and lost consciousness. Unused to wine, it had gone straight to their heads.

As the tide of the estuary receded, it was the gentle rushing lap of water that reminded Fearn where she was in that bleary state of half-sleep when the blackness of night hid everything from them. Vaguely, she wondered how it was that warm furs now covered her, wondering, too, about the something else she had been going to do and why could she now feel Barda's length at her back? *Barda?*

Feeling the shock throughout her body, she swivelled and tried to leap away at the same time, but was pushed back down by a man's arm, bare, warm and as hard as steel. Still disoriented, her head reeled as a large hand was clamped over her mouth, holding her down to prevent her scream for help, while her own hands tried to make sense of what was happening and failed to recognise the body they knew.

It was the deep commanding voice of Aric that broke through the panic, soft and reassuring, and close enough for her to feel his breath as the sounds touched her skin. 'Shh…hush, lady. Steady. There's no danger. You're quite safe. Quiet, now. I'm taking my hand away, so don't scream. I'm here to keep you safe, that's all.'

She let the words find a niche in her memory as his hand slid away, its wrist held tightly by her fingers that found the linen bandage. 'Where's Haesel?' she whispered, hoarse with fright.

'Fast asleep behind me. You go back to sleep now.'

There was a part of her that craved sleep, accepting that her body was indeed safer than it had been from Barda's selfish demands. Yet somehow she had let the enemy get this close when to keep him at a distance, in every respect, had been her one intention from the start. Reasoning deserted her in the dark warmth of his nearness, in the kind of safety she had known only when Haesel had shared her bed, in the comfort she had felt as a young child with an adult nearby. She felt sleep overwhelm her again while breathing in the outdoor scent of his body, feeling his breath on her shoulder and the surprising softness of his short jawline beard. Almost asleep, she turned towards the haven of safety and was scooped up, gently, to lay with her head on the crook of his arm, her mouth against the bare skin of his chest that rose and fell like the rocking of the ship.

In the starlit darkness and with the sounds of lapping water to remind him of the tides, Aric smiled at his success. But in this game, one could not afford too much self-congratulation, experience having taught him that it would take more than this to bring this rare bird to his hand, nor would he be able to rely on wine again to foil whatever plan she was hatching. If she remembered anything of this episode, she would be doubly on her guard, no doubt hating him more than ever for his ploy. This had been her last chance to make a run for it with the open sea just round the bend and Northumbria left behind. To meet up with King Swein and the rest of the Danish fleet, it would take them quite some time to reach Lundenburh, sailing south, then west along the great River Thames. It was a long time for her to be caged up with a crowd

of woman-starved warriors. She would have to
become accustomed to his methods of safety and
he would have to be on his guard against her
methods of resisting them, as she surely would.
Having just found a release from a husband's
brutish thraldom, she would not take kindly to
his, however different.

She awakened slowly to the sounds of activity around the ships and to a painful thudding in
her head quite unlike anything Barda had been
responsible for. Frowning, she squinted at Haesel's pale unsmiling face and knew that she, too,
was feeling the effects of last night's indulgence
while folding blankets and furs with nothing like
her usual deftness.

The maid saw that Fearn was awake. 'Come
on,' she said. 'They need us to take the shelter down. They'll be moving the ships into the
water soon. Please, lady. Move!' With no time
or energy for discussion on whatever it was that
nagged her memory of the night's strangeness,
Fearn forced herself into action. To catch the
tide was all important to the men and, even as
she clambered into place loaded with furs and
rugs, there were men aboard pulling on ropes to
raise the mast which, until then, had been lying
along the deck.

Nestling like two birds into the curve of the prow, the women listened to the men's roar as they pushed in unison, felt the lurch and dip, the lift as the ship righted itself, kept steady by a few of the oarsmen, then the hasty scramble of men on to the deck. With his leather-clad feet on their platform, Aric yelled and waved his arms at the helmsman, whose task was to steer them safely between sandbanks and mudflats while men unfurled the sail from the yardarm, waiting for orders to hoist it to the top of the mast. Beyond the stern of their longship, Fearn could see the three others following on and, by the way the sandy dunes flattened and disappeared altogether, she knew they would soon be on the open sea that lifted the ship with a rhythmic swoosh. Aric made as if to leave the prow, but then dropped to his heels until his eyes were level with Fearn's. Above them, the striped sail cracked as the wind filled it. 'The gods are with us,' he said. 'We have a fair wind, but we shall be staying within sight of land, and make better progress if we keep going and sleep on board.'

'I'm relieved to hear it,' Fearn said, looking steadily into his eyes to find some change there after her disturbing thoughts of the last hour. 'I believe cold food and buttermilk suits us better than wine. We both prefer to eat and sleep as we did before. We feel safer that way.' The problem was, she could remember very little of what had happened last night except that something had and that she had been kept safe, whatever she might be implying.

His eyes gave nothing away, nor did the straight line of his mouth. 'Having got this far with you, your safety is of concern to me. Are you telling me that you did not feel safe last night, after what happened on the sand?'

'No, but…'

'Good. None of my men wishes you any harm. Neither you nor the maid. But they've been away from home now for over a year, wintering in Lundenburh, and they would see little wrong in taking advantage of women's presence amongst them unless I and my two companions reminded them who you belong to.'

'*Belong to?* You? Then you can remind them, Dane, that I belong to *no one*.'

'Yes, I could do that, if that's what you wish. Shall I tell them now and give them something to look forward to at the end of their day's work? There'll be some competition, of course.'

It was Haesel who brought her mistress to her senses. 'Lady!' she said, grasping Fearn's arm in a vice. 'Think what you're saying, for pity's sake.' She shook the arm, aware that the after-effects of the wine were still causing some problems. 'Tell the Jarl that you need his protection, however it comes. And so do I. *Think*, lady.' Her voice was breathless with fear.

Aric knew what else Haesel was trying to say. 'You are still a maid?' he asked her.

Looking at Fearn, Haesel nodded. 'Yes. And last night…'

'You felt safe?' Aric said. 'With…?'

'Yes.' Her eyes left Fearn's with the admission that her memory of what happened was the clearer of the two. The younger of Aric's two companions had whispered to her that he was known as Hrolf and that she was perfectly safe with him. Which indeed she had been. There had been no sign of either men as Haesel awoke, though she guessed who had guarded the lady.

'Haesel? You slept with—?' said Fearn, angrily.

'I was kept safe, lady. As you were,' Haesel interrupted.

Fearn's face paled with the shock of realisation that the hazy memories of last night were as she had suspected. Haesel, too. Her young maid. Glaring at Aric, she winced at the pain in her head as words flew at him like arrows. 'You play a wily game, Dane. My maid does not understand…'

'Your maid understands more than you think, lady. She is…how old?'

Haesel answered. 'Sixteen, my lord, to my lady's three-and-twenty.'

There was a distinct huff of annoyance from Fearn as the information she had been pleased to withhold was now given freely and for no good reason. At the same time, she could tell that Haesel's reading of the situation was quite different from her own, for she had heard a certain note of pride in the maid's voice in stating her age. Clearly, she was not as averse to his method of being kept 'safe' at night as she herself was. She could not look at Aric as she spoke, though her voice was gruff with fear at the way matters were unfolding beyond her control. 'I would ask you to remember,' she said, 'that my freedom from the demands of a husband lasted only a few hours, most of those without me knowing it. And for two years I longed for that freedom, for reasons you will…already…know.' The words almost disappeared beneath the slap of water on the bows, as Aric leaned forward to hear them. 'Naturally, my maid is curious, but I am *not*,' she said.

But the Dane had no time for that kind of conversation. Pushing at his knees, he stood up, uncompromising in his parting shot. 'Such is the nature of thraldom, lady, even for one year. You should thank your god you were not taken by a savage.'

She watched him make his way through the bustle of men, giving directions on what to put where, but leaving the sailing of the ship to his shipmaster. She had said she lacked curiosity, but knew it to be less than the truth, for she *was* in fact curious to know how he had come to her last night and exactly what had taken place. That curiosity fuelled her imagination, for she had seen him half-naked and had already felt the strength in his body, though she knew he had not abused her in any way, as Barda certainly would have done. Even so, she had now lost her hard-earned freedom, his severe words making it clear beyond any doubt that she was to be his slave of one year or forfeit his protection, such as it was. Travelling like this with so many lust-ful men was too dangerous for her to indulge in a surfeit of pride, but the thought of the price she would eventually have to pay filled her with nothing but dread and revulsion.

The offshore wind took them out of the Humber Estuary and into the wide expanse of the open sea with the sails bellying and the ropes straining while men swung the ship round time and again to tack down the eastern coast.

* * *

It was some time before Aric himself brought
bread, butter and cheese to the two women, with
a pitcher of ale, which was when Fearn noticed
that his hand was no longer bandaged. Proudly,
he showed it to her, both sides of his thumb
completely healed and showing only the faintest marks where yesterday the wounds had been
red and sore.

'I don't know what you did, lady,' Aric said,
leaning on the bulwarks, 'but I've never healed
as fast as this before. Do you have healing powers?'

'Skills, not powers,' she said. 'I was taught
well by my Benedictine friends.'

'You treated Earl Thored's men?'

'Many times.'

Aric looked along the ship, his eyes searching for a man to whom he beckoned. 'Einar!' he
called. 'Come!'

The man took some time coming through the
crowded deck stacked with chests and sacks,
with men and caged hens, slowed down by a
clumsy bandage round one foot on which he
limped, his face wrinkled with pain. A red-faced
hoary old warrior with long flowing hair and a
plaited beard hiding all but two red cheeks and
two bright blue eyes, he eventually accepted the

arm of a comrade for the last few steps, collapsing with a grunt on to a chest.

'Put your foot up here,' Fearn commanded without waiting for an introduction. Quickly, she began to unwind the smelly bandage, stiff with blood. 'How long has it been like this, Einar?' she said.

Clasping his leg with both hands, he puffed with pain as the linen came away. 'Two…three days, lady. Gathering laver from the rocks. Stood on something sharp. It's underneath. I cannot see.'

The wound on the soft pad of his foot gaped open and raw with grains of sand covering the deepest part. 'My lord,' she said to Aric, 'I need a bucket of seawater to wash this in. Then some clean linen strips and some of that laver he was gathering. Or has it all been eaten?'

'There's some left, lady,' Einar said. 'You want me to eat some more of it?'

Laver was a favourite food for sailors who plucked its floppy pinkish fronds from the rocks all around the coast. Other kinds of seaweed were sought, too, to be boiled, then rolled in oatmeal and fried with bacon. Without a fire, men chewed it raw. Having washed the foot clean of sand and blood, Fearn was able to see into the wound. Delving into her leather purse that hung

from her girdle, she brought out her bronze twee-
zers, at which Einar made no protest. A crowd
of men craned their necks, three deep, to witness the proceedings as Fearn probed the wound
and, after three attempts to grasp the hard edge
of the splinter, she carefully drew out a sizeable
shard of white cockleshell that had been lurking
in there for the best part of three days. Holding
it out to the patient, she smiled at him. 'There's
your problem,' she said, placing it on his hand.
'Now, where's the laver?'

The last of the laver had been boiled to a pulp
the night before, while there were fires but, as
Fearn told her patient—who happened to be the
cook—the pulp was perfect for a poultice. Covering the wound with a thick layer of the gluti-
nous substance, she bound the foot rather more
expertly than before with strict instructions that
it must not touch the floor for a day and a night.

'Shall you not be saying a charm over it?'
Einar wanted to know.

'Not a charm,' she replied, 'but I will remember you in my prayers, if you wish?'

'Yes,' Einar said. 'My thanks, lady. If I can
do anything for you…?'

'I like shellfish,' she said, 'but next time, mind
where you put your great feet.'

She won a friend, that day, and a crowd of ad-

mirers hugely impressed by her expertise. On a
more personal level, the little act of mercy gave
her a sense of purpose and worth, and a certainty
that the men on this ship, at least, would be unlikely to threaten her safety, or Haesel's, as long
as she could cure their ailments.

Even with this new awareness, Fearn knew
that the sleeping arrangements of the previous
night would, without the wine, be the usual way
of things and that to make a fuss would be coun-
ter-productive. Perceptive as ever, Haesel tried to
calm her fears, knowing more than anyone else
of Barda's ugly manners which, over the years,
had made Fearn quite unable to show him any
affection. As darkness approached and anchors
had been dropped within sight of the shore, food
was shared out and lanterns lit, men sitting in
'rooms' between the ship's supports, eating, talking and singing. Haesel rigged up their curtain to
provide some privacy as well as warmth, helping
her mistress to comb her hair and remove girdle
and pouch, shoes and jewellery.

'My knife,' Fearn whispered. 'I think I might
keep it with me, Haesel.'

Haesel placed a hand over hers. 'No, you
won't need that.'

'But you…did you…?'

'Need a knife? No, lady. I was in no danger, nor will you be.'

'How do you know that?'

'Listen. The man called Hrolf was with me, just as the Jarl was with you, but all he did was lie at my back and keep me warm with his arm. That's all. They're not going to do more than that here, are they? In this space?'

The picture of 'more than that' in the confined triangular area made them both smile, for although Haesel was a maid, the doings of lovers was no mystery to her. 'Did he not try to kiss you?' Fearn wanted to know.

'No, not once. I was more awake than you. Most of my wine went into the sea. So you should take what comfort and warmth is offered you, lady. I saw the cloak and felt the winds, didn't I? And that turned out to be so. But I've had no signs of you being hurt, so perhaps when he comes you should think of him as just another fur rug to keep you warm. One of those blond costly ones from the northern lands. You've always wanted one of those.'

'I'm glad you're with me. You say the funniest things.'

The gentle rocking of the ship on shallow waters soon lulled Haesel to sleep, but Fearn's thoughts churned over and over as she fought with all the emotions of the past few days, ever since the news of the Vikings' presence on the river. Twisting the gold ring on her little finger, her mother's last gift, she could not prevent tears of sadness at the void left by her parents' sudden departure, a sadness that had not abated since then. Pushing away the furs, she crept out on bare feet through the makeshift curtain on to the deck crowded with recumbent forms like long parcels of sealskin. The deck lifted and rocked beneath her feet and water slapped the sides of the ship as she leaned over the side to watch the moon's reflections rippling like silver ribbons. She wiped a tear away before it fell, wondering if the moon was shining on her loved ones as it was on her, and how far she would be from them, in Denmark. Would Mother Bridget still be there in Jorvik when she returned? There had been no time for a proper farewell to the nuns. Lifting her head from her hands, she sensed a presence behind her. 'You!' she whispered. 'No, leave me alone. Go away!'

'Aloneness is in short supply on a ship,' Aric said, quietly. 'The best we can do is to try to help each other through the problem.'

'Help?' she croaked. She would like to have screamed and hammered at his wide chest for making such a useless offer. 'Help? You are the one who created the problem and each day in your company makes it worse. You must know that.'

Stepping like a cat over a sleeping man's feet, he came to stand by her side, leaning on the lower curve of the prow. 'Tell me about them. Your parents.'

Angrily, Fearn stared at him. 'How do you know I'm thinking of my parents, Dane?'

'Well, you'd hardly be weeping for anyone else, would you? That husband of yours, his screeching mother, your foster mother and father? Don't tell me you're missing them already. And although I hardly created the problem of your parents, I am probably guilty of taking them out of your reach. Whereabouts are they, exactly?'

'That is part of the problem. I don't *know* where they are,' she replied sharply.

He took a moment or two to accept this unlikely-sounding tale. 'You really don't know? Has Earl Thored never contacted them? Have you?'

'From the day they were sent off, away from Jorvik, I have heard not one word. They may have died for all I know.' Seeing things from a negative viewpoint came naturally to her just then. 'How would I contact them?' she whispered.

'Don't you know why they were banished?'

'I was five. It may have been something to do with their faith, but I can't be sure. My foster father was baptised, but I know it was only for political reasons, not because he truly believes. My father, Earl Oslac, was deeply committed. He would have been appalled at the idea of his daughter having to spend her days and nights with a Danish heathen, especially the one responsible for her husband's death.'

'I thought we had agreed, lady, that you are well rid of him. Perhaps your father might thank me for doing what he would not have been able to do. As for spending your days and nights with a Danish heathen, there must be worse things that could happen to you. Earl Thored would have chosen your second husband, I seem to remember. What's more, you would have fared worse if you'd had bairns, for then you would have been parted from them, too, wouldn't you? How long were you married to that man of Thored's?'

'If you are asking why there are no children, Dane, it's both a mystery and a blessing to me, for he was not fit to be a father. If my own father had still been Earl, I would have been allowed to choose my own husband. Knowing what you do of him, can you wonder that I want a celibate

life with the nuns where I can make use of my
healing skills?'

'No, I cannot wonder at it. But your body may
tell you differently, in time.'

'My body is my own to do with as I will. You
should know this, Dane.'

By the light of the moon, his expression was
fully revealed to her, serious and thoughtful, and
as understanding as any man could be at the
workings of a woman's mind. 'Interesting,' he
said, quietly. 'And here was I, thinking that as a
believer in the new religion, you would be bound
to accept whatever your god wills for you.'

'What my God wills, yes. Not necessarily
what *man* wills. Men tend to confuse the two,
as I have no doubt you will, too.'

'Fortunately, lady, the issue is not one that
concerns me. For one year I have taken over the
responsibility for your body, ceded to me by Earl
Thored. At the end of that year, you may be left
wondering whether the experience was willed
by your god or what you people call *wyrd*. Fate.
Destiny. *What will be.* Isn't that how they put it?'

'Whoever or whatever willed it,' she said,
sharply, 'it was not me.'

But as she spoke the words to him, face to
face, the voice at the back of her mind cast
doubts over them. Had she not willed it in some

small degree, the voice told her, she would have fought him tooth and nail, used her knife to better effect, thrown herself over the side of the ship, *anything* to prevent the thraldom he was so intent on. There, in the darkness lit only dimly by the moon's hazy glow, her senses were alive to his nearness, to the potent power of his masculinity, the aura of strength and virility that surrounded him like a mantle in which, she knew, he could swathe her, easily, in a manner beyond her experience. Her body's responses were already giving the lie to her assertion, just as something in his manner told her he did not quite believe her, either. Her eyes slid away from his, unable to withstand his examination.

Turning from her, he took the curtain and lifted it high enough for her to bend beneath his hand and enter the dark space beyond, without question or protest. Immediately, he was beside her, moving her away from the cool wooden side towards the middle where the furs were peeled back, ready for her re-entry. Removing his boots and tunic, he pulled the furs up over them, laying his arm over the top of hers to pull the soft covering up, keeping it between them.

Fearn could not move away without disturbing Haesel but, as the unfamiliar warmth of Aric's bulk spread slowly into her back, the trembling of her body eventually lessened. Dark memories of Barda's hot mead-reeking breath and fumbling hands on her breasts kept her alert for the slightest movement, but the Dane was perfectly still, if not altogether silent. 'You have nothing to fear from me,' he whispered close to her ear. 'Tomorrow we should reach Lundenburh and meet the rest of the fleet, and our King Swein. He's been negotiating with your King Ethelred.'

'How best to fill your ships with English treasure, you mean,' she whispered back.

'Yes, I hope so.'

'The Queen and I know each other. I wonder if we shall be allowed to meet.'

'I don't see why not. Remind me, what relation is she?'

'None of mine. Queen Aelfgyfu is the only daughter of Earl Thored and his first wife, who died in childbirth. She and I were brought up by the Lady Hilda, his second, until Aelfgyfu was given in marriage to King Eethelred in 984. I was just fourteen and she was seventeen, the same age as her husband, poor girl.'

'Why poor girl? Would you not be a king's wife?'

'Wife to a *seventeen*-year-old?' she whispered, fiercely. 'Having bairns one after the other until she's worn out, for the sake of politics?'

'In politics, a woman's role is as peace-weaver. Is that not a worthy calling?'

'I know *you* think it is, Dane. Elf was a dutiful daughter. She knew that the King must always have the Earls on his side and that the most binding link is to marry the daughter of one of them. Particularly when they're as remote as Northumbria. And for the Earl to be able to say he's the King's father-in-law puts him in a very strong position. I missed her when she left. I still do. We were like sisters.'

'Have you not been able to send messages to each other?'

'We were both taught to write. We send letters whenever anyone travels to where the royal court is.'

'So…you *write*? Well then, I got the best of the bargain when I took you instead of young Kean, didn't I? In Latin *and* English?' He felt the sudden pull of her shoulder as she turned back into the pillow, telling him that the conversation was at an end.

'Patronising *oaf*!' she muttered. 'You suppose women are hen-brained?'

Still, he made no move and it was not long before the sound of her breathing and the relaxing of her body next to his told him that she slept. It was some time before he did the same, for now

he had managed to find out more about this remarkable creature, and what a pity, he thought,
that he had bargained for only one year of her
life. Would it take that long to get her to accept
him?

During the night, a stiff breeze blew the sea
into waves beneath them, rocking the ship and
gently throwing Fearn against the buffer of Aric's body to be caught in his arms. Sleep became
difficult. 'Turn towards me,' he said. 'It'll be
more comfortable for you this way, lady.'

'No…no! I can't. I'm all right. I'd rather…'

'You need to have more sleep. Come on, now.
I've told you, you have nothing to fear from me.
Trust me. I shall not touch you, except to keep
you from rolling about.'

Reluctant, and still drowsy, she turned herself
into his arms and felt them close around her, rolling her gently with him instead of against him,
her head tucked beneath his chin. Cautiously, she
lay a leg over the top of his to anchor herself and
felt the soft leather of his breeches. He had told
her to trust him and, though she could think of
no reason why his word was any different from
the three other men in her life who had let her
down badly, she allowed herself to be rocked like
a child until sleep returned. Her last ponderings

were about the *wyrd*, the three sisters who spun out the thread of one's life, measured it, then cut it and decided on the use to which it should be put. The priest at Jorvik had derided the notion. It was their God, he said, who decided that, not three mythical sisters. But Fearn thought, as did many others, that the priest would have to find a way of combining the two views, for she doubted that the notion of 'what will be' would ever fall out of favour, being so much easier to accept than God's will and all its ambiguities. She dreamed of rocking a child in her arms, a dream so powerful that she felt the ache of emptiness deep inside her waiting to be fulfilled, and she half-woke, weeping, but was rocked to sleep again in Aric's arms.

Under the command of Aric the Ruthless, the four longships reached Lundenburh just as the sun disappeared over the flat horizon ahead of them. From well inside the mouth of the Thames, the sails had been lowered and tied away in favour of the oars, making good speed with the tide to help them over the miles to where the huge Danish and Norwegian fleet lay at anchor. It had been a long and hard day's sailing and the men were exhausted, but not enough to prevent the noisy celebrations at having won a massive pay-off from the dithering English King Ethelred, whose refusal to make a stand against the aggressors had his court tearing their hair out with frustration.

From where she and Haesel stood in the safety of their ship's curving prow, Fearn could see Aric and his men laughing with a crowd of comrades, guessing that the jest was against the English. She had asked to be allowed to meet with Queen Aelfgyfu once more before her own departure from English shores and Aric had arranged it with his king, Swein Forkbeard, who had seen no harm at all in his trusted commander abducting a foster daughter of Earl Thored while fleecing him at the same time. If Aric thought that was a better deal than taking Thored's own son, then one look at the woman in her crumpled finery told Swein all he needed to know about the probable reason.

Putting all associations with Barda aside, Fearn had decided to wear the beaver-fur cloak, partly because she was proud of having made it and partly to cover herself against the admiring stares of the Vikings who crowded the wharves of Lundenburh. A clean white veil covered her hair, held in place by the gold circlet studded with garnets, though the indigo-blue kirtle remained as testament to the conditions on board a shipload of men, still creased and muddied round the hem, and spotted with blood from Einar's wounded foot. That morning, he had come to show her how, in one day and a night, all signs of the wound had completely vanished, a fact that he needed her to verify since he himself could scarcely believe it. Since then, she had been held in awe as one man after another was shown the healed foot and Aric realised that she was not only remarkable, but a singular asset to have at his disposal.

Night had fallen as Fearn and Haesel were escorted to the royal palace, a large timber-and wood-tiled building not unlike the great hall at Jorvik in size, but more embellished by carvings of dragons and intricate knotwork than the northern Earl's. Guards, polished and business-like, stood at every entrance to demand the identity of the guests whose escort had been provided by the Queen herself, as for the first time Fearn was able to appreciate the grandeur surrounding the dear friend whose letters never described her lifestyle, only domestic matters as if she were still only a nobleman's daughter. Torches and beeswax candles threw light upon the colourful wall-hangings and shone upon the gold-threaded silken kirtles of the Queen's ladies, shimmering as they moved.

As the heavy door opened, one lady passed her infant over to one of the others, coming forward with open arms and a happy smile to greet Fearn. 'Dearest one,' she whispered. 'Ah, my dearest friend.' Her arms closed about Fearn's shoulders, holding her face to face to see how nine years of separation had treated her, while a wave of spicy perfume wafted between them.

'Elf…oh, Elf, I've missed you so,' Fearn whispered, searching the lovely face to refresh her memory, but seeing there a maturity imposed by years of childbirth and anxiety. 'I never expected to be seeing you in this situation. What's happening to us, Elf? These Danes are running circles round us.'

Hands reached up to caress faces, to find more detail through touch than mere eyes and voices could convey. Tears welled up and threatened to run down cheeks until embarrassed laughter stopped them, for it would not do to show this weakness before the court ladies. 'What's happening to *you*, more like,' said the Queen. 'The message I received was that the Lady Fearn was with the Danes and wished to see me. But surely my father has not allowed them to take you? Has he?'

Fearn nodded, letting Aelfgyfu lead her to one side where she sat upon a silk padded bench with Haesel beside her, telling what had happened over the last few days, including her new widowed state. The Queen sympathised, hugging Fearn as no one else had done for years. 'It's a relief,' she said. 'Your letters mentioned your unhappiness, dearest, but I never thought you'd be freed so soon. God punished him as he deserved.' Realising how that sounded, she revised her words. 'Oh, what am I saying? Now you've lost your freedom again and to a Dane. So *cruel.*' The ice-blue eyes, so like Earl Thored's, sparked with a rare anger. Elf had never been a wilful child—her calming influence on Fearn had been one of the most missed aspects of her absence. Fearn would never have hit a woman nor fought with a man if Elf had been there that day. Elf would have intervened to prevent it. Elegant and still slender, with a long braided plait of white-blonde hair, she was every inch the stuff of which queens were made and, at twenty-six, was the fecund mother of five children. Her letters to Fearn had indicated, more than once, that she loved her husband, Ethelred, who many men criticised for his indecisiveness. Fearn wanted to know if her declarations of love were true, or were her letters more diplomatic than heartfelt?

'It's the truth, Fearn. You have suffered at the hands of your man, but I have known nothing but tenderness from mine. Ethelred and I were both only seventeen when we were bonded, but our love has grown since then. I try to be a good wife to him. His troubles have increased since the Danes returned, yet he is reluctant to fight and lose men. He'd rather lose wealth than lives, yet whatever he does or doesn't do is criticised. For my part, I give him what I can.'

'You've done well, dearest one. A girl and four boys, now.'

They looked over to where the infant lay in his nurse's arms, gurgling at her soft talk. 'Would you like to hold him?' the Queen said.

'May I? This one is… Edred?'

The child, a tiny bundle wrapped loosely in linen and soft wool blankets, waved his arms as he was given to Fearn, smiling up at her, full of trust. 'You don't swaddle him?' she asked.

'No. I believe children grow perfectly strong and straight if they're left free. Besides, I don't need to hang my infants up on a hook on the wall while I get on with my work, do I? I have ladies to tend their needs, though I've always suckled them myself. He likes the look of you, Fearn. See, he's smiling.'

The Queen could not have known how her

child's smile almost broke her friend's heart at that moment. The little fingers closed warmly round Fearn's as if they belonged together, tugging the adult knuckles towards the little petal-like mouth that opened to suck greedily, sending a ripple of motherly desire through Fearn's body that made her gasp at the sweetness of it. Sobs rose in her breast at the overwhelming ache to nurture, while hot tears of emptiness poured down her cheeks, shaking her with the pain of guilt at not wanting to bear any child of Barda's which, as a dutiful wife, she ought to have done. This, the tears told her, was what had evaded her, quite naturally, time and again, and now she must accept the anguish of being childless through no fault of her own.

Haesel came to her aid, gently removing the babe from Fearn's arms, handing it back to the nurse before helping her mistress to catch her sobs in the end of her veil. In the two years of Fearn's marriage, Elf had naturally assumed that the joys of motherhood had eluded her, so far, and had no idea that the urge was so painfully within her, or that it had been so thoroughly stifled. Rocking Fearn in her arms, she made comforting sounds while wondering how her friend would keep herself chaste in this terrible situation. 'For one year,' she whispered into Fearn's veil, 'just a year. It may not happen in that time. Then you will return and find a good man to give you the family you never had. Think on that.'

'I shall go to the nuns at Clementhorpe,' Fearn said, wiping her cheeks. 'I do not want any man, Elf.'

'That's your recent experience speaking,' Elf said, gently. 'I know what you fear, but really it can be the most wonderful thing with the right man. You are still young, dearest, and things change for the better as well as for the worse.'

'May I see the other four?' Fearn said.

'Well, the three boys will be asleep now, but I can send for Gemma. She's seven now and thinks herself a lady already.' She made a sign to one of her ladies, pronouncing the name of her daughter 'Yemma' since the G was soft in their language. 'But Fearn, love… I must warn you…are you all right…you're sure? I don't want you to be upset.'

Thinking that Elf referred to her recent bout of weeping, Fearn nodded, bracing herself to see an adorable child the sight of whom would show her again what she had missed. What she saw was indeed an adorable child with long fair hair like her mother's, with the same regal bearing, too, with the same lovely features Fearn would have expected Elf to produce. Except for one outstanding oddity. Her eyes. One was as blue as bluebells and the other a deep mossy green, exactly like her own.

The voices came from a long way off and the room gradually disappeared from view. It was the first time Fearn had ever fainted.

Chapter Four

'Forgive me, dear one,' the Queen was saying, holding a beaker of wine to Fearn's pale lips. 'Forgive me. I could not tell you of this. Not while you were with my father. He obviously doesn't wish you to know of your parentage, or he'd have explained, wouldn't he?'

'I'm completely lost, Elf. What does it mean? That my parents are not my parents? That I'm related to you and to the Earl?'

Elf did her best to excuse her father's silence on the matter. 'I don't suppose for one moment he thought you and I would ever meet again. He wouldn't have known your Dane would be here in Lundenburh while the royal court was here. We might have been anywhere. Winchester. Hamwic. We rarely stay anywhere for long. King Swein did his deal with Ethelred months ago and, had it not been for the storms, they'd have been away to Denmark earlier. So my father had no reason to think you'd ever have chance to find out that we're half-sisters, love.'

'So he doesn't know that Gemma and I have the same eyes?'

'No, indeed. I haven't told him. That would be to admit that I know he's your father, for obviously this oddity runs in his family. Like red hair, it doesn't affect everyone. But I realised we were half-sisters ever since Gemma was born. Even at birth, her eyes were not the same.'

'No wonder Hilda is such a bitter woman. Earl Thored has not been true to her, has he? I'd never have known about young Kean, either, if the Dane had not come for him. But Elf, who *is* my mother? Surely it cannot have been Clodagh, Oslac's wife, the ones who were banished? They were devout Christians. She would never have…oh, it doesn't do to think of it, Elf.'

'I remember Clodagh and Oslac. I was eight when they were sent away. They were always kind to me, more so than Hilda.'

'They were good people, but now this has stirred up a lot of questions. Why were they sent away? And *was* Clodagh my mother?'

'She had black hair like yours. And she was lovely, like you.'

Fearn did not answer the compliment, but laid

a hand over the Queen's, hearing the past instead of the present tense and wondering if she would ever discover the truth of the matter. Wondering, too, if Clodagh and Oslac had suffered the same fate as Jarl Aric's sister, whose husband had been quietly removed by Thored, yet in Clodagh and Oslac's case had lived to tell the tale. 'Elf,' she whispered, 'I refused to say farewell to him. I refused his blessing. That must have hurt him badly.'

'He didn't want you to know, dearest. Perhaps he was ashamed. In any case, he's hurt *you*, hasn't he, by letting you go? But I also think this must be kept from the Dane. It would not do for him to know he's abducted the Queen of England's half-sister, for then you would be even more valuable to him. He would demand a ransom for your return.'

'Elf, the Danes are already bleeding us dry. I don't think…'

'I know, dear one, but the less he knows about your parentage, the better. If you take my advice, you'll not tell anyone. Not yet.'

'Does your husband the King know?'

'Not having seen you, love, there's no way he could know either and, for the time being, I shall say nothing. What's he like, this Dane?

Some of them are utterly ruthless. I hope he's not ill-treating you.'

'That's what they call him. The Ruthless. And I suppose in war, he is. So far, he's treated us reasonably well, but I cannot wait for the day I'm allowed to return. Heaven only knows what I'm supposed to do when we reach Denmark. Whatever it is, I shall make him regret this insult.'

'Don't, Fearn. Life is too short to be spent avenging insults. Men cannot help themselves, but we can. Did you bring your tablet-weaving?'

'Yes, but…'

'Then spend your time making beautiful things and in healing the sick, as you've always done. You must not make this an excuse to let your skills go rusty. They were God-given. Use them on everyone who needs them, as Mother Bridget does. And write to me. Let me know where you are. Will you?'

'Of course,' Fearn said, feeling the soothing energies of Elf's advice.

'Is that kirtle the only one you've brought? Have you nothing warmer?' Anticipating a negative reply, the Queen was soon directing her ladies to re-clothe and groom her half-sister and maid in beautiful warm kirtles of softest lambswool. In a chest they packed more kirtles for

her and Haesel, girdles, fine leather shoes, linen
veils and undergarments, lengths of wool, linen
and silk for her to make more, with a pile of
linen, silk and gold threads for embroidery, a
box of sewing tools to add to her own and parchment for her letters. They also put in strips of
worn linen, a necessary addition to any travelling woman's accessories that Haesel had not had
time to prepare in readiness for their monthly
courses. A pile of exotic furs went on top. It was
a perfect antidote to the heart-rending emotions
earlier in their meeting, and by the time they had
made their farewells, a messenger had arrived
to say that Jarl Aric was waiting for her in the
great hall.

'This I must see,' said the Queen, pinning the
beaver-skin cloak under Fearn's chin. 'Sounds as
if he's impatient to reclaim his trophy.'

'Oh, Elf! Hardly a trophy.'

'You think not? Well, then, you watch his face.'

Fearn had been escorted to the palace not by
Aric himself, but by Englishmen of the Queen's
own household. Perhaps, she thought, her visit
had lasted rather longer than expected and the
Dane had become concerned that she might have
begged to stay there. So whether the expression
that passed over his face as the great carved
doors opened was one of relief or undiluted ad-

miration, Fearn was unable to decipher except that, deep inside her ribcage, something thudded softly, as if trying to escape.

The Queen was the first to recover her surprise, having expected to see a large bewhiskered, overdressed Viking like King Swein Forkbeard, who fancied himself, rather than the tall, good-looking, neatly dressed younger man who met her with a respectful bow of his shining blond head. Aelfgyfu had never cared much for fair-haired men, but this one was quite exceptional, so her quick glance at Fearn implied.

'So, you have come to take away my dearest friend,' she said to him. 'I dare not tell you what this costs me, Aric the Ruthless, but you should know that you will have the custody of a jewel beyond price for one year only. Nor need I tell you what will be likely to happen if she should be damaged before she is returned to us.'

'Lady,' Aric said, 'your threat is unnecessary. If anyone is damaged, I believe it might be me. The Lady Fearn has already warned me of her intentions and I have no reason to disbelieve her.'

'Good. Then I have one favour to ask, before you deprive me of her company. Allow her to send me letters and to receive mine. Regularly. Do you have ink and quills where you live?'

'There are a few followers of the new faith where I live, lady. They will have the necessary tools. I will see that they are made available to Lady Fearn.'

The Queen nodded. 'It will no doubt be something of a novelty to have a slave who reads and writes. Look after her well.'

Aric was not inclined to get into a discussion with the Queen about whether her friend was his slave or his woman, although either term would be correct. The Queen wished to shame him, naturally. 'I intend to, lady,' he said, holding out his hand to Fearn. 'Come. It grows late. We must catch the next tide.'

The doors behind Fearn and the Queen were still open, giving Aric a view of the royal apartment, of her attendants, and the little seven-year-old girl whose curiosity was getting the better of her. While her mother's ladies were attending to the baby, Gemma sidled quietly through the door to stand just behind the Queen and Fearn, listening to the exchange and sensing the restrained animosity behind the politeness. With the open regard of a child, she stared at the handsome Dane and, as her mother embraced the Lady Fearn, saw how the Dane looked at her intently and smiled. To a self-confident child such as Gemma, this was the kind of attention she enjoyed so, returning the smile, she sidled back into the company of the attendants ready to tell them, at some later moment, what they had missed. Haesel was the only one to see what had happened.

Drawing on all his resources not to betray, even by the lift of an eyebrow, what he had just learned from that exchange of smiles, Aric bowed again to the Queen and led Fearn out of the palace complex into the dark night that reverberated to the noise of thousands of Vikings. Crowded into the port of Lundenburh and making their presence felt in true Viking style, they were drinking all the mead and ale they could lay hands on. Now Fearn understood why Aric had thought it necessary to bring her back with his own escort.

'Your men?' said Fearn, keeping close to Aric and Einar the cook. 'Are they carousing, too?'

'They're all on board, waiting to go,' he said. 'I told you.'

'I thought you meant tomorrow. You mean... now?'

'Yes, now. Can you imagine what it will be like for ninety-four longships all trying to catch the same tide? Our ships sail tonight. Last in, first out.'

'Alone?' she said.

He looked at her, trying to read her expression by the light of the torches.

'You'll hardly be alone with seventy men on board, will you?' he said. 'Yes, if you mean my ship, we shall be alone. Your friend the Queen thinks highly of you.'

'She is a good woman and dear to me. She is generous, too.'

'So I see. Those furs alone must be worth a fortune.'

The oarsmen were already in place as they climbed aboard where there were some smiles of welcome for the two finely dressed women and some silent admiration for the lady who could claim a personal friendship with her Queen. For her part, although her short time with Elf had been both happy and sad, Fearn's return to the ship was not as distasteful as she might once have thought, for the dangers she had feared had not materialised. Nevertheless, she warned herself not to place too much trust in these men, being the enemy intent on winning her beloved country for themselves, taking every advantage of Elf's weak husband, King Ethelred. His unreadiness to defend England was now causing havoc all over the country, of which her abduction was just such an example.

Fearn and Haesel had been asleep for several hours, lulled by the rhythmic sound of oars dipping and lifting, when the ship dropped anchor at the wide mouth of the Thames, just as it reached the sea. Padded with an extra layer of furs, Fearn felt the change of temperature as Aric joined her, too tired for conversation, but reluctant to waste the opportunity offered by Fearn's recumbent form to make him even more comfortable. Spooning himself into her back, he encircled her waist with his arm, made a deep growl of contentment and fell instantly asleep. She also slept, but awoke briefly when all was still to find that his hand had slipped beneath her breast and was cupping it, tenderly. The ship rocked, bringing back thoughts of her meeting with the Queen, of the shocking discovery that somewhere, somehow, Earl Thored had taken yet another woman who was not his wife and had not seen fit to make her, Fearn, aware of her true parentage. She could not imagine how it could have happened, or why, when neither Clodagh, her mother, nor Oslac, her father, would ever have condoned adultery.

Laying her hand over Aric's, she prised it carefully away from its snug position under her breast and placed it on his leg, reasonably sure it had arrived there in his sleep.

'What is it, lady?' he whispered.

'Go to sleep,' she replied.

'Tell me.'

'Are you married, Dane?' The question emerged before she could stop it.

There was a pause, in which she knew he smiled. 'If you agree to call me by my name, I will tell you whatever you want to know.'

'If I call you by your name, you will take it as a sign of friendship. And I am not your friend.'

'I think you should take the risk. We shall be together for a year and a lot of men will answer to the name of Dane. It could cause some confusion.'

'Aric, then,' she mumbled, unwillingly.

'Lady?'

'It is only fair that I should know something about the man I must be shackled to for a whole year. Wives are not usually best pleased when their husbands arrive home with female slaves. If there's going to be trouble, I need to be prepared.'

'There will be no trouble of that kind. I have neither wife nor children.'

'And lovers?'

He smiled again in the darkness. 'Now why on earth would you need to know that?' he said.

'I don't *need* to know. It makes no difference to me. No reason.' All the same, she had revealed the direction of her thoughts to him. That was a

mistake. She tried to rectify it. 'Just wondered.'
But it was too late.

Lifting himself up on one arm, he hung over
her and moved her head to face him so that she
felt his warm breath upon her cheek, the weight
of his arm on her, bringing back the memories,
still too recent, of a man's insistence. There was
barely time for him to say, 'Wondered what?'
before her breathless plea,

'No…no! Please don't. Let me go…please…
let me go.'

Immediately his hand lifted away as he rolled
back, taking her hand in his and holding it, hearing the fear in her voice, feeling her body begin
to tremble. Challenging one minute, fearful the
next. What a conflict of emotions, he thought.
What kind of abuse had brought her to this point
where a man's closeness crossed the boundary of
acceptance and caused a reaction close to panic?
She would have heard, he was sure, of the violence of Viking raids, the abuse of women and
nuns, the savagery of warriors venting their war
rage and lust upon innocents, the pointless de-
struction, the desecration of holy places. He had
never indulged in sexual depravity, nor did he
approve of his men showing that kind of mad-
ness, though he knew it happened, even so.
But this woman had suffered not at the hands

of Vikings, but her own husband, and now she was bound to believe that she had moved from one kind of violence to another. Interestingly, though, she wanted to know more about him, about wives, children and lovers. And if that was not a positive sign, then he did not know what was. 'Hush, lady,' he whispered. 'Lie quiet. You wanted to know about my lovers?'

Snatching her hand away from his, she turned her back to him with a loud, 'Tch! No, I don't. I've had my fill of that kind of boasting. Go back to sleep and keep your hands to yourself.'

This time, his smile was more audible, which did nothing to soothe Fearn's ruffled feathers, and it was some time before sleep returned, long after those conflicting emotions had been mulled over countless times. Why had her heart thudded so when he had come to the palace for her? Why had she secretly been pleased for Elf to meet him? Why had his looks of admiration mattered to her and why did she care if he had lovers, when experience told her that most men did, particularly pagans? And how would his family react to her, even over a limited time? What could she do to counter the rough ride they would be sure to give her? And how could she prevent Aric from taking the ultimate revenge on Earl Thored and doing to her what Thored had done to Aric's sister? If she could believe that the act would be in the name of love, then she would be able to bear it. But for revenge? Insidiously, the memory of holding Elf's infant stole into her thoughts as if to change her mind and once again her body trembled with longing. Until that moment with her own little nephew, she had never allowed the powerful urge of motherhood to take hold. And now it had, how would she manage to contain it?

Haesel's prediction of wind in their faces came true once more as the great Viking longship ploughed its way through the North Sea, this time heading north-east with the sails billowing and men hauling on ropes to angle them precisely. There was no time for conversation, for it seemed to take every man's concentrated effort to keep the ship on course, to look out for dangerous sandbanks, to navigate at night by the stars, to snatch food and sleep, and to avoid accidents on board. They happened, even so, when heads were clouted by beam or tackle, ankles twisted, hands cut by ropes. Then they were sent to Fearn and Haesel for treatment, always with miraculous results that kept the crew in awe of them to the point of veneration.

Yet there was hardly any contact with Aric himself who was on duty night and day, sleeping whenever he could, but not with Fearn. The difference between rowing up rivers and sailing on the open sea was now apparent to the two women and the feeling of being totally at the mercy of the elements was brought home to them constantly. Any contact Fearn had with Aric was brief, curt and impersonal. She and Haesel were no more than cargo who happened occasionally to be useful. Meals, in spite of having stocked up at Lundenburh, were spare and unpredictable, and each day spent on that leaping, bouncing ship was permanently damp, noisy and none too warm, despite the furs. And although neither she nor Haesel suffered from sickness, they were bruised by the continual lurching of their cramped quarters.

Although Aric had no time to speak to Fearn, Haesel and Hrolf managed to exchange a few words every now and then, changing the young man's 'protection duty' into a pleasure that benefitted the maid in many small acts of kindness, though he, too, slept where and when he could. It was this new experience, combined with the all-consuming effort of getting through each day and night, that drove from Haesel's mind the little scene she had witnessed at the palace when young Gemma had been, for a moment, in Aric's presence.

So while Fearn's relationship to Queen Aelfgyfu, to Earl Thored and to Kean was now known to Aric, Fearn herself was certain that the secret was hers. It was a disturbing element that remained on her mind constantly, for if it affected her status, it could also be seen as a danger, as Elf had pointed out.

Not surprisingly, conditions on board the sea-tossed ship were worse at night than by day, when obstacles could be seen. Once, when Fearn stumbled back to the shelter in the prow, ducking her head to avoid a diagonal rope, her foot slipped on the deck and sent her crashing down on top of a sleeping man swaddled in a walrus skin, hitting him with the empty wooden bucket she'd been carrying. Unfortunately, it was Aric who, with a loud oath and a yelp of pain, sat up to grab at her then, realising who he had hold of, struggled to his feet. 'Ye gods, woman!' he yelled, holding her. 'Is this how you try to kill me?'

Furious that it was him and not one of the sixty-nine others, she fought off his helping hands while trying to find somewhere to place her feet, darkness preventing her from seeing what she was doing or how to right herself.

Glimpses of his wild pale hair whipping across his face came as a shock, never having seen him without his tidy plait, and now a streak of dark blood on his forehead showed where the bucket had hit him. Resentment flared up inside her for all the times he'd ignored her needs and left her to her own devices. Lashing out at the wet face and tousled hair, she yelled back at him above the noise of the waves, venting her anger and frustration, her extreme discomfort and exhaustion. 'If I wanted…to kill you… Dane,' she panted, 'I would not…choose…a bucket…would I?'

She stood no chance of fighting him off, there on the wet deck that shuddered and bucked in the dark chaos of sleeping bodies with men pushing past to loosen ropes. Completely disoriented, she was thrown heavily into his arms and held fast, with no time to see how to evade him as his mouth found hers, stifling her cry of surprise and fury and stopping her hands in mid-air, quite missing their intended target. To be kissed was the very last thing she had expected, experience warning her that any violent reaction she could offer would invariably result in painful failure, as it had always done in the past. But now, as the deck shuddered beneath her feet, she was being supported by his iron-hard arms and submerged in the cool movement of his lips over hers, removing her from the chaos as no words could ever have done.

Her mind closed to everything happening around her, bringing her senses to bear on the soft dampness of his beard on her skin, the salt taste on his lips, his loose hair lying across her eyelids and the urgency in his kiss. His grip on her was still strong as he spoke, though his voice was hoarse with tiredness and want. 'Go back into your shelter,' he said. 'Go on…over there. You've disturbed my rest and half-killed me, so now you can offer me some compensation.'

'What?'

'Don't argue. Just get under cover.'

Not understanding what he could mean by compensation, she could not believe he intended more than the comparative comforts of her fur bed, but the choice of refusal was denied her as he manoeuvred her bodily into the shelter of oiled skins where the spray missed them by a man's length. Falling on to the damp furs beside Haesel, she found that Aric's intention was to join her, as he had before, landing with an ungainly thud by her side and pulling her towards him as the prow rose up on the crest of a wave. Fearn felt, however, that it was rest he needed, not what his searching mouth was telling

him. Nor did she intend to offer him any kind of
compensation for what had been no more than
an accident. Pushing him away with arms and
shoulders, she made her intentions clear. 'Get
off me!' she whispered, trying not to wake her
maid. 'Lie still and go to sleep. I do not want
you, Dane. Not now. Not ever! Will it take another blow to the head to make you understand?'

His slurred words were little more than a whisper on the wind as he flopped back, half-asleep.
'By all the gods, what was in that bucket?'

'Nothing. Unfortunately.'

His response emerged as a squeak as he lost
consciousness but not before he'd appreciated
his narrow escape and the humour of it, too. But
Fearn was able to see how close she had come to
a danger she had been dreading from the start,
which now seemed nearer after that spontane-
ous search for comfort when nerves and tempers
were frayed by days of hardship. Lying close to
him for the little warmth he could offer, she visited that brief moment again to savour the surprising tenderness of his lips that was so far from
her experience, the tingle of excitement it gener-
ated against her skin, the unfamiliar desire for it
to last longer, so new to her. Elf had assured her
it could be wonderful with the right man. And
that, Fearn supposed, was at the heart of the mat-

ter. The man to whom Elf was married loved her as an equal, whereas the man lying beside Fearn was out for revenge and, for one year, they were certainly not going to be equals. Slaves had no rights whatever.

It was the sight of seagulls that first alerted the men to the fact that land was not far away, that and the long dark line on the horizon ahead. With a good chance that they would reach the Danish coastline before noon, the men began a frenzy of washing, combing hair and beards, laughing and teasing, tidying the deck and coiling ropes. Haesel hung their bedding out to dry in the wind, smiling shyly at Hrolf who helped her to lift water buckets over the side. The egg-sized swelling on Aric's forehead had turned blue-grey under a veil of hair that he left unbound to cover it, careful not to disclose to anyone how the injury had been caused. On the few occasions when Fearn had seen him, he had not looked her way, although she had only realised how she was staring when Haesel nudged her. 'His hair,' Haesel said. 'I think he's washed it. It's so pale. Paler than mine.' Her own blonde curls were sticky with salt spray, framing her face like coiled springs. 'Do you want to keep your veil on?' she said. 'You know the Danish women don't wear them.'

'All the more reason for me to keep mine. I shall not try to look like them. I shall stay as English as I possibly can.'

'Mother Bridget said we should make ourselves useful,' Haesel reminded her, 'to whoever we live with.'

Fearn leaned over the side of the ship, watching the dark line of land in the distance. 'I shall not be making myself useful to anyone,' she said, though her defiance was lost in the thud of waves and wind. Anxious thoughts occupied her mind almost constantly, for although she knew much about the Danish ways from the women in Jorvik, hearing their language, seeing the way they dressed and ate, the anticipation that she would soon be a part of that life was less than appealing with new faces and names, new relationships, too. And although she tried to reason with herself that the expected hostility of Aric's family was not her concern, she knew how easily she could become the target of spite. The Dane had no business bringing her into a situation so loaded with problems. His revenge would be sure to rebound on her, rather than on Earl Thored. No, she would not co-operate with him, or make herself useful. Why should she, when the Dane had ridden roughshod over her right to freedom?

No doubt sensing Fearn's reception to any attempt to explain where they were, Aric left it to Oskar, his companion, to point out the various features as they sailed between headlands into a wide stretch of water. This, he told her, was known as a fjord. Fearn refused to be impressed. The land was flat, dotted with farms and squat, thatched dwellings. Small fishing boats rocked sleepily on a mirror of water and, on Aric's longship, the rowers took over from the slackened sails. At last, Fearn said, the constant wind would give them some respite from its force.

'It's brought some colour to your cheeks, lady,' Oskar said, smiling.

She held back the sharp retort. Oskar was a good-natured, pleasant-faced man doing his best to ease her transition into a new country. 'Have you any family to greet you?' she said, expecting a roll call of names.

'Not at Aggersborg,' he said. 'My wife and child are at Lindholm, lady. We shall reach them tomorrow, but not on this ship.'

'So why do we go to this… Aggersborg?' she said, turning to him.

'It's a new fortress town,' he said, 'where

some of the King's fleet is based. The men will return home from there, like us. At Aggersborg, we shall sleep on dry land at last and eat a good meal. Then we'll pick up Aric's ship and sail on up the Lindholm Fjord. It's not so far.'

Without this explanation, she assumed that Aric would have let her believe that his relatives would be there on the quayside at their first stop. There was, however, a large crowd of people there to watch the huge longship coming in, rowed precisely by more oars than they could count. Smoothly manoeuvring alongside the jetty with oars held upright, the men looked as if they'd been out on a day's jaunt instead of battling against the ocean. Every man was well groomed and clean, helmets and swords shining, the epitome of efficiency. Fearn's shelter had been dismantled and all her belongings stored in chests ready to be carried ashore and she as tidy as she could make herself, with Haesel's help. She longed to take a bath, to wash away the salt that clung to every part of her.

To Aric the Ruthless, who had achieved so much on that voyage, the moment was understandably precious to him and, as the crowds cheered and crowded alongside the ship, it was not Fearn who was uppermost in his mind, but the well-deserved reception for him and his men.

Not wishing to divert the attention to herself, Fearn stayed back in the curve of the prow from where she could see how proudly he stepped on to the quay followed by his men, the hugging and backslapping, the shouts of recognition and the squeals of young women delighted by his return. She saw their smiling eagerness to make him acknowledge them, which he did, telling herself it was none of her business, yet experiencing a certain irritation that he was ignoring her, at that moment. She knew that he would, eventually, show her off as the prize he had won, to applause, curious stares and questions. They would assume, of course, that she was a high-ranking slave and he would not contradict that. 'Haesel,' she said, turning away from the side, 'get ready. We're getting off this boat our way. Look, every one of them has his back to us. We can easily climb over the side on to the quay. The gap is only small.'

It was true. With the level of the quayside considerably higher than the water level, one large stride over the side would take them easily to the back of the crowd and, while they were looking in the opposite direction, she and Haesel could stroll away towards what looked like a market-place. 'Right,' Haesel said. 'Take your veil off and stow it in my bag. I can't stand being in this thing a moment longer.'

With everyone else caught up in the excitement of the moment, it was easier than they could have believed to clamber on to the quay and sidle round behind the seething crowd, then to saunter away, quickening their steps towards the stalls where foreign traders displayed their wares, direct from the sturdy merchant ships. In many respects, the merchandise was similar to that which they saw every day in Jorvik: barrels of wine from the Rhineland, cloth from Frisia and beautiful glass drinking vessels from the Far East. Although they were unable to trade without money, the relief of being upright on dry land, seeing familiar objects and women's clothes instead of men's, mixing with people other than warriors was like a drug that made them giggle at their own audacity, not caring how their freedom might end.

A group of stout merchants wearing huge fur hats caught their attention by their loud voices and waving hands as they stood almost knee-deep in furs of all colours, boxes of beeswax, barrels of honey and swords in tooled leather scabbards. Eyeing the furs, Fearn and Haesel discussed what animal had first worn them, not noticing how they were being quietly surrounded by large dark-skinned men with beards and exotic gowns, whose interest in Fearn's beautiful black hair became obvious when one reached out a hand to touch it. He grinned broadly as she whirled round to protest. 'Where you from?' he said, in very broken English.

'Lady,' Haesel said, grabbing Fearn's arm, 'come away. These men are looking for slaves.'

Fearn had seen their kind before in Jorvik, but never without the Earl's escort. In her eagerness for a few moments of freedom, she had forgotten the dangers facing young unprotected women, especially in a place like this where they were not known to anyone. 'Leave us alone,' Fearn said sharply to the richly dressed merchant. 'We are with the Jarl Aric.'

The men apparently found this amusing, their laughter showing expanses of discoloured teeth. 'Eh…no!' one of them told her. 'Aric…he always have the blonde women…not like you… I take you with me…yes?' He reached out again for her, but she reacted quickly to prevent it, pulling out her knife with one hand while holding Haesel out of the way with the other. At the same time, she glared at the man with the full force of her eyes and saw with satisfaction how his face reflected his utter astonishment, and some fear. 'Dah!' he whispered. 'This one…worth a *fortune*!'

The situation grew more serious, for now Fearn's most unusual feature was seen as a valuable asset and, as the danger grew, so she became more aware that the crowd of onlookers was dispersing, leaving them to deal with it as best they might. Even the other merchants were more curious than helpful. It was not Fearn's knife that saved the situation, but Haesel's uncanny premonition that they were at that moment being looked for and that, if she screamed loud enough, Jarl Aric, Oskar, Hrolf and Einar and others would know where to find them. Consequently, Haesel's screams were the loudest ever heard in the Aggersborg marketplace in living memory, surprising even Fearn, who used the nearest man's temporary shock to slash his fat be-ringed hand across the knuckles with her knife. His scream of fright seemed to echo Haesel's, and although it seemed like hours before help came, it was only seconds before Aric himself brought a group of his men, pushing through the swarthy merchants who had ringed their prey, scattering them like autumn leaves.

Furiously angry with herself for not having the foresight to see what was a common enough problem wherever merchants came and went, but never thinking it might happen to her, Fearn could have wept with relief at the sight of Aric

and his companions. She knew, however, that
Aric would also be furiously angry with her and
that he would have just cause to show it. So when
he took hold of her firmly by her upper arm,
he not only demonstrated his exasperation with
Fearn, but made his ownership of her more than
clear to the slave merchants.

'Mine!' he yelled at them. 'Idiots! Hands off
my property!'

Fearn gritted her teeth as she was hauled
along beside him, recalling how she had made
matters worse by not wearing her veil, as English ladies did, and by not wearing the neatly
coiled plait of Danish women, either. Wearing
one's hair loose was only for very young girls
and women of low morals. She made no protest
at Aric's rough treatment but, from the corner
of one eye, saw how Haesel's wrist was now in
the keeping of Hrolf, whose drawn sword was
ready for use.

Aric's message to the merchants needed
no elaboration, all except one of them putting
up their hands while backing away. The man
whose hand dripped blood was determined on
compensation, holding it up for Aric to see
and finding several oaths to hurl at Fearn, but
grunting his satisfaction as Aric found two
shining coins in his pouch to give him. Then,

still gripping Fearn in one hand, he turned the group back towards the longship where the very situation she had wanted to avoid awaited them, with an extra element of ownership made even more apparent.

All the way through the crowds' murmurs of approval, Aric marched Fearn, grim-faced and unrelenting in his hold on her, while she refused to protest even as she noticed the smiles and sniggers of those young blonde Danish women the merchants had mentioned. Clearly, they would not have minded being in her shoes, guessing where his possession might lead. Nor did Aric protest verbally at her foolishness as he led her up towards the high ramparts of the Aggersborg fortress, through the tunnelled gateway and out into the circular grid of wood-paved roads that led past workshops to the domestic area at the very centre. Her humiliation could not have been more public, but by now she had ceased to let it trouble her when all that mattered was her rescue and the man who had rushed to claim her. Not that she believed there was any more to his hasty response than ownership. Having brought her safely this far, he would not let her go so soon and so easily.

But she had been living at close quarters with this enigmatic man now for at least a week, enough time for her to rely on him for her safety and whatever comfort he could provide, and enough time also for her to experience the kind of reliability no other man had shown her in all her twenty-three years. The memory of his kiss was never far from her mind, though even that was hard to find a reason for, except the exasperation of a woman-starved man who'd had a heavy bucket dropped on him. He had kept well away from her as they crossed the ocean and now, to her, even his hold on her arm was somehow more acceptable than that.

Steering her into a massive building more impressive in size and furnishings than the one at home, Aric used his grip on her to make her face him. 'You and your maid will stay in this building. Don't try to escape again. My men guard all four entrances.'

'I was not trying to escape,' she retorted, putting up a hand to comfort her arm. 'If I had been, I would not have been hanging round the market stalls.'

He looked as if he had not heard her, but summoned a grey-haired woman who had waited nearby. 'This woman will see to you. Your chests will be in your room. Ask her for anything you need. She speaks your language.'

'We need a bath of hot water,' Fearn said, 'and

some food that doesn't taste of salt and a room without men in it, and we—'

'Ask her!' he cried angrily, turning to go. 'And do it politely.'

Chastened, she tried a shy smile of apology on the woman who, to her relief, smiled back with understanding. 'You are tired,' she said. 'Come this way, if you please.'

'What is this place?' Fearn said, following her to a corner of the hall.

'One of King Swein's palaces,' said the woman. 'It's used for administration mostly and for protection from our Norwegian neighbours. Here is your room.'

Of newer construction than her own small chamber in Jorvik, the room was more comfortable and spacious with rush matting on the floor, warm hangings on the walls, rug-covered chests and a curtained bed built into the wall. Her chests of clothes were already there and, at the first mention of a bath, a huge half-barrel lined with leather was carried in, soon filled with buckets of steaming water while Fearn and Haesel peeled off their sticky salt-soaked clothes.

Sweet-smelling herbs in the water released an aroma into the room, bringing them back to some semblance of normality after days of exposure to wind and sea spray, and when their hostess brought bunches of soapwort for them to make a lather, the cares of those cramped uncomfortable days dissolved into the steam. Lathering her mistress's hair, Haesel washed out the stiff tangles at last, leaving a shining mass of black curls to drip down Fearn's back and face as she stood to receive a linen towel to wrap around her head.

Feeling a rush of cool air on her shoulder, she assumed it was the woman returning with more water. Haesel's yelp alerted her to her mistake yet, instead of snatching at the towel, Fearn turned to see that it was Aric who stood transfixed in the doorway with the latch in his hand and an expression of incredulity on his face at the glorious sight of her body, naked from the waist upwards. Water and lather ran in rivulets over her breasts, with spirals of black hair sticking to her skin which was bronzed in areas where the sun and wind had caught it. Only an hour ago, she would have yelled angrily at him to wake him from his trance, but the warm aromatic luxury of the bath had soothed her rattled nerves and, instead of an angry reaction, she simply turned her back on him to receive the towel from Haesel whose horrified face almost made her smile. The door closed with a soft clack of the latch. 'Serve him right,' Fearn whispered, 'for walking in without knocking.'

'Lady, he saw you *naked*,' Haesel said, helping her out of the tub.

'Half-naked,' Fearn corrected her. 'As much as I've seen of him. Now it's your turn. Come on, get in before it cools.'

The sheer indulgence of having clean linen next to her skin at last, of having firm earth beneath her feet and the fresh scent of herbs around her, while not banishing all her cares completely, at least put them into a context where they could be thought about, free from the added complications of bodily discomforts. For one thing, she had perhaps underrated her need of Aric's protection, this being a foreign land where things would be done differently and where her standing as an earl's foster daughter would carry nothing like the weight it had in Jorvik, where she was known to everyone. In spite of her show of courage, the episode in the marketplace had shaken her more than she wished to admit and now Aric had made it plain that he thought her a foolish creature on whom he need expend no particular courtesies, not even to knock on her door.

Unsure of how to convince him that she was still a lady, she tried to summon some kind of strategy while standing by the small window which, covered with oiled linen, showed only that the light was fading. Haesel had gone with their hostess to bring a torch to light the lamps and to visit the kitchens for food. Behind her, the sound of the door latch made her turn in expectation of light and food but, against all her hopes, saw that it was Aric who entered and closed the door, waiting for her to speak.

But now too much had happened between them since she had been taken captive for her to think of him as simply the brutal overlord responsible for her husband's murder. He was more than this, yet possessing qualities that even she was bound to recognise, as his reception on the quay had demonstrated. And while each day for him had been taken up with the effort of keeping them all safe, for her the elements had stolen away many of her emotions and left her with resentment, confusion and fear of the future. Now, just when she had been sure of his continued avoidance, he was here again to see what had changed in her, now she was in his country.

'Well?' she said. 'Have you decided yet?'

'Decided what?'

'Whether I am to remain a noble-born earl's foster daughter or your slave to do with as you will. My ignoble march to this place would seem to indicate that I have already lost whatever status I once had.'

He moved slowly towards her while she pressed herself backwards into the wall below the window, trying to dodge sideways when he came too close. His body prevented hers from moving, so that she felt his breath on her face just before his mouth sought hers, his kiss giving her no answer except that it was careful enough for a noblewoman yet masterly enough for a slave. Still moist, sweet-smelling and more relaxed, her body bent into his, feeling the strength of his arm across her shoulders and his other hand in the bright loose curls of her hair, steering her head closer to his mouth for as long as he wished it. 'Woman,' he whispered, letting her breathe, 'don't ever run from me again. Swear it.'

'I told you,' she said, looking into the cool grey eyes, 'we were not running away. We wanted to get off that damned ship, that's all.'

'And you couldn't have waited?'

'For what? For you to parade us in front of that crowd, like booty?'

'Which I did. You yourself made that happen, impetuous little fool, and nearly got taken by slavers. Next time, you wait for my command.'

As if to reinforce his instructions, his kiss was hard and searching like that of a man suffering the same impetuosity.

Pushing at his shoulders, she prised herself far enough away to speak, though he would not release her. 'I have a mind of my own, Dane,' she said, 'and I shall find it very hard to obey your commands unless they suit my purpose. I have warned you, I shall do all I can to make you send me home early.'

His hand moved from her hair to roam over the soft curves of her hips and buttocks, telling her how much he wanted her after a year of celibacy. The bruise on his forehead could no longer be hidden by the lock of pale hair that hooked into his eyes and Fearn could not help thinking how much more vulnerable he looked with his hair loose, though his words belied that image. 'Listen to me,' he said. 'You cannot have it both ways. This is Denmark, not England, and if you want my protection, which you *do*, then you must do as I say. You will be here for a year…'

'As what?'

'As my woman. So it will be best for you to forget your grievances and try to learn something from the experience. You may even begin to enjoy it.'

'In your bed, you mean,' she said, struggling against him.

He held her, easily. 'Yes, in my bed. Or yours. Or anywhere else.'

She hated his flippancy when, to her, it meant so much more. 'Of course, you would say that, wouldn't you? It's what you implied to Earl Thored, isn't it? Did you think I would find that amusing?'

'No. That was crude. Forget that I said it.'

'I wish I could, but unfortunately, you see, that kind of remark has more effect on a woman than on a man. They would think it amusing. But I do not want it to happen to me. I did not want to bear my husband's child and I don't want yours, either. But you have answered my question, even so.'

'Which one?'

'Whether I remain as an honoured noblewoman or become a slave. You have removed the difference, Dane. It is *you* who wants it both ways, isn't it, by calling me *your woman.*'

'Take it whichever way you want, lady. The distinction clearly matters to you more than it does to me,' he said, too casually for her peace of mind. 'But I would remind you of the good manners you were taught as a noblewoman, which is to show due courtesy to those whose hospitality and help you accept.'

'Your family?'

'You will live with me in my house, with our servants. My younger sister and her husband, my uncle and cousin all live in Lindholm, too. They will help you to settle in.'

'I see. And you intend to haul me there by one arm, then, do you?'

'Do you want me to?'

She sighed, suddenly tired of an argument she was clearly not going to win. 'No,' she said, 'I don't.'

'Then either cover your hair or wear it as the young women here do.'

She nodded, closing her eyes as he kissed her again, tenderly.

'At last, I think we're getting somewhere,' he whispered. 'You will eat in here this evening. I shall eat and sleep in the hall. Tomorrow, we shall be away at daybreak.'

'I'm so tired. May I not sleep through the morning?'

'No. My men need to get home to their families. They cannot wait on your sleep, lady.'

'Yes, of course. I shall be ready.'

'Tonight, there will be a guard posted outside your door.'

'Oh? In case we try to escape?'

'In case of sleepwalkers,' he said, turning to go as the two women entered.

'Sleepwalkers?' Haesel said. 'Does he mean us, or them?'

'I have no idea,' Fearn said, sleepily.

Chapter Five

Despite her exhaustion, the days of discomfort, the nights without sleep, there were issues demanding Fearn's attention that kept sleep away long after she might have given in. The bed was like a warm cloud, the sheets dry and clean, her skin soothed by the woman's deft oily hands, yet still the memory of Aric's recent kisses, which she had done little to resist, returned in waves of guilty pleasure. After all she had said, after all that had happened, she found it quite impossible to pretend that his lovemaking bore the slightest resemblance to what she'd been used to, as a wife. Quite the opposite—his lips searching hers, his closeness, his arms and hands gripping her shoulders had made her forget everything that had gone before and to experience again that melting warmth flooding into her thighs. A small voice at the

furthest reaches of her mind suggested to her
that those brief moments when he had held her
might make up for the worst happenings of the
last few days, but, no, she would not let that
pass. He was the enemy and she had sworn to
make him regret what he had done. There must
be no weakening of her resolve in that. Even
that determination, however, provided no an-
swers to the problem of how to keep herself on
course when he would certainly do his utmost
to become her lover. He had already hinted to
her that she might begin to enjoy it, even against
her will, and a year was a long time to withstand a siege as potent as that.

The other issue to prevent her immediate
sleep was the meaning of Haesel's omen, the
second to have come to her since Barda's murder. It was as if her premonitions had suddenly
been released by the absence of his ill nature, a
consequence she put to her mistress as they prepared to sleep. 'You may well be right,' Fearn
said. 'Your sightings may not have been the only
qualities to be squashed. I can think of several
of my own. Tell me what you've seen.'

Haesel came to sit on the bed, her hair now
a halo of pale curls newly washed, her badly
scarred neck partly covered by her hand, hiding it from sight. 'It's a bit odd, my lady. I saw

something like the infirmary at Clementhorpe, you know, beds in a row with people in, all clean and tidy and with rushes on the floor. There was a lovely fresh smell like Mother Bridget used to have in her place.'

'Could it have been Clementhorpe you were seeing?'

'She was not there. You were not there either. None of the nuns, just beds. But it was not Clementhorpe. No, I'm sure it wasn't. Could they have an infirmary where we're going?'

'I doubt it. There won't be many Christians and there won't be any nuns. They do their own kind of healing and, from what I've seen of it, it's none too effective. The men on the ship were impressed by our remedies, but you know as well as I do that it was only the kind of thing we learned from Mother Bridget. We don't know exactly what your omen means, love, but we'll soon find out. And tomorrow, we both wear our veils and circlets when we go out.'

Haesel smiled and removed her hand from her neck. 'Yes,' she said.

No more had been said about the vivid picture in Haesel's mind, but it stayed with Fearn for some time, bringing back Mother Bridget's advice not to hold on to her resentments, but to make herself useful. Was this what she meant?

* * *

Their short journey to Lindholm a few miles further up the Limfjord was taken aboard Aric's own ship, a smaller, more streamlined craft than the great longship that had brought them across the sea. This one, he told Fearn, could not have done that with its shallower sides and smaller rudder. She had nodded her interest, used to hearing details of men's prized possessions, though to her shame she realised how her interest was focused more on his appearance that morning, how the early sun shone on his sleek fair hair now tied back again into the pigtail and how a sprig of pale pink cowberry blossom had been tucked into the top of it. To her annoyance, she knew that only a woman would have done such a thing and that he would not have known it was there, most likely. The bruise on his forehead had completely disappeared, surprising even her. Such injuries usually lasted over a week, in her experience. Was this another female talent suddenly to emerge after the withdrawal of Barda's malevolence? It was certainly beginning to look that way.

The fjord was at least as wide as the great River Ouse that flowed through Jorvik and was in many ways similar with low-thatched farm houses on either side, animals grazing, fields of wheat and barley, rich green meadowland, fishing boats and nets hanging up to dry. As the fjord narrowed round a small egg-shaped island, a dense cluster of wooden houses spread backwards from the water's edge to make a sizeable settlement without the dense pall of smoke that hung over the rooftops of the town she knew in England. Here, the air was clean and fresh, the water clear blue, shimmering in the northern light.

The sound of Einar's horn blasted across the water, alerting the settlement to the arrival of the Jarl's ship, at last. 'That should wake 'em up.' He grinned. On board were Aric's closest companions and those others who lived at Lindholm, among them the young warrior who had teased Fearn and been threatened by her, now one of her most respectful admirers. As before, a crowd had gathered on the quay to greet them, women with infants and excited children, men with sleeves rolled up come from their work, older relatives and a scattering of younger women with eager smiles to greet their lovers. Fearn felt their curious stares and knew that inevitably she would be seen as the Jarl's English captive, for his mission had been quite specific, to make demands on the English and to return his nephew to his own kin. Their eyes searched for the boy.

She was helped on to the quay by Aric's strong hand, the object of scrutiny from dozens of strangers whose smiles gave way to open stares, then to frowns and murmurs, then to hands over mouths as they saw not only her beauty but her most startling feature, to them a sign so unusual that it must mean she was an enchantress. Even the man to greet Aric first, obviously a senior relative, had a barely concealed frown for Fearn. His eyes were pale and icy, his voice heavy with suspicion. 'Who's she?' he asked. 'And where's the boy?'

'We'll not go into that now, Uncle,' Aric said, clasping the older man by the arm. 'This is the Lady Fearn of Jorvik, daughter of Earl Thored of Northumbria. She will stay with us for a year.' He drew Fearn forward by the hand, expecting his uncle to take it in his, to welcome her with a smile, at least.

There was no contact, no smile. Instead, the uncle drew a young woman forward by the arm, though she was clearly unwilling. 'And this is your cousin Freya, young man, or had you forgotten it in your thirst for novelty?'

'Freya,' Aric said, ignoring the cutting sarcasm. '*Hej*. Are you well?'

'Never mind asking her how well she is,' the uncle snapped. 'Perhaps you'd better explain—'

'Uncle, the explanations will wait until later. I ask that you greet our guest.'

But Fearn had seen the distress in Freya's eyes and knew with the instinct of a woman that she preferred not to be a part of this confrontation. Reaching out for Freya's hand, she smiled at her stricken face. 'You have nothing to fear from me, Freya. I am a complete stranger here, but I can understand what's being said. We have a large Danish population in Jorvik, you know, and I would be glad of your friendship.' She watched the relief spread over Freya's sweet face and the warmth change her eyes to a smiling blue. Like so many Danish women, she was fair-haired and neatly dressed in a white pleated kirtle over which was wrapped a length of blue fabric held up with a pair of huge bronze brooches, and though she could not have been called a beauty except by one who loved her, her figure was perfect. It had not taken Fearn more than a moment to detect the ambition for his daughter in the uncle's tone, a development that Fearn would do nothing to upset, if she could help it. If Freya was meant for Aric, then so much the better.

The greeting from Aric's brother-in-law and two young nephews was less confrontational. A bear hug from Olof, his younger sister's husband, squeezed the air from his lungs and the squeals of joy from the two lads took no account of Aric's guest or her strange eye-colouring. 'They hoped you'd be bringing Tove's lad back with you,' Olof said, glancing sideways at Fearn. 'Wenda's going to be very disappointed.'

'Where is she?' Aric said. 'And little Kol? Where is he?'

Fearn listened carefully. Her reception was not unexpected, in the circumstances, but so many nuances of tone suggested that there were complications in these relationships no guest could foresee. Instantly, the two boys watched their father's face to see how he would answer. 'At home,' Olof said. 'Kol has been ill for months. All winter through. It's his breathing. Wenda's at her wits' end.' There was some resignation in his words that disturbed Aric. He was aware of his sister's expectations and knew that her disappointment would be very great.

'Perhaps,' Fearn said, 'we should go and see her and the child?'

Understanding what she meant by this, Aric hesitated, his eyes searching hers for the optimism he hoped to see, yet knowing of the resistance they would encounter to Fearn being there instead of Kean and also the superstitious nature of his people. He thought the risk was worth it. 'Yes,' he said to Olof. 'The lady is a healer.

Would Wenda allow her to see Kol? Surely there can be no harm in it?'

Olof shrugged as if the decision was not his to make. 'I have no objection, but she might have. She's set her heart on having her sister's bairn to live with us.'

'We're wasting precious time,' Fearn said, tiring of the prevarications. 'Show me the way, if you please. Haesel, come. Stay close to me.' Her businesslike tone seemed to motivate them and so, cutting a swathe through the crowd, Olof and his sons led the way on wood-planked pathways between the timber houses to the upper end of the settlement where the fenced gardens and dwellings were larger, many of them surrounded by outhouses, huts and paddocks. Clearly, this was where the wealthier members of society lived with servants and slaves and more space to keep domestic activities separate.

One house of medium size had fewer extra buildings set around it and, as they walked up the pathway to the door, the two young lads burst into the house, letting out a cloud of blue smoke that made Fearn turn aside to catch her breath. Holding a hand to her mouth and nose, she followed the men inside, adjusting her eyes to the gloom in which the only source of light was the roaring fire on the floor hearth in the centre of the room, filling the place with woodsmoke. Fearn was used to the smoky rooms of Jorvik where the doors were left open during the day-time and the smoke found its way out through the thatch. Many people suffered from bronchial problems, but Fearn had seen nothing as serious as that of the red-faced child who lay in his moth-er's arms, gasping for air and coughing feebly.

Aric crouched down before his sister, pecking her on both cheeks with a smile of deep concern. 'I'm back, Wenda. See? What's to do?'

Wenda's bloodshot eyes filled with tears. 'Kol,' she whispered. 'He cannot even sleep for coughing. I don't know what else to do. Close the door, one of you. He'll catch the cold and I'm trying to keep him warm.'

'Will you allow this lady to see him? She's a healer. From England. She can help.'

For the first time, Wenda appeared to see the other woman silhouetted against the open door-way. When it closed, Fearn became just another shadowy figure, an adult where there ought to have been a ten-year-old boy. Wenda's arms closed more tightly around the child, making him cough again, protesting, 'No! No…no!'

Tapping Aric's shoulder, Fearn signalled to him to change places with her. Then, crouching where he had been, she asked, 'How old is Kol, lady?'

There was a hint of hysteria in Wenda's frantic rocking and now the tears ran freely down her cheeks on to the child's overheated body. 'Three years,' she sobbed. 'You cannot do anything for him. I don't know who you are. Best for you to leave.'

'Never mind who I am, just tell me about your child. Does he cough blood?'

Her head shook. 'Just coughs. Cannot sleep nor eat. He's slipping away.'

'Will you trust me to touch him, lady? I have some experience with little ones. See, let me feel his forehead…there…like that.' The child's skin burned under her touch while his mother watched Fearn's hand like a hawk. 'Look at me, lady,' Fearn said. 'Look into my eyes. There's nothing for you to fear. This is not magic, but healing. There are things the child needs, all of which are here around you. Will you let me hold the child and start the healing? See, I have no charms, no spells, only my hands. Let me take him…there… he's quiet now.' Gently, she took Kol into her arms and stood up, telling the dazed mother to come with her to the door, but anticipating her resistance.

'No! Not outside!' Wenda protested. 'He's so frail and it's cold.'

Again, Fearn turned to her. 'Kol needs to breathe fresh air,' she said. 'Come with me. We'll make him better together. Just do as I say.' Soothing the mother with her voice and matter-of-fact manner, she took her and the child out into the sunshine, followed by Aric, Olof, Haesel and the boys, who watched with interest as, layer by layer, the infant was peeled of its furs, woollens and bindings that reeked of stale, eye-watering urine. As Fearn sat on a log, Kol lay quietly on her lap, gasping deep lungfuls of clean air, while his red cheeks changed visibly to the palest rosebud pink. 'Haesel, look in my bag and find the balm we use for breastfeeding mothers. That's it. Now, lady,' she said to Wenda, 'take a good dollop of that and smear it round his little bottom where all the red is. Give him a week and this little fellow will be galloping round out here, learning to pee into the grass instead of into your best linen.'

'Oh,' Wenda said, wiping her eyes with her apron. 'He's stopped coughing.'

'Get the boys to gather those cowslip flowers over there,' Fearn said, 'by the bagful. Make an infusion and spoon some into Kol three times a day. Do you have marjoram?'

'Yes, it lasts all winter here,' Olof said.

'Then gather the flowering tips and infuse that, too. He can have that between meals to soothe his throat. Then, put his bed out here, wrap him loosely and let him sleep outside until he recovers. Look, he's nodding off already.' Sure enough, Kol's eyes were rolling into heavy eyelids and, as Fearn re-covered him in a loose blanket and rocked him gently, the child slept at last without another cough.

'And at night?' Olof said. 'We have to keep the fire going.'

'Then find a way to let the smoke out,' she replied, handing Kol back to his mother. 'Feed him some gruel when he wakes, lady. Little and often until he recovers his strength. Will you allow me to come and visit you tomorrow?'

'Oh, yes…would you?' Wenda said. 'Thank you…*thank you* for coming.'

'I'm glad to be of help,' Fearn said, though as she walked away towards the complex of buildings that was Aric's home, she wondered what might have happened if she had not, if she had refused, because Kol was Aric's nephew.

Aric was more positive. 'Well,' he said, 'that's at least two of my family you've managed to impress in the first hour of your arrival.'

'Only two?' she retorted. 'Then I must try a

little harder. Though I don't know why I should try at all, when my only reward is captivity.'

'Are you not rewarded by your success in healing the sick?'

Fearn stopped in her tracks, whirling round to face him. 'You must know, Dane, that there was little wrong with that child that common sense could not cure,' she said, angrily. 'That was not healing. That was about giving the child air to breathe, that's all. Swaddling a child of three winters like a babe and then wondering why it cannot sleep for soreness. Keeping it in a dark smoke-filled room for three years. Why could not Olof fix the problem? It doesn't have to be like that. Were the two boys kept like that, too?'

'Calm down,' he said. 'Wenda is Olof's second wife. Kol is her first child with him. She won't take advice from anyone about rearing the babe. That's why I'm amazed she listened to you. Perhaps now she'll let Olof fix the smoke problem. She thinks the air is too cold for infants and Kol is not the most robust of children. You handled her with tact. That was clever of you.'

'Yes,' she said without thinking. 'Clever of me not to have taken advantage of the situation. I might have killed the child. Is that what you're saying?'

Aric grabbed her arm, holding her back when

she would have stalked off. 'That was a stupid thing to say. You could no more kill a child than fly,' he scolded. 'Don't put words into my mouth.'

'So who did?' she retorted. 'Why did you introduce me to your uncle as Earl Thored's daughter when you know that I am not?' Did he know the truth? she wondered.

'A slip of the tongue. I should have said foster daughter,' he said, releasing her. 'Over there, look. That large house with the shingled roof. That's where we live.'

She looked, but would not let him know how very impressed she was. 'That's where *you* live,' she said, sullenly. 'I shall *exist* for a year.'

'That's entirely up to you,' he replied. 'I don't mind if you exist, as long as you cure us all of our ailments. And if you can control your sharp tongue, start to call me Aric.'

Fearn had assumed that, in material and style, the houses of Lindholm would in most respects be similar to those in Jorvik, so she was not surprised to find that the long hall with the central fireplace and wooden platforms running along each side was essentially the same except for the richness of the materials. Which, she thought bitterly, they would be, wouldn't they, with all that silver looted from England? No hard earth floor here, but smooth timber planks to walk on, timber to line the walls and a large shelf running under the roof where she saw sacks and boxes for storage. Bunches of herbs, wormwood and lavender hung from the beams, giving off a clean scent so very different from that in Olof and Wenda's all-purpose room.

'Is this where you sleep?' Fearn said, looking round at the piles of furs and cushions covering the low platform. She thought she knew the answer already.

'The servants and slaves sleep here in the living quarters,' Aric said. 'I've had more chambers built into the far end. One of them will be ours.'

It would have been useless, she knew, to make a fuss about sharing a room with him for, in the end, that was what he intended. A middle-aged woman stood with her back to them, her hands busily working on the vertical threads of a large upright loom that leaned against the wall, her hair covered by a white scarf knotted at the back. The door at one side of her was wide open, letting in the sunlight and a couple of chortling brown hens.

'Deena!' Aric said in a loud voice. 'She's deaf,' he explained to Fearn.

The woman turned and smiled at them, placing a hand flat over her heart and looking at

Fearn with interest until Aric told her, 'Lady Fearn. English.'

Deena nodded, then pointed a finger from one to the other. 'Your woman?' she said.

Fearn's *no* collided precisely with Aric's *yes*, bringing a broad smile to the woman's homely face as she understood the situation, as if it would only be a matter of time. 'Ah!' she said, turning back to the loom.

'If you think saying it will make it happen any faster,' Fearn said, crossly, 'then think again. It won't.'

'She's a slave,' Aric said. 'It doesn't much matter to her one way or the other.'

'It matters to *me*, one way or the other.'

'Me, too,' he retorted, smiling. 'Come and see our room. Over here.'

The chests and baggage brought from Jorvik were already in the room and, even though several chests belonging to Aric were there, there was still plenty of space for the handsomely carved bed with dragon-headed posts, several stools and a table on which rested a magnificent gold gem-studded reliquary casket, obviously stolen from a Christian monastery. Aric saw her astonishment. 'Yes,' he said. 'It's Irish. Like Deena. Amazing, isn't it? Worth a lot.'

'To those monks who made and owned it,'

Fearn said, holding back her anger, 'it would have been beyond price. But I suppose you killed them to get it.'

'Somebody did. I bought it and Deena from the same merchant. Now, I shall leave you here to arrange things as you wish while I go over to my uncle's house. It looks as if I might have some explaining to do.'

'That was inevitable, wasn't it? So what do you intend to do about your cousin Freya? It looked to me as if you had an obligation there. Do you?'

A mischievous look crossed his face as he answered, 'My uncle thinks so.'

'And Freya? Does she think you have? Would you marry her?'

'I might. D'ye think she'd make me a good wife?'

'Your own cousin? We Christians don't advise that but, as a pagan, you'll do whatever you wish, I expect. But if I were Freya...'

'Which you're not.'

'If I were, I'd not wait for a man like you who brings home another woman.'

Before she could turn away, he caught her round the waist and drew her in hard against his body, pressing her against the bulge of his rising desire. 'If you were my little cousin Freya,' he said, touching the tip of her nose with his, 'you would do exactly as your father bids you, as she does. She would not refuse me, if I made a bid for her, because she goes with her father's farm and whoever takes her takes the farm. And he wants me to do that because he knows I'm the best.'

'The best at what?' she whispered over the loud thud of her heart.

'At breeding quality horses. That's what he does. He's not going to hand that over to a man he doesn't know, believe me. I've been doing it with him since I could walk.'

'So Freya doesn't have a say in it?'

'In theory, she should. In reality, no.'

'I see!' she cried, pushing at him to escape. 'So go and make your peace with them both. I wish you well of it.' Her struggles did not have the desired effect, for he was too strong for her and they were too near the fur-covered bed to avoid falling on to it with a soft thud, with Fearn trapped beneath him and no chance of avoiding his kisses. For her, the room darkened into the sensuous warmth of his mouth moving over hers, stopping all those peevish thoughts at the talk of him marrying his cousin, as if such an important step meant nothing more than the gain of a stud farm. Her resistance melted with a sudden sweet urge of desire when his hand strayed boldly on to her breast, possessing it, kneading it gently over the loose linen of her gown. And although memories floated through her consciousness like ghosts, she let them pass by without stopping, for this was different in every respect, especially in the tenderness that brought neither pain nor fear. It would have been so easy, then, to let him go on, to go with him to the end and to discover for herself what she had never yet experienced, for she knew now that if anyone could teach her, this man could. 'Stop,' she whispered, grasping his wrist. 'Please…stop!'

'Why?' he said, kissing her neck.

'Because I'm pleading with you. I'm not ready for this yet. Give me time.'

He sighed and rolled away, leaving her empty, relieved and disappointed, too, and quite unsure of when the right time would be. Standing up, he held out a hand to pull her upright, a small gesture that had never been offered to her before, easing her again into his arms. 'Can you feel that?' he whispered.

She could, hard against her womb. 'Yes,' she said, trembling.

'I shall not force you,' he said. 'That's never been my way. I can wait.' With the pad of his thumb he wiped away the single teardrop from the corner of her green eye. 'I'll be back before supper. Don't go away. You hear me?'

'Yes, I hear you.'

'Deena will prepare it. The kitchen is outside. Go and take a look round.'

She nodded, then he was gone.

It was some time before she could rouse herself, wondering how it might have been and for how long she would be able to hold him off. Their room was not dark, lit by what at home they called 'a wind eye', cut in the wall with a wooden shutter like an eyelid which could be opened and closed with a rope pulley. Outside this, the shingled wooden roof overhung the walls all round to make a dry walkway where, in bad weather, the animals and hens took shelter. She wondered why Olof and Wenda had not built their house in the same way, with the kitchen outside and a covered pathway between. Looking round outside with Haesel, they saw that there were storerooms with fish drying on racks and hams hanging from the ceiling, sacks of grain ready for grinding and boxes of spices imported from foreign lands.

They discovered two more slaves, one a young man named Ivar, who did the heavy work, and a girl of Haesel's age named Eve, a Christian brought from Cornwall who spoke a dialect they had difficulty in understanding. Such a pity, Fearn and Haesel agreed, that people should be owned by others to do with as they wished, but how far was these people's plight from her own and how much better had they been before? Thinking of her own life as the wife of a brute and the daughter-in-law of a scold, not to mention the father who had given her away, perhaps her own degree of slavery was preferable, in many ways.

Aric strode on towards his uncle's house, half-closing his eyes against the bright glare of the sun on the fjord where, in the distance, the small island of Egholm lay like a green-herb pancake. His uncle was expecting him and, as Aric had anticipated, his uncle's sister Astrid, too, a woman of mature years and huge self-importance. They were waiting for him, leaning on the gate to the paddock where a herd of beautiful riding horses cropped the grass. 'Took your time, young man,' Uncle Uther said, taking the stem of hay out from between his lips and looking Aric up and down as if he knew exactly what his nephew had been doing.

'Aunt Astrid,' Aric said, kissing her cheek dutifully. Her skin was as wrinkled and as brown as old parchment, her white hair scraped back tightly from her face and tied securely in a knot. Loaded with brooches, necklaces, arm-rings and bracelets, the impression was one of high status and wealth, which was not far from the truth, but had never intimidated her *jarl* nephew. 'Are you well?' he said.

'No. I'm getting old and my legs ache. What's all this about a woman? You were supposed to be bringing your nephew back with you, not an earl's daughter. Did you not manage to find him?'

Aric leaned on the gate beside his aunt, who had never married and who had taken over the role of matriarch in her widowed brother's household, having simply marched in one day with all her belongings, whether Uther and his daughter liked it or not. They had not dared to argue. 'I did find him,' Aric said. 'He's a handsome lad, being fostered by Earl Thored's man and his wife. And perfectly happy.'

'Well, *he* may be,' said Aunt Astrid, 'but his family are not. This is where he belongs. We thought you understood that.'

'Couldn't keep his mind on the job with that skew-eyed young thing there,' Uther said, sourly. 'She's charmed him all right. And what about my Freya? How do you think *she* likes it? Eh?'

Again, Aric ignored his uncle's bitterness. 'I do understand,' he said. 'I have brought her away for one year, that's all. I shall take her back after that and bring Kean home with me. They know that. It's expected. It gives the lad time to make adjustments. Besides that, it pays Earl Thored back for taking Tove and having her man killed. He has my nephew and I have his daughter. That's a just revenge.'

'Aye,' Uther said, spitting a sliver of hay out of his mouth, 'and I suppose you think it gives you nice time to do with her what bloody Thored did to our Tove, do you?'

Aric had had enough of his uncle's insinuations. 'Uncle, I think that my plans are my own business, not yours. You can suppose what you like, but I have my own good reasons for doing what I did. Kean will come to live here with my sister and her family eventually, but if you insist on trying to arrange everyone's lives for them, don't be surprised if they object. I am a king's *jarl* now, Uncle. No one but the King may tell me who to marry or, for that matter, who I take to my bed.'

'Hmm!' Astrid murmured, glancing at her brother's glowering profile. 'There now. That's you told. So, *Jarl Aric*, may one venture to ask what your plans are for your cousin Freya? Does she continue to hope, after a year of waiting for you, or does she start to look elsewhere?'

But before Aric could answer, his uncle slapped a hand down hard on the gate. 'Freya goes with the farm, Astrid! I've told you that. It's his for the asking, but he'll have to take Freya as well. It's her home. It's what she wants.'

'How do you know that?' Aric said.

'Because I do. You grew up together. She'll make you a good wife.'

'And if I don't make her a good husband, what then?'

'Argh! Men have their diversions, we all know that. The woman from England is not going to make a fuss, is she, not just for a year, and I don't suppose Freya would, either. She knows you've had women.'

'I've heard enough!' Astrid snapped, pushing herself away from the gate. 'I sometimes wonder what you've got between your ears, Uther Borgsen, when you can knowingly put your own daughter into that kind of situation. A minute ago you asked him how he thought Freya might like him having another woman in his bed and now you're urging him to go ahead and do just that. Don't tell me this is all about the stud farm, Uther. Where is she?'

'Who?'

'Freya, of course!'

'She's…er…around somewhere.'

'Huh!' Astrid marched off, limping a little whenever she remembered.

Uther sighed, heavily. 'Tell me about this woman of yours,' he said. 'And tell me about young Kean, too. Does he resemble his mother?'

Together, Fearn and Haesel explored the large plot of land on which Aric's house stood, soon realising that it was indeed the largest and grandest in Lindholm with not only more cultivated land, but also the houses of Aric's tenants, each with a vegetable plot attached. Beyond that was a patch of woodland from where the villagers had obtained their timber, but which was sure to be the source of berries, nuts and mushrooms, so necessary to Fearn for supplementing meals and for healing, too.

'Let's take a look,' Fearn said. 'We may find something we need to start a new stock of herbs. I can already see elder and hawthorn and rowan, and there are brambles for blackberries and—'

'Shh! Wait!' Haesel whispered. 'Look, over there.'

Fearn looked where the maid pointed, keeping the thick trunk of an oak tree between her and two figures walking one behind the other, stealthily, their hands linked like lovers. 'It's Freya,' she whispered, feeling her heart begin to hammer as she saw how a narrow shaft of sunlight caught the fair hair of the man who led her into the woods. 'But who's the man? Can you see?'

'Yes,' Haesel said. 'You know him. Remember the one who tried your circlet on and teased you to get it? The Jarl knocked him over.'

'Him!'

'Yes, that's him all right. His name is Loki. Did you think it might be…?'

Fern nodded, riveted by the sight of Freya, Aric's sweet cousin, stealing a few precious moments alone with one for whom she had waited a whole year while he was in England and while Aric assumed she was waiting for him. Knowing they ought to turn away to respect the lovers' privacy, they remained instead like statues to watch how Loki turned to catch her in his arms, bending her body, their fair heads merging into one blond mass. Then, as they watched, the lovers sank down into the soft litter of the woodland and disappeared behind a huge clump of ferns, and Fearn found that she was trembling with a relief she could not begin to understand. 'Let's go back,' she whispered. 'We have some unpacking to do.'

Chapter Six

Aware that the discovery of Freya's secret lover must not be allowed to influence her attitude to Aric, Fearn found that she could think of no good reason why it changed anything, only that, in some way, it did. She could not say why she was relieved, but then spent the next few moments imagining an unwilling Freya in the arms of her cousin, loving another man but being pressured into obedience to her father. Despite the lip service to women's choice in who to marry, the facts were often quite the opposite, as she knew from personal experience. Poor Freya. What a dilemma she faced. As for Aric's reaction to Freya's preference for one of his own men, that would be hard to imagine, but whether he would insist on marrying his cousin in order to acquire her father's stud farm was a question she could not even guess at. He had not been named 'the

Ruthless' without good reason, so much was certain, having seen and experienced that particular trait for herself.

He had taken her up to the top of the hill that evening from where they could see the settlement of Lindholm extending down to the fjord, each plot neatly fenced and tended. The hillside itself was the burial ground for countless ancestors, each cremation enclosed by stones, triangular, circular and boat-shaped, casting long shadows in the evening sunlight. Sand blew in from the shore like a fine veil meant to conceal them, silently gathering around their feet, and although Fearn knew she was meant to admire the views of the flat, lush fields and sparkling water, it was the stealthy encroachment of sand that made a more lasting impression.

To her relief, she had been allowed to sleep with Haesel that night, finally to catch up on those hours of wakefulness.

Refreshed and washed in clear water from the well, they relished the touch of dry linen on their skins, dry shoes on their feet, hair silky and clean. Then, by themselves, they went to the house of Olof and Wenda, reasonably optimistic about the child's progress and relieved to enter an almost smokeless room where work was in progress above their heads to remedy the problem. Through the door at the far end, they could hear squeals of laughter as Kol played his own version of skittles with his two older brothers while his doting mother leaned on the doorframe smiling encouragement, her spindle whizzing on a long thread.

Half an hour later, Fearn and Haesel sauntered away with Olof, who had climbed down the ladder to tell them more of Kol's miraculous recovery and the first night's sleep he'd had in three years. It was, he told them, entirely due to whatever kind of magic Fearn had worked. She had been sent by the gods.

Fearn let the reference to magic go. 'I had not realised,' she said, 'that Kol was your wife's first child. Perhaps it was some sound advice she lacked, more than anything?'

Olof stopped, not wanting to go beyond the plot. 'He's her first child with *me*,' he said. 'Kol is her second. She had a previous relationship.'

'Oh, I'm sorry. I've got it wrong, haven't I? May I ask what happened?'

Sadly, he shook his head, looking beyond her. 'She was not married at the time and the father would not accept it.'

'Not accept his own child? Why ever not?'

'It had a deformed foot, for one thing and, for another, it was a girl. He said it could not be his. He said it should be exposed. Left out to die.'

A shiver of cold horror wrapped around Fearn's shoulders like an icy blanket while, beside her, Haesel let out a wail of anguish, stifled in her hands.

Olof noted their reaction, but went on with the terrible saga. 'She had no choice, poor woman. Her father agreed. He didn't want her and her deformed child living with them any more than the child's father did. They took it from her. Days old, it was. She nearly went mad with grief. I'd lost my wife a year earlier, so I took Wenda to live with me and the boys. They needed a woman and so did I. And I thought the lads would be good for her. Then Kol came along and she was so…well…possessive, you might say. Wouldn't let him alone. Wouldn't let him go outside. Cossetted him till…well…you've seen. If you'd not talked some sense into her, lady, the lad would have died. You wouldn't think her own father would be so uncaring, would you? But he was. A hard man, that one.'

'That's Aric's father. So…he died?'

'Aye, soon after I took her in. He's up there on the hillside.'

Aric had not identified the particular boat-shaped stones where his father was, but Fearn had seen him hesitate, then move on. 'And their mother?' she said.

'She divorced him when Aric and Wenda and Tove were young. Went off to live in Iceland. Made a new life for herself. He's not told you?'

'Aric? No, to be fair, I've never shown any interest. It doesn't concern me.' She spoke the words with a certain defiance although they were not altogether true. It concerned her very much that he had been brought up to believe that such appallingly cruel practices were acceptable methods of dealing with deformity and unwanted girls. Did he still believe that? she wondered.

'Where did they take it?' she said. 'The infant.'

'Up there, in the cemetery. It disappeared.' Olof was reluctant to go into any more detail, so omitted to tell her how the woman he had come to love had had to be forcibly restrained from running after them to find her child. It was a dark period of their lives that would never be erased from their memories.

Fearn wondered what effect the tragedy had had on Aric, abandoned by his mother, a witness to the mental distress of his sister, the loss of an older sister and then the loss of his fearsome father. And in spite of all that, he had shown himself to be capable of leading men in the King's following and had been created Jarl, with all the many responsibilities and benefits that went with the position. How could she not spare just a small measure of admiration for such a man? If she had not been abducted by him and forced into this humiliating position, she would have done so but, as it was, her anger was still too raw to listen to anything like reason. It was her body's responses that were refusing to conform, for now she could no longer deny watching for his shadow to fall across the doorway, hearing his voice in the yard or hall, or watching his movements while pretending to do just the opposite.

Partly to boost her hostility again after those moments of more tender reflection, she took advantage of his presence in the yard where he held a beautiful filly by her halter while talking to one of the grooms. Dismissing the man as she approached, he fondled the filly's velvet nose and waited for Fearn to speak, but when she did not, he saw that her eyes were troubled. 'What is it, lady? Is the child not improved?'

'It's not that,' she said. 'Kol is quite recovered. Wenda cannot thank me enough. Olof believes the gods sent me. They didn't. It was partly the

smoke and partly your sister's over-protective-
ness after the loss of her child.'

'Ah! So she told you.'

'No, Olof did. I wonder why you did not. It
might have helped.'

The hand continued to fondle while the filly
rolled her eyes at the intruder. 'The short answer
to that,' he said, 'is that we…you and I…haven't
yet reached a position when we can talk about
ourselves, have we? You are too angry to ask
anything and I am waiting for you to soften some
more.' He noted the way her eyes swung away
from his. 'Just in case you bite my hand off.' He
smiled. 'You tried once, remember? Once bit-
ten, twice shy.'

'I need to know,' she said, 'whether you still
approve of exposing unwanted babies. I find the
practice barbaric, and totally unnecessary.'

'It was not up to me to approve or disapprove,'
he said, softly. 'It was my father's decision and
the man Wenda claimed had fathered it. He denied it was his.'

'But it was, wasn't it? Olof believed her.'

The filly tossed her head at the sharp tone.
'Shh!' Aric said. 'I've told you, it was not my
business and I was not able to influence my father's decision. It's not unusual here to reject
girl infants, lady. They're not as useful as boys,

and dowries are expensive. And what chance would Wenda alone have had to provide a dowry for a lass with a twisted foot? Who would...? Fearn...?'

Her name was flung after her as she stalked away into the house, her eyes blazing, her mind wondering, not for the first time, about the kind of God who allowed such things to happen to women and about the kind of society who saw the arrival of new life in terms of usefulness and cost. In her chamber, she found Haesel sitting on a three-legged stool, holding her head in her hands and sobbing as if her heart would break. Placing her hand upon her maid's back, Fearn had no need to ask what the matter was, for Haesel, too, was feeling the mother's breaking heart, the helplessness against men's decisions, the senseless waste of life after months of hope. Fearn drew her maid up to clasp her in her arms. Was it better, she wondered, to remain childless than to see a life squandered so needlessly?

Aric ran a hand over the filly's satin chestnut back, then led her to the field and let her run. The conversation with Fearn had not been comfortable, for he suspected that his views on exposure were important to her not only for Wenda's sake,

but for her own, too. It was only natural, he supposed, when he had made it clear to her that, as
his woman, she would share his bed to a more
intimate degree than she had so far. On the other
hand, he told himself, her two-year marriage had
produced no child, for whatever reason, so why
should she think he would be more successful?
Unless, of course, the problem had been her husband's, not hers. The question was not a simple
one to answer and only time would tell. Even so,
he regretted stretching the truth about his failure
to involve himself in Wenda's tragedy. She had
looked up to him and he had failed her.

'Astrid Borgsen,' the large lady said, hoping to make an impression. Without waiting
for an invitation, she swept past Haesel into the
hall where Fearn was sitting on the low platform, attempting to unravel her tablet-weaving
threads from the jumble that had come about
during the journey, perhaps irretrievably. Holding one of the tablets away between her teeth,
Fearn glanced up past all the pleats and folds, the
fur trims, brooches, chains and double chins to
find two fierce blue eyes under a pair of heavy
white eyebrows drawn together in a frown. 'Astrid Borgsen,' the lady repeated, clearly used to
some positive reaction at the sound of her name.

Removing the tablet carefully from her mouth, Fearn knew without being told that this was Aric's formidable aunt and had already decided on the exact degree of respect she would dispense, when the time came. It was not as if she was unused to this kind of thing. 'And I,' she said, politely, 'am Lady Fearn of Jorvik. Please do come in, Astrid Borgsen.'

Since the lady was already well inside, she could hardly miss the reprimand, pursing her lips and bending as much as she was able to scrutinise Fearn's lovely face and to see for herself the curiosity about which her brother had been so scathing, as if it had been a fault similar to a calf born with five legs. Her own eyes widened under Fearn's bold stare. 'May the gods have mercy!' she boomed, standing up straight. 'Uther was right. They *are*!'

With a sigh, Fearn laid the jumble of threads aside and stood up to face her visitor. 'Not one in the middle of my forehead, I fear. Now that *would* have been something, wouldn't it? May I offer you some mead?'

Not used to being answered so readily by a younger woman, Astrid blinked back her surprise. 'Yes, you may. I am Aric's aunt, you know.'

'Yes, I do know. But you are not *my* aunt, are you? And I am not a permanent fixture here, so I shall not mind if you address me as Fearn, plain and simple. And this is my woman, Haesel. She is not a slave and I do not treat her as one. Shall you bring our guest some mead, Haesel, love?'

'Well!' said Astrid, watching Haesel depart. 'You seem to be settling in. Haven't been in here since Aric's father departed this life. It's cleaner.'

'Ivar and Eve are very efficient,' Fearn said, placing a cushion stuffed with goosedown on the platform for Astrid to sit on. 'Please, will you sit a while?'

With a breathless grunt, the white-haired aunt lowered herself down, grumbling that she'd never be able to get up again. 'There now,' she said, smoothing the pleated linen kirtle over her knees, 'tell me something about yourself.'

Fearn sat on the opposite side of the glowing embers, noticing how Astrid's chubby fingers flashed with gold rings, with garnets, obsidian and cornelian. She was unhealthily overweight, making her lungs wheeze noisily. There were no thanks for Haesel as Astrid took the beaker of mead from her, yet the honeyed liquid was downed in one long gulp as if it was water. Fearn preferred to direct the conversation herself. 'I can't tell you anything you won't already have heard from your brother and your nephew,' she said, sweetly, accepting her beaker of well water with a smile. 'So why not tell me the real purpose of your visit, Astrid? Did you perhaps wish to tell me about your plans for your niece Freya and her cousin Aric? Oh, it's no surprise to me. Did you think it would be?'

Astrid's eyes narrowed. 'So he's told you, then?'

'That he's expected to take Freya as his wife? Of course. Why would he not?'

'Because, I suppose… I assumed he…you… might be planning…' The thought fizzled out completely as Fearn leaned back, laughing quietly.

'Planning?' she said. 'I'm not planning anything, Astrid, and I don't believe Aric is, either. I'm here for a year and then you'll get your young Kean back. Revenge over. All honour restored. That's the last you'll see of me. Freya is a delightful young lady. Is she as keen on this partnership as you and your brother are?'

'Freya is an obedient girl. She will do as she's told.'

'Freya is a *woman*, Astrid. Had you overlooked that?'

Impatient with the word-juggling, Astrid looked away before coming back to Fearn with a hard stare. 'What are you suggesting? That she may go against all our wishes?'

'I'm suggesting that she may actually have a mind of her own, as women do.'

'I was not allowed a mind of my own when I was her age,' Astrid said, sullenly.

'Ah, so is that why you've remained unmarried all these years?' Fearn knew the question to be impertinent, put to one of Astrid's generation by a much younger woman, but before she could regret it, she saw how Astrid sank down into her bulk and how the heavy folds of skin above her eyes drooped like shutters to keep the pain inside.

'My parents,' she whispered, 'expected me to…' Again, the sentence faded.

'To marry a man of their choice?' Fearn said. 'Not your choice?'

Astrid nodded. 'I refused. Said I'd rather stay single all my life. I would like to have had children, so I mother Freya as if she were my own.'

'And now you're going to insist on your choice for her? As your parents did?'

'No. Not if she doesn't want it. Of course, I cannot speak for Aric, or Uther.'

'Then all you can do is to wait and see what happens, isn't it? Time has its own way of resolving this kind of problem.'

'And what about you, lady? Are you waiting to see what happens, too?'

'I have no choice. I am not free, as you know. I am simply the means by which the Jarl Aric is taking his revenge on Earl Thored. Not an ideal situation for any woman to be in.'

'Especially not you. You are widowed, I believe. Are you still mourning?'

'Not at all, Astrid. But that doesn't mean I'm ready for another relationship.'

'Then refuse to let him take advantage of you, Fearn. As I did with men when I was your age and lovely to look on.'

Between women, so much could be read into a silence, in the direction of the eyes, a sigh, the movement of a thumb, even. So Astrid knew without being told that, for all her claims of detachment from this affair of family honour, Fearn's heart had already begun to thaw towards the man who had dared to abduct her from beneath her father's nose. An English earl, no less. Not a mere nobody. And knowing her nephew as she did, Astrid could not believe that he would tire of her in one year, promise or no promise, for she was the most beautiful creature she had ever seen and intelligent, too. She had heard about little Kol's recovery. So had half the village.

'I'm putting on a feast tomorrow,' she told Fearn, 'for Aric's safe return. You'll come, won't you? As Aric's partner?'

Fearn smiled at the sharp blue eyes. 'Thank you, Astrid. I'll come as his newest trophy.' Their leave-taking was quite different from their introduction, concluding in a warm hug at the wicker gate to Aric's large compound.

'I think,' Astrid told her, 'you and I will get on well together.'

Re-joining Haesel in the hall, Fearn delved deep into the chest given to her by Queen Aelf-gyfu containing so many treasures that replaced those she'd left behind in Jorvik. Her wax writing-tablet and stylus had been included, for safety, with a few sheets of writing parchment intended to encourage Fearn to write to her. Goose feathers for quills were easy enough to come by and oak galls for ink could be found if one knew where to look. 'Haesel,' she said, 'if you love me, sort out that tablet-weaving for me?'

Haesel's smile was angelic. 'I do,' she said, 'for not treating me as a slave. And to show it, I shall untangle that lot. Where are you going, lady?'

'To find some oak apples. There'll be plenty in the woodland.'

'Without your veil?'

'Without my veil,' Fearn said, picking up a wicker basket.

'Hussy,' said Haesel, affectionately.

* * *

The tangled mass had begun to take shape at last as Aric appeared, took a look round, and enquired where her mistress might be. 'Gone to pick oak apples in the wood,' she said. 'For ink.'

'Oak *apples*?' he said, frowning. 'Do you mean acorns?'

'No,' Haesel said, not daring to take her eyes off the blue and red threads. 'They're growths. Round things like crab apples, only dark. Wasps make them.' When she finally looked up, Aric had gone. 'Oh,' she said.

Going over, word for word, what she and Astrid had said about choices and the right to refuse, the thoughts Fearn had previously held about not wanting another relationship, especially after her disastrous marriage, now began to waver. Would she spend the rest of her life like Astrid, who both regretted and defended her choice to remain single? Would she continue to crave a family, as she did, to hold a downy-headed infant in her arms and know that it would never be hers? And what if, like Wenda, she gave birth to a deformed child and a girl? The poor woman had still not recovered from the trauma. What right had any man to use a woman so and then to abdicate all responsibility, as Wenda's man had done? And yet, even as she asked herself the question, she knew the answer to be fashioned by the body, not the mind. Longing for physical comfort, and perhaps an escape from her father's home, Wenda would have given herself with little thought as to the consequences while her mind was overruled by desire. And because he had been a man of little worth, it was she who had paid the price, not him. Could she imagine Aric the Ruthless taking the same course of action, or herself remaining childless for ever, when her body had begun to yearn for fulfilment night and day? Should she go to him and offer herself, after all her denials? Would she find out at last what making love was all about, before it was too late? Before bitterness set in? Before Astrid's kind of self-indulgence spoilt that loveliness she had spoken of?

No, how could she entertain such an idea? The man was arrogant and too sure of her. He had probably had several women already since their arrival; the blossom in his hair attested to that. Astrid's advice to refuse him would pay him back for all the indignities she had suffered for the sake of men's revenge. Reaching the woodland, she soon found a plentiful supply of oak trees amongst the ash, elm and beech, many of them with oak galls, commonly known as apples, fixed to their branches, rough round growths that came off in her hand with only a little persuasion. Dropping these into her basket, she stepped over a carpet of bluebells that spread deeper into the forest, reminding her of home and the way spring moved so reassuringly into the first days of summer, as it was doing here. She and Haesel had been concerned about the differences between the two countries, but now she saw only the similarities, even in the language.

When the loud chink-chink of a blackbird and the quick flutter of startled sparrows made her aware of another presence besides her own, she turned to look behind her and saw, silhouetted against the distant edge of the woodland, a man's shape, instantly recognisable. Aric. Come to look for her, taking advantage of her aloneness and the privacy offered by the woodland. Just as Freya and Loki had done.

Stealthily, with her heart beating a pulse into her throat, she stepped back to place herself behind the nearest wide tree trunk, knowing it would easily hide her. But the forest floor was littered with dry twigs and, with a loud crack that echoed into the canopy of new leaves, she revealed her position, her dull-green kirtle blending with the leafy bushes, but the white shift

showing at her neck making her as visible as
her veil would have done. She saw him begin
to move towards her, then she turned to run,
her basket of oak-apples clutched in her arms,
leaping like a deer over the bluebells and wood
anemones, swerving round low bushes and ducking under branches, yelping with anger as her
hair was snagged, time after time.

His footsteps pounded and cracked behind
her, his long legs covering twice the ground,
she hampered by her long skirt that constantly
slipped from her hand as she pushed at clinging branches. A clumsy squawking pheasant
flapped from beneath her feet, tripping her up
and launching her, face down, into the soft leaf
mould. From the corner of her eye, she caught
sight of Aric leaping over a bush like a stag in
full flight almost within touching distance and,
as she clambered to her feet, she tripped again
on the hem of her kirtle. The basket flew ahead
of her, scattering the contents and bouncing
them away just as Fearn fell heavily on to her
side, knocking out the words she had been ready
to scream. 'No…no! Leave me alone! I don't
want…' she gasped.

But it was too late for protests when his
weight was already holding her firmly to the
forest floor, his hands easily catching hers be-

fore they could reach his face, like bands of steel around her wrists. His pale hair had been loosened by the clawing branches and now it hung in fine wisps through which he laughed down at her, as if this chase and capture had been planned for their enjoyment. He was not even out of breath, she noticed. 'Let me go, Dane,' she panted. 'I did not come here for this.'

'No, my beauty,' he said, 'I know you did not. But you agreed once not to run from me again. Didn't you?'

'You surely didn't expect me to agree to that. You know how I feel about this. It's too soon. I need more time. In my country, widows are allowed a decent interval….'

'I know all about that, too,' he whispered, touching her chin with his lips, 'but that's for grieving widows, and you are not a grieving widow. Yes, you are angry about all that's happened, with your father, with me, and with yourself for wanting me, in spite of your denials. Oh, yes,' he went on, ignoring the quick turn of her head away from him, 'I've seen you looking at me, imagining, curious.'

'I have *not*! Arrogant brute!'

'Wondering what it will be like. And you may well have come here to gather stuff for your ink-making, but that was not the only reason, was it?'

Slowly, she turned her head to look at him, to see if he had read her mind accurately. As a wife, intimacies had only ever taken place in the so-called privacy of their chamber where disturbances were not unknown and where, through the wickerwork partition, the rowdy yells and raucous laughter of men, the squealing of women and the yapping of hounds almost drowned out the noisy rutting of her insensitive husband.

Aric waited for her to deny it. When she did not, he released her hands while nudging at her chin again with tender lips. 'This,' he said, softly, 'will be good. Here we have peace and privacy and time for you to discover things you could not have imagined.'

'You *are* arrogant!' she whispered.

'Sure of myself, yes, and sure of you, too. I doubt you've ever been told that you're the love-liest woman in all England, have you? I've seen a few, but nothing to compare, so far. Nor in Denmark. I've seen how men's eyes follow you, my beauty.'

'Lust. That's all. They do it—'

'After all women? No, they don't. And there's nothing wrong with lust. It's not so different from your curiosity. But sometimes it means more than that.'

'And you're going to tell me that this is one of those times, I suppose.'

'Hush, woman. Let go of your anger, or it will make a shrew of you, and a year is a long time for a man and a shrew to live together. This is more than simple lust. I want you because you're a match for me. Courageous, fierce, passionate, impetuous. You have the body of a goddess, made for loving, and I can give you pleasure, if only you'll allow it. Let me show you.'

His hand and voice quietened her, luring her thoughts away from her rough capture towards the warm invasion taking place along her thigh, stealing upwards, lingering slowly, timed to the kiss that gentled her mouth. Forbidding any more insincere protests, Aric moved his lips over hers, his hand finding a way beneath her kirtle and linen chemise, sliding tenderly over smooth undulations of skin, coming at last to the luscious curve of her breast.

Trembling, she caught at his hand through the fabric, remembering a distant nightmare, then letting it go along with the exquisitely gentle touch that brushed over her nipple, sending waves of delicious pleasure into her thighs of a kind she had never experienced before, melting her body. She took his head between her hands to hold it where she could look into his eyes, at the same time feeling the softness of his hair hanging in wisps over her face, teasing her eyelids and cheeks.

His eyes darkened, now serious, roaming over her skin as if to take his fill of her loveliness, but also to see how well he had banished the distress they had both feared. He saw the growing desire there, lurking beneath the heavy lids and the thick sweep of black lashes, and her lips, not scolding, were parted and waiting for more of his kisses with the added sensation of his soft beard on her skin. So different from her wifely episodes when every move was intended for her husband's enjoyment, rushed, brutal, and always devoid of any kind of comfort, Aric's loving was leisured and tender, his caresses, though hampered by clothing, were designed to show Fearn what she had missed. Exploring the sensitive skin of her inner thighs with languorous sweeps of his hand, he was tuned to receive all those signals that would indicate her readiness for him, her long sighs and moans mingling with the fragile sounds of the forest around them, the hesitant touch of her hands on his face and neck, inhibited by never having explored a man before. At the art of making love, Fearn was still a complete novice in the hands of a master, a detail now pushed to the back of her mind in the face of so many exciting discoveries.

The signal he had hoped for came just as his hand reached its goal, instantly parting her legs for him, yet still with a trace of fear lingering in the hard clutch of her fingers on his shoulders, prompting him to whisper reassurances with his kisses. 'Yes…yes, I know…it's all right…just let go now. We'll take this slowly, my beauty. There…am I hurting you?'

'No. Go on,' she whispered against his mouth.

He smiled down at her, bracing his arms on each side of her body, almost losing himself in the sheer beauty of the moment and in the exultation of having, at last, won her trust. He had never really doubted it. He had noticed her interest, but she herself had made it happen, which was as it should be, and now it would be up to him to turn the tide of her anger into a raging desire. That would be revenge indeed.

Whatever Fearn had expected, she now realised that her imagination had come nowhere near reality when each of Aric's slow thrusts made her gasp with pleasure, never hurried but apparently meant to make their first time a discovery of lingering delights and sensations, undisclosed until now. The world slowed to a halt. The echoes of the forest faded with her thoughts, only broken by the soft rhythmic sound of Aric's breathing that accompanied each powerful pulse of his body deep into hers. Neither of them spoke, for there was nothing they could have said to enhance the experience. For Fearn, this alone was a revelation she wanted to continue, having no idea that for her it could develop into something even more wonderful. So when the exquisite heat flared through her body and flooded her limbs, she moaned in an ecstasy of uncontrolled excitement, helplessly adrift. Aric responded, elated by his success, urged on by Fearn's wildly tossing head and mewing cries, her amazing eyes opening only once to bore into his, then closing before his next burst of energy.

Then Fearn understood for the first time what the fierce conclusion signified and that she was not only a physical part of it, but that it was also for their mutual pleasure, a pleasure she had never known existed until now. Riding on the crest of a mighty wave of sensation, she was swept along by the intensity of Aric's vigour in which his caring was all for her, never for himself alone. She had known he could be the one to teach her, but this was a lesson to exceed everything and now, no matter what complications might follow as a result, she knew the joy of being a complete woman at last.

Exhausted by emotion and sated by her ardour, she felt the last slowing pulses of his body inside her before he carefully withdrew and rolled aside with a groan, leaving her feeling bereft and at a loss when there was no word of praise, no touch of hand, no caress. Puzzled, she thought to prompt some kind of response, framing it in the same kind of tone that had begun the encounter, more familiar to them than compliments. 'You are disappointed,' she said, turning her body towards him, thinking he might do the same. 'Well, I have nothing like the comparisons you'll be able to make, but never mind. You've taken your revenge, Dane, and that's what this was about, isn't it?'

'Yes,' he said, very quietly. 'That's what it was about. Come on, we'd better go back.' Abruptly, he sat up to adjust himself and then stood to offer her his hand. 'I'll help you pick up your oak apples.'

Fearn felt as if an ice-cold shower of water had doused the glow simmering inside her until the moment when he'd replied, straight-faced, to her half-hearted spitefulness. But pride kept her on course, refusing to ask for an explanation. Angrily, she sat up, ignoring his offered hand, turning her back on him. 'You go,' she said. 'I can find them myself.'

'Fearn…' he began.

'Go! Leave me alone! You've done enough damage.' Still with her back to him, she felt him hesitate, then heard the snap of twigs as he walked away, echoing through the chilling numbness of her mind.

But, no, she could not allow this to happen. She was an earl's daughter and sister to England's Queen, and worth more than a quick tumble on the forest floor. Why had she allowed it? Why had she not drawn her knife on him? Why was she allowing him to walk away without even an attempt at an explanation? Had she fallen so far from the standard he'd been expecting, after all his flattery woven around her character and looks? She had a right to know. Now. While the memory was still alive. 'Revenge, Dane?' she yelled after him, clambering to her feet. 'Is that really the best you can do, then? So where was the pleasure you were going to show me? Was that *it?*'

She saw his shoulders droop as he half-turned and waited for her to come within speaking distance, his hair raked back off his forehead, catching the dappled sunlight on the folds of his soft woollen tunic to which bits of the woodland clung. This was far from the arrogant man who had pursued her half an hour ago.

'You knew that was what this was about,

Fearn,' he said as she drew near. 'We both understood that. It was never about anything else. Only revenge.'

'Anything else? Like what?' she cried. 'Like love? Did you—?'

'I didn't imagine *anything*,' he said, harshly. 'But such things happen when a woman discovers what her body can do. I don't want that to happen to you. Our time together lasts only one year. That's all. You will have served your purpose and my family's honour will be satisfied. Then you'll be returned.'

'Like used goods. So what's to stop me from returning home now? Does your revenge need a whole year? Isn't once enough?'

'That was the time we agreed on. My sister was with your father for that time. At least you'll be alive at the end of it.'

'Your sister. Yes, of course. You should have brought her child back instead of me, Dane. Think of the empty flattery and energy you'd have saved.'

'But I brought *his* child back, didn't I?'

Fearn had intended to ask him again about how he knew this, but had been waiting for an appropriate moment. The first time, he had been evasive. 'So perhaps *now* you can tell me what you know of this,' she said. 'Did he tell you?'

'Your father? No, of course not. But it doesn't take much to see how his mind works, does it? It's sons Thored wants, not daughters, so why would he have kept you away from your parents to remain with him? Because he sired you, woman. Because you are his own. Then when I saw your sister's child in Lundenburh, I was sure of it. I took you instead of Kean to make your father suffer as our family did when he took Tove and used her. Only she didn't return and you will.'

But now Fearn's emotions had endured too much for caution and words were thrown out like daggers. 'Oh, don't be too sure of that, Dane. I can keep a family feud going for another generation without too much effort.' She had given no thought to the reaction this would provoke after so little success with the previous ones and his long stride towards her across a bright patch of bluebells took her completely by surprise. His gold-circled arm flashed and she was grasped and pulled with a thud hard into his chest, her head pulled round too close for comfort into the fierce glare of the steel-grey eyes.

'Is that what Christians do, then, when life goes hard for them? Eh? Opt out of life altogether?' he snarled, bending her so that her thighs pressed against him. 'Or is it that the

healer can turn killer? Either way, you will remember that you are my woman still, like it or
not, and you will do nothing to injure me or my
property. Do you understand?'

Glaring at him with the full force of her amazing two-colour stare, she saw how he flinched
before holding them with his own. 'Your
woman?' she said, scornfully. 'Still? After that
sad performance?'

'Stop it!' he said. 'That kind of jibe is unwor-
thy of you. I know exactly what you felt just now.
You cannot conceal that from me. I saw it in your
eyes and felt it within your body, and now you
will have to learn how to deal with it and not
become its slave. In this kind of arrangement,
there is no place for sentiment.'

'You should have warned me,' she whispered,
remembering.

'Yes, I should. You have a rare natural ability. I should have been prepared.' Slanting her
mouth under his, he kissed her with an expertise
that seemed to remind them both of the quality
of their loving, and perhaps as a comfort, too,
for the harsh words that had sought to blemish it.

She was trembling as he released her, still not
knowing whether her role as his woman would
include more such episodes, or whether he would
be satisfied with having awoken in her what he'd

called a natural ability and leave it at that. There was no mistaking, however, the hard pressure of the bulge beneath his tunic. Stepping back apace, she summoned all her courage to bring her body back into her control, instead of his. 'Then the answer is simple, isn't it?' she whispered, trying to prevent her voice from shaking. 'Having done what you set out to do, you can now leave me alone. You have shown me nothing new that I cannot live without, Dane. Did you think you had?'

His look held both disbelief and disappointment as he answered her. 'You are a noblewoman, remember? An earl's daughter. Lying does not suit you.'

His message stung and she could no longer face him. They both knew that what he had shown her that day had lain dormant within her for years, waiting to be brought to life, and that the effects of it would take hold and make every other experience less than worthless. Unless it was with him. Turning away, she left him standing there. 'Where are you going?' he called.

'To get my basket. I've wasted enough time here already.'

Some time later, it was Haesel who found her, sitting on a log, clutching the empty basket, her streaked cheeks showing where tears had been, now dried. Questions, too, had come and gone, few of them answerable, not even Haesel's concerned, 'Lady, are you all right? Shall we go back?'

No going back. I've come too far. I should never have let him show me.

When she did not answer, Haesel set about recovering as many of the oak apples as she could find and placing them in the basket, seeing by the bed of flattened bracken that what she suspected had in fact happened. Then, taking a piece of linen from her pouch, she touched it to her tongue and began to remove all traces of tears from Fearn's cheeks like a mother with her child. 'There now. Can you stand? Come, lady. We'll leave this place,' she said, taking Fearn's hand.

'Elf told me,' Fearn whispered, allowing herself to be led. 'I didn't believe her.'

'Told you what, lady?'

'That it would be so wonderful. With the right man. Now I know what she meant.'

'So why the tears?'

Fearn's steps slowed as she felt once more the coldness that he had put between them, even before a single word of admiration to pair with the compliments he had showered on her beforehand. 'Because… I suppose…it meant nothing to him and everything to me, and because he would not even pretend, for my sake, that there was anything more to it than simply to pay my father back. He would not even allow me to think for one moment that it might have changed anything between us, no tenderness, no emotion, just an act that had to be concluded there and then. He probably gets more excitement from his mares and stallions.'

Facing her, Haesel gently shook the hand she was holding. 'Perhaps it was a mistake to hope that he might begin to feel the way you do, lady,' she said.

'Does it show? I've tried not to let it. I told him I didn't want him.'

More than anyone, Haesel understood her mistress's needs and how, after being starved of even the smallest husbandly kindness, Fearn's heart had begun to open like a flower in the warmth of Aric's presence. To give her credit, she had resisted for as long as she could what she knew to be inevitable and yet, in her moment of weakness, had forgotten that, for him, this had less to do with affection between a man and a woman than retribution for past wrongs. If she had held that in her heart with more conviction, Haesel thought, sadly, perhaps she would have prepared herself better for something beyond her imagination. This, of all times, was when Fearn needed her mother's advice most.

Intending to return to the great hall, Aric took a detour instead by way of the sloping field behind the settlement where the ancestors of Lindholm lay, marked by stones. He had taken Fearn up here on the previous evening to show her the extent of his property, though he could tell how her thoughts were more of the home she had left behind than her new one. Sand piled up in drifts around his feet, some of the stones half-covered already like the ploughland they'd had to abandon, too sandy to grow crops.

Fearn's acid words burned into his mind, fading each time he recalled her soft body beneath his, responding to him in a way far beyond his expectations, especially after her previous ordeals, urging him on to scale new heights of sensation as new to him as they were to her. He had not been prepared for that. He had always thought there was no more for him to discover. Countless women had dulled his performances except, perhaps, after a long voyage. So although he had seduced her with words she would not have heard before, he had felt that he was saying them for the first time and meaning them.

He picked up a handful of sand and let it blow away from between his fingers, like words lost in the wind. His hand had taken her breast, felt the silken skin, the instant hardening of her nipple, heard the soft moan, the gasp of surprise. Everything he had done had brought him delight in her awareness, telling him that this glorious woman might as well have been a virgin for all she knew about lovemaking. Except that her journey with him to the end was by no means virginal and that, too, was something he had not been prepared for. Yes, he had fully intended to turn her anger into desire for him, to make the revenge that much sweeter, but he had expected that to grow over a period of time, not to burst into a conflagration that had scorched him as much as her. In his experience, a conclusion such as that came only rarely and it had taken all his pretence not to let her know it. So much so that, with his unkind words, he'd brutally inflicted a double wound on the heart of a courageous woman. She had been right, of course, when she'd said he ought to have brought Kean instead. Life would have been simpler if he'd stuck to the plan. Now, he could not even ransom the lady as long as Kean remained with Earl Thored for, earl's daughter or not, she was of less value to him than his son.

Shielding his eyes against the distant glare of the fjord, Aric picked out the movement of figures below him: women washing clothes in the stream, men moving sheep into pens for shearing, builders raising a wooden cruck frame and children getting in the way. He recognised his cousin Freya's petite form and blonde hair as she carried a pail of milk across her father's yard, almost hearing her squeak of surprise as young Loki rounded the corner of the byre, catching at the pail before it slopped its contents. But what he saw next was so unexpected he could hardly believe his eyes; this sweet, mousy, obedient young maid being steered into the open doorway of the byre and held against the frame for a kiss which lasted too long for it to be a simple greeting. With the milk pail on the floor beside them, the two lovers were oblivious to the world until Uther's distant shout made them both jump apart, Loki to skip away like a sprite into the shadows and Freya to pick up her pail, her face as composed as before.

It was quite some time before Aric stood, dusted the sand off his tunic and walked down to his uncle's farm to talk to him about the horses.

Chapter Seven

Avoiding the blaze from dozens of lamps shining through the open door of the great hall, Haesel kept to the shadows and well away from the streams of servants carrying platters of steaming food to the feasters inside. From the hall, shouts of laughter rose and fell on waves of merry music—pipes, whistles, drums and harps—to which few people listened except to join in, now and then, with some hearty table-thumping. Haesel knew she would not be missed. These feasts usually lasted until the early hours and the Lady Fearn was in the good company of Oskar and his charming wife, Ailsa, and Einar and his lady, putting a brave face on the kind of event she would rather had avoided. Celebrating a Viking homecoming was, however, a way for Aric the Ruthless to reward those men of Lindholm who had left their families and risked their lives to be at his side, and to thank those who had been left behind as caretakers. But Haesel saw no reason to be a part of this, especially since hearing yesterday the terrible tragedy of Wenda's infant. Such heartlessness was impossible for her to understand, even from a society where any abnormality was looked on with suspicion.

It was the issue of Wenda's infant that drew Haesel to the cemetery on the hillside that night, following the sandy path by the light of the full moon, not knowing exactly where the child had been left, but needing to make some kind of sympathetic connection and to feel something about its pitiful destiny. Then perhaps the worst images in her mind would fade and restore to her some peace. As if some unknown force was leading her, she picked her way through the marker-stones to the top of the slope where she halted, sinking to the ground obediently in answer to a silent instruction. As she waited in the darkness the scent of newly cut grass drifted strongly on the night air, bringing snatches of laughter and the roar of men in their eternal preoccupation with contest and rivalry.

A prickling sensation stole along her arms, even before she saw the shadowy figure of a young girl climbing the path towards her, too young to be anyone she knew so soon after her

arrival in Lindholm. At her approach, Haesel
spoke, for it looked as if she had not been noticed, sitting there alone. But her words had not
the slightest effect and it was then that Haesel
saw her transparency and knew with the certainty of experience that the girl was of the past,
not the present. She was even more convinced of
this when the filmy figure reached the stones just
beyond Haesel's feet and bent to touch a bundle
that Haesel had not seen, lifting it off the ground
and into her arms, cradling it as a mother would
have done. Except that this girl was too young to
be a mother, but not too young to sense that she
was in danger, standing for a moment to listen
and to look before moving away. She did not take
the same path back to the settlement, but seemed
to skirt the edges of the plots before fading into
the moonlit landscape of stones.

Shivering with emotion and relief, and close to
tears, Haesel stood on shaking legs, then slowly
made her way back down the hillside, reflecting on what she now knew and must keep secret,
that some five years ago, a young lass from the
settlement had rescued Wenda's infant and that it
probably still lived where it would be safe from
mistreatment. Opening the wicker gate into the
croft, she was relieved to see a familiar figure

coming from the hall to meet her. 'Hrolf!' she whispered, smiling shyly.

'Where've you been?' the young man said. 'I missed you.' He stood before her as if to insist on an answer, then took her tenderly into his arms and held her head against his chest. 'You're trembling,' he said.

'I needed some fresh air,' she said against his woollen tunic. 'Will they stay in there all night?'

'All night and half tomorrow, too, if I know anything. The Lady Astrid doesn't do things by halves. Listen! That's your lady tuning her harp, isn't it?'

The hall had fallen silent as they walked in together, respectfully waiting for Fearn to listen to each string whilst twisting the pegs, then to ripple her fingers across the strings in preparation for a song. Haesel knew which one it would be, a haunting song of her Northumbrian homeland, its hills and streams, the sun and shadows on the fells, its wild moorland. Fearn's voice was husky and low rather than bright, and there was not one who listened who could doubt her longing to be home. There was one man in particular who, instead of watching her dark head and the fall of her hair, looked down at his hands clasped together, clearly taking on the responsibility for her sadness and deeply moved by her performance. Beside him sat his cousin Freya, glancing anxiously from time to time at her hoary old father, Uther, whose fist was pressed hard against his heart, his face drawn into a frown of pain.

'Aric's uncle is unwell,' Haesel whispered to Hrolf.

'Aye, he's getting too old for this kind of thing,' he replied, 'but try telling him that.'

'It's his heart,' she insisted.

'Nah! He doesn't have one. He and his brother were a heartless pair.'

The applause for Fearn's recital drowned out any reply Haesel could have made to that enigmatic remark, although she was left with the impression that Uther Borgsen was not well liked by Aric's men. She and Hrolf stayed close to Fearn and her new friends for several hours after that, but the time came when the women asked to be excused, Fearn amongst them. As she rose from her cushioned bench, Aric came across to her, slipping off one of his heavy gold arm-bracelets and laying it on the table beside her beaker. 'For you,' he said. 'For your singing.'

Their eyes met as others looked on to see how she would accept the gift, but Fearn simply turned away to go, leaving the gold bracelet where Aric had put it, glinting with blood-red garnets. He watched her leave the hall, then snatched the weighty gold piece and thrust his hand through it. 'Women!' he said to those near enough to hear, though all could see that his clumsy gesture had misfired enough to anger him.

The linen cloths that the Queen had supplied for Fearn's monthly courses now flapped on the line round the back of the great hall, pegged there with split twigs by Haesel and the slave girl Eve, neither of them regarding this task as anything but a routine duty for their lady. But Haesel had seen something disturbingly familiar about Eve's movements, something she could not identify except, maybe, by asking the girl about herself. 'Do you find it hard to be a Christian amongst so many pagans, Eve?' she said, taking a peg out of her mouth.

Eve picked another cloth out of the bucket. 'At first I did,' she said, 'until I found that there are others here.'

'Here in Lindholm? Where?'

'Just a few. They keep it quiet. Down on the edge of the village by the merchants' quarters. I go to see them several times a week. They'll be glad to know we have you and the lady with us. I can take you to meet them, if the lady wishes it.'

'I'm sure she would. But how long have you known them, Eve?'

'Since I first came here,' Eve said, picking up the bucket. 'About five winters, or thereabouts. I was about eleven when I was stolen, but I can't grumble. Life in England was a lot harder and I had less to eat. I think you might be about my age.'

'Sixteen? Yes, something like that. Without someone to remind you of when you were born, it's a bit difficult to tell, isn't it? Did you wear your hair loose then?'

'Oh, yes, like all children. But now I prefer to keep it covered with a scarf. It keeps men's hands off it.' She grinned. 'One of the problems of being a slave is that men think they have a right to you.'

'Jarl Aric?'

'No, not him. But I hide when his uncle comes here.'

Haesel could understand it. Eve was darkly pretty, a dainty young woman with perfect white teeth and a ravishing smile, and a swinging long-legged walk that rocked her hips seductively. They walked together back to the hall, and although Haesel had not asked Eve directly if she had rescued Wenda's child that night, she was reasonably certain that, about five years ago, that was what had happened and that it was not hard for her to guess where Eve would have taken it.

Later that day, Eve took Haesel and Fearn through the maze of timber walkways between houses and plots across to the far side of the settlement where merchants' boats were tied up at the jetties. Hrolf was also with them, which Fearn took to be a sign that they would not be allowed to go far without an escort, but whether for their safety or as a curb on their movements she was unsure. Nevertheless, she was glad of his presence when, with a group of merchants haggling over a shipload of slaves, there was the large fur-hatted man whose hand was still bound up from Fearn's knife-wound.

The part of the wharf known as the merchants' quarters was a hive of activity where living went on side by side with buying and selling, storing and exchanging, making money and trading in every kind of commodity, where now Fearn could see the pathetic state of people who, tied together and half-naked, were being sold straight from the ships. Watching the scene from the distance of a large warehouse, they saw how the slaves, some children with their mothers, some women obviously pregnant, younger men and boys stumbled on to the jetties in bare feet, their hair filthy, clothes damp and dirty, eyes staring in fright or half-closed with exhaustion. Herded like sheep, they shuffled into a wicker enclosure to the sound of men's shouts and children's pitiful screams.

'No, lady! Don't go!' Eve said to Fearn as she made a move towards them. 'Wait, you'll see... there...over there...those people will take them. They're some of the Christians. Watch!'

As they watched, a group of well-dressed Danish men and women appeared as if from nowhere, the women's long hair tied up in elaborate knots, large bronze brooches on their shoulders, fur edges around their cloaks. Three of the men were already speaking to the dealer as if they knew exactly what each slave was worth, shaking heads, walking away, returning to look again and haggle some more. 'Will they buy them all?' Fearn said, sickened by the sight of so much distress. If this kind of thing happened in Jorvik, she had never seen it. 'There must be at least twenty, including babies.'

'They usually manage it, because the slave-traders want our cloth,' Eve said. 'They can't find anything like it elsewhere. See those bales on the wagon?'

For the first time, Haesel and Fearn noticed a horse-drawn wagon behind the group, stacked high with bales of cloth in a tantalising array of colours ranging through deepest blues, browns and black to every dye colour that the women knew, and more, bright reds and yellows, greens and the softer tones produced by lichen, bark and heathers. Eve explained that not only were these people expert dyers, but weavers, too, for the fabrics were of fine wool, locally grown linen and imported raw silk, skilfully woven into the expensive diamond twill pattern, embellished with gold-threaded tablet-woven bands and embroidered with threads made here in Lindholm by their own goldsmiths.

'But who makes it?' Fearn asked. 'There must be years of work on that wagon?'

'No, just a lot of willing hands. In exchange for their freedom, the slaves who come here from Russia, Ireland and England are happy to share what skills they have. They're fed and clothed and looked after by the Christian couple and their helpers, and eventually they recover and set to work. Some teach the others who come and some go to work for other families.'

'But not as slaves?'

'No, this will be the last time they're bought or sold.'

As they listened to Eve, the bolts of cloth were being spread on tables, billowing and shining in the sun, fine transparent linens next to the sheen of silk and the comforting warmth of lambswool, and Fearn could see by the merchants' patting and stroking hands, their greedy eyes and fast bargaining that they found the exotic fabrics of far more interest than the miserable half-starved creatures whose bonds were already being untied. It was a busy time and not one to be disrupted by curious visitors, so although Fearn would like to have made contact with these compassionate Danes there and then, it was the poor slaves who needed their attention rather more urgently. 'No matter,' said Eve. 'Now you know where they are, you'll be able to find them on your own. But keep well away from the Russian merchant with the hat. He has a reputation.'

'We saw him at Aggersborg,' Haesel said. 'But where do the slaves go to be tended? Is there a separate house for them?'

Eve pointed to a large longhouse with a series of smaller huts nearby, well back from the trading area. 'Over there is a special place where women can go to give birth and be looked after. And anyone else who needs healing.'

They had begun to walk away, but Haesel felt a pressing need to see this place that had already taken shape at the back of her mind. 'Might we just take a quick look?' she said. 'I'm curious.'

It was only a few moments' walk to the spruce well-tended plot where boys turned the soil with spades and others gathered armfuls of young kale. Unlike the busy great hall on Aric's plot, the interior of this one was quiet and neatly furnished with rows of beds along both sides, each one occupied by a mother and her infant, rocking and crooning, feeding or sleeping, and so close to Haesel's vision that she had to cling to Hrolf to stay upright. 'What is it?' he said, supporting her.

Her face was almost white as she smiled an excuse. 'Just women's things.'

Later, Fearn was able to ask more, though she, too, had seen the connection. 'Then this has something to do with us, doesn't it? Your seeings always do,' she said.

'They might be glad of some help with the healing,' Haesel said. 'Perhaps we should go back there later on and introduce ourselves. This has come at a perfect time for you, lady. Just when you need to talk about things, as you would with Mother Bridget.'

'Danes,' said Fearn, dismissively. 'A poor substitute for Mother Bridget.'

'No, Eve told me that the couple who run the place are English, like us. That's how she got involved. She says they're elderly now, so they leave the buying and selling to the Danes, but they're the ones who started it all.'

'What else did she tell you?'

'Nothing much. No use telling her we're from Jorvik when she thinks that Cornwall is all there is to England. She has no idea where she is now, except that it's a long way from home. Er… lady…' she said, looking sideways at the figure in the doorway, 'the Jarl wishes to speak with you, I think.'

Deliberately, Fearn took her time to adjust the gold circlet over her veil, to pull her girdle into place and to slip her feet into the loose leather sandals. She would not look at him, but sauntered past him on to the pathway, debating whether to speak, and how, and of what, when there had been only the briefest contact between them since the previous day, and that acrimonious, to say the least. Walking together in silence, they entered the paddock where four mares and foals looked up from their grazing to come to them, breaking the tension that Fearn had no wish to relieve with the slightest courtesy. Even so, it was impossible for her not to speak to the delightful foal who sniffed at her face as if to offer some comfort, her low words listened to, their tone understood. 'She likes you,' Aric said, pulling at the mare's ears. 'If I gave her to you, would you accept her? She'll probably be a grey, like her dam.'

At any other time the idea would have given her great pleasure, never having been offered a gift of such value before. But now was too soon for the hurt to be salved by a gift of any value and she clung to her pride like a limpet to a rock. 'No, I thank you,' she said. 'You have nothing I could ever want.'

The reply clearly shook him as he realised how deep the rift between them had grown and that he had no kind of policy to deal with such a calamity when he had never had to placate a woman's self-esteem before this. Placing a hand on the mare's withers, he used it as a prop while he groped clumsily for the right approach. 'Fearn,' he said, 'last night, my attempt with the arm-ring…to thank you for…'

'Was quite unnecessary,' she replied, coldly. 'Don't give it another thought. I don't need your thanks. Not for anything. My song was for me, not you.'

'You are sounding more like a petulant child than a grown woman,' he said.

'Yes, life can be so confusing,' she retorted. 'Yesterday, you came to me as a man and walked away like a bewildered youth who didn't know the value of what he'd just won. But be very sure, Dane, that you'll never win it from me again. Or, if you do, you'll have to fight for it, for I'll not suffer your scorn a second time.'

'Fearn, it was not like that. I admit I was confused. I did not expect to feel the way I did. It took me by surprise. But it was not scorn I felt. And somehow I have to win you back to me.'

'I have never been yours. Nor will I ever be.'

'Yesterday, there was a moment when I felt you might have been.'

'Mistaken. That's your arrogance speaking.'

'And you have not been over any part of…of our lovemaking…and thought…?'

'No, I haven't. Your walking away was the most memorable part.'

'Fearn,' he said, softly, 'you're lying again.'

A heat rushed into her nose as tears stung behind her eyes and the foal pushed its velvet muzzle against hers, absorbing her distress. 'It's the truth,' she whispered. 'If you want to give me something, give me a boat to sail me back home.'

'In a year, I will. But I cannot live with you for that time and not have you in my bed.'

'And suffer all that dreadful confusion?' she said, pouring scorn into her voice. 'Just think what *I* shall have to suffer.' If tears of anger had not filled her eyes just then, she would have moved quickly to evade him as he stepped towards her, reaching out with gentle firmness to hold her close to him.

'This is what you will have to suffer, my beauty,' he said, slanting her head against his to receive his kiss, so potent that Fearn felt the effects of it travel down as far as her knees. Moving, searching, this was not the attempt of the bewildered youth with which she had taunted him, but a reminder, if she needed one, of the virile male who had won her with such ease, and with her co-operation. Now, effectively contradicting all she'd been saying to him, her arms disobediently reached up to his shoulders, her fingers finding his plait of hair and holding on to it like a lifeline, bringing back to her memory certain elements of their loving that she had thought never to repeat. She did not even protest when his hand took her breast to feel its heavy roundness, so tender at this time of the month, so aching for more than he could give, so sensitive to the gentle kneading motion of his fingers. Vaguely, the picture of that mothers' room with the suckling infants came and went in an instant, exciting a response from her lips like a wail of intense desire, causing a deep throb of pain in her womb, making her push at him and plead to be released. 'No,' she gasped. 'No more.' One hand pressed against her body below her girdle and immediately he knew why. Lack of privacy and two sisters had informed him well.

'Put your arm around my neck,' he ordered, bending to lift her into his arms. 'Come on, it's all right. I'm taking you back.' Striding down to the house, he caught sight of Haesel and called to her to open the door, swinging Fearn through into her chamber and laying her carefully on the fur-covered bed. 'Tend her,' he said. 'Hot drinks? Honey? Do you have charms for this kind of thing?'

Haesel smiled kindly at his concern. 'Er... no, but I've just gathered some chamomile and feverfew, the first of the season. That usually does very well.'

It was not usual for Fearn to be unwell at times like this, but the last month had been exceptional in every way, and so it was a week before she felt like repeating her visit to the Christian community over on the far side of the settlement. Again, Eve accompanied them, but Hrolf had not been told of their plans so had gone with his family to the marshland to make a ritual sacrifice.

To house a new influx of slaves, tents of hide had been erected in the nearby field where the occupants had already taken on a more normal appearance, clean, better clothed and no longer half-starved. Eve took her guests into the large building, a thatched roundhouse where barefoot children scuttled between adults, fetching and carrying, stirring pots over the fire, playing board games or helping to feed several sick people who lay under furs round the sides. Near the doorway, two huge looms leaned against the walls, worked by women who did not look up from their weaving as Fearn, Haesel and Eve entered, but a call from the far side of the room was in English instead of the usual Danish. 'Eve! We've missed you! What happened to you, lassie?'

'A bit more to do than usual,' Eve said, hugging the lady who, although English, wore a Danish woman's costume. Her hair, still dark, showed many streaks of silver in the thick knot of plaits behind her head and, although her bronzed skin was lined with age, the beauty remained in the high cheekbones and black-lashed eyes, the wide mouth and full lips. She had once been a beauty and now, standing before her, was a replica of the younger woman she would once have been. Neither of them had been…could *ever* have been…prepared for this moment, assuming that the intervening years and distance were the same as death, though even that dreadful thought had not stopped them from imagining how each would look.

Both of them gasped as recognition filtered into their memories, the shape, the scent, the greater height that was Clodagh, the womanliness that was Fearn, the hands that reached out, faltered, then went up to cover mouths distorting with anguish and mews of disbelief mingling with certainty. It must be...yes...no..it *must* be her. Surely. 'Can it be?' Fearn whispered. 'Mother?'

That was the one word Clodagh had convinced herself she would never hear again. The room was silent. Even the children were still, watching the miracle, watching the tears spring to the eyes of mother and daughter, watching the hands reach out to touch, then to grasp, pulling gently with trembling fingers. 'Fearn...my... Fearn?' Clodagh whispered, her voice breaking with emotion. 'Is it really...my little girl?'

'Yes, Mother. It's me. Yes...look, we have found each other.'

The beginning of a wail started in Clodagh's throat before she was clasped in her daughter's tender embrace and, for a time, no recognisable words were spoken, only fingers tracing delicately over features, the same but different, their eyes taking in every detail to make up for lost years of heartache. Tears coursed down their cheeks and dripped off their chins. 'A miracle,' said Clodagh. 'I never ceased to pray for it, lassie. Even now I can scarce believe it. I worked His will here to atone for my sins, but I never thought…oh…dearest, *dearest* child.' Now came the rush of words, the release of emotion, the torrent of guilt that made little sense to Fearn, who had to ask twice about her father before the answer came. 'Your father? Oslac? Yes, he's here somewhere. He helps me here. There would have been little point in coming all this way to sit around looking miserable, would there? But what of you, child? They said the Jarl had returned with a woman. Was that you? The Jarl's woman?'

Turning her hand over inside her mother's grasp, Fearn showed her the gold ring on her little finger, too small to fit any other. 'I came with him, yes. But look here, Mother. I've worn this since we parted. Shall we go outside and talk a while? There is so much I need to know. Will you tell me what happened to break us apart?'

Palming away her tears, Clodagh nodded. 'The ring. Yes. It's all I was allowed to give you. And to leave you behind was the greatest punishment of all, my darling.' They went outside to sit

on cushioned logs in sight of the busy merchants'
stalls and Clodagh, wife of the once-powerful
Earl Oslac of Northumbria, wept while she explained that what to Fearn had seemed a simple
matter of banishment had been nothing of the
kind. 'Yes,' she said, holding Fearn's hand on
her lap, 'your father *was* banished because it was
felt he was allowing his duties to the new church
to come before his duty to the King. The Archbishop of York supported him, but that wasn't
enough. Thored was his chief *thegn* and he was
told by the King to take over from Oslac and to
send us away out of Northumbria so as not to
cause trouble. As if we *would*,' she said, dab-
bing her eyes.

'But Oslac is *not* my father, is he?' Fearn said
gently. 'Earl Thored is my father. So what happened there? Why could someone not have told
me? Is this the sin you mentioned just now?
Adultery?' In spite of her gentle tone, she could
not keep out a hint of censure. Clodagh had always been a devout Christian to whom the sin
of adultery would be the last thing on her mind.
Or so Fearn had thought.

'You were much too young to understand,
love,' said Clodagh.

'I was not too young to understand that you

left me,' Fearn said, reproachfully. 'I cried myself to sleep every night for years.'

'Was Thored not kind to you?'

'As much as a man like him *can* be kind. He
was not kind to his wife Hilda, was he? And she
was not kind to me. Since I learned that Thored
was my natural father, I've been able to understand her resentment, but too late for it to make
any difference.'

'You deserve an explanation, Fearn. I never
thought I'd be given the chance to explain, but
my prayers have been answered. It was never my
desire to leave you behind, Fearn, my dearest. It
broke my heart, but…'

'But Thored insisted? Because he fathered
me? Because he wanted to take me from Oslac?
Were those the reasons?'

Clodagh shook her head, her beautiful sor-
rowing face expressing profound guilt as well
as grief. 'No, love. It was Oslac who insisted on
leaving you behind, not Thored.'

'What? My…? Why? He loved me, didn't he?'

'Try to understand our predicament, Fearn.
Oslac and I were a childless couple for many
years. We desperately wanted a family, but nothing happened. Oslac knew that Thored was at-
tracted to me and it was he who suggested that
Thored should try to father a child on me. It

was a risk. It might have been my problem,
rather than Oslac's, but we were desperate and
Thored needed no encouragement to do what
was needed. Oslac truly believed that, as long
as it produced a child, it was the right thing to
do. He really intended to adopt Thored's child
as his own.'

'Mother…that was a *terrible* risk to take.'

'Too risky, as it happened. Thored was handsome and strong, and a good lover, and it was no
particular hardship to either of us, only to Oslac.
Then I found that I was expecting you and we
thought then that everything had turned out for
the best, that Oslac would accept you as his own
kin. He tried. He tried hard, poor man. But he
could not put aside the fact that he had failed and
Thored had succeeded. You know what men are
like with their pride. He turned to the church for
help and there were those who grumbled at his
priorities, looking more and more to Thored for
leadership. So when we were told to leave Northumbria for good, Oslac decided he could not
take you with us. He saw all the affection I lav-
ished on you as being a substitute for Thored.
No, of course it was not true, but that's how he
saw it. He wanted us to go back to the beginning
as a childless couple and to go somewhere well
away from England.'

'But you loved Thored?'

Clodagh's voice became a whisper. 'Yes, love. I did. I couldn't help myself. But I also owed a duty to Oslac and I had to obey him. It tore me in half, but I had to leave both my beloved child and the man I loved. After five years of watching you grow like a beautiful flower, I had to… oh, Fearn, my dearest.' Burying her face in her hands, Clodagh sobbed as she remembered the pain of separation, her daughter's distress and total inability to understand what was happening except that her world was being turned upside down. 'Can you ever forgive me, Fearn? Can you try to see how it happened?'

There was no easy answer to any of this while it was still so new to her, and so very unexpected, as well as being contrary in almost every detail to the explanation Fearn herself had applied to a set of circumstances no one could have imagined. Once more, love had played havoc with all their clever plans and left a tangle of rights and wrongs that would take years to unravel.

For several more hours, the two of them sat close together to exchange years of information of which both had been starved, healing the wounds caused by enforced ignorance, false supposition and the small stale crumbs of hazy memories. Fearn told her mother about her life, about Aric's visit to Jorvik and the reason for her being here at Lindholm. She told her about Kean, the product of Thored's liaison with Aric's widowed sister, now dead. She told her of the meeting with Queen Aelfgyfu and the moment when Fearn's relationship to her was revealed, and how Haesel had predicted some events, including the care of sick people along the same lines as Mother Bridget in Jorvik.

'We buy any slaves who are brought here,' Clodagh told her. 'Many of the women are pregnant by the time they arrive, abused by the traders, so we have a place where they can give birth and recover their strength. Then we teach them our cloth-making skills, although most of them already have some knowledge, even if it's only the wool spinning. The Irish are always good at making linen. We have good embroiderers, too, and men skilled in making the gold thread. We try to show them better ways to live. We have a priest and a deacon, and we've converted dozens of pagans over the years. Ah…here comes our little Meld.'

Returning from the jetties where she had been to look for Oslac, a very small blonde child was being held by each hand, Eve on one side and

Haesel on the other, her inward-twisting foot making progress slow and rather lop-sided, though her beaming smile and sparkling blue eyes gave no indication of pain. The elderly Clodagh and little Meld, a shortened form of Raegenmeld, ran towards each other with arms ready to catch, swinging the child up into her embrace just as Fearn had been when she was five. 'She's our little God-gift,' Clodagh said, nuzzling the laughing face. 'Eve found her one night and brought her here, and she's been with us ever since. These pagans have the strangest ways of treating human life,' she said. 'It's no wonder so many of them are interested in our beliefs, but we still have quite a problem explaining why one thing is right and another thing is wrong. Of course, we don't always get it right ourselves, do we, when we want something very much?'

Walking more slowly a little way behind was the shrunken but wiry old man whom Fearn barely recognised as Oslac, his brown arms ornamented with pure gold bracelets and, round his neck to show off his status, a flat collar of beaten gold that flashed in the sun and reflected light on to his white beard and hollowed cheeks. One look at Fearn brought a choking sob to his throat and hands that held hers, fiercely tight, followed by a plea for forgiveness that wrung her heart with pity, for he was a modest man, and full of remorse. White-haired, he still retained some of the authority that had once been his as Northumbria's senior statesman, and while he admitted that he had no right whatever to offer Fearn his fatherly advice, it was clear that he *would* be glad to offer it, as she would be only too happy to ask.

There was, however, a limit to the time the three young women could spend there, though there was still so much more to be said. But as they left, more tears of joy flowed, with promises to return and discuss the future, leaving Fearn with the euphoric sensation that, on that momentous day, a miracle had happened to lift her spirits from a very low place. For Haesel, the day's events had been a personal triumph although, exercising her right to choose which parts of her 'seeings' to divulge, she saw little point, this time, in telling Fearn about having seen Eve in the cemetery five years ago when she had now seen for herself that Wenda's child lived happily with her adopted family. There had been more than enough for Fearn to assimilate that day without adding her own small miracle. As it happened, Haesel had judged correctly when she observed how the discovery of Clodagh and

Oslac affected Fearn so deeply that she was unable to respond to any attempt at discussion, as if the miracle was still working its power in her consciousness. For so many years, the problem had occupied every corner of Fearn's mind, waking and sleeping. Now, not only had they found each other at last, but the complex machinations behind the separation were almost too bizarre to take in immediately, for what had happened was well beyond the understanding of a five-year-old, even in the smallest degree.

But Fearn's emotional development had come a long way in the intervening years, some would say *too* far for a young woman of twenty-three winters, and what her mother had told her about falling in love with Thored seemed to echo around her own recent experiences with Aric. Since that day one week ago when he had exposed her feelings for him, she had stopped denying them so vehemently, even though she was convinced of the folly of it. Aric's plans for his own future did not include her. She had nothing to gain and everything to lose. Only the discovery of her long-lost parents would make the year remotely bearable. That, and the infrequent occasions when she would be allowed to share more of that amazing loving in the arms of her abductor, the man she had tried, and failed, to hate.

A glimmer of hope had appeared that day, nevertheless, when Oslac had told Fearn of his connections with merchants, most of them amicable, and of the ease by which he and Clodagh could send messages back to England. They had even sent slaves back to their homes and as messengers and ambassadors to other Christian communities, to make essential contact. As to why, then, no word had ever been sent to Thored to tell him where they were so that he could put Fearn's mind at rest, Oslac admitted that he had not allowed it. What would be the use, he'd said, of telling the man who had usurped his place where he could be found? What use would it have been to keep alive the child's hope of being able to see her mother again? In Oslac's jealous mind, Fearn belonged with the new Earl of Northumbria, her natural father, who would be able to arrange a good marriage for her. He had failed to see what both Fearn and Clodagh could see quite clearly: that the bond between mother and daughter was stronger than time or distance or the plans of men, or that hope and love were not so easily banished.

Though the possibility had not been discussed at the time, Fearn stored this information in her mind for consideration as a way of shortening her one-year stay in Lindholm. So one of the first things she did on reaching the longhouse was to make use of her newly made ink and quill pens to write to her half-sister Elf in Londenburh on the parchment sheets she had supplied. She was still writing it when darkness fell and the lamps were lit.

Fearn had been asleep for several hours when she felt the soft feather mattress dip and the linen sheet move over her skin. 'Haesel?' she murmured, sleepily. But instead of Haesel's whisper of reassurance, an arm was laid heavily along the sumptuous curve of her hip and thigh, the hand already smoothing a pathway into the secret hollows that were now more easily accessible than the first time when clothing had come between them. She felt his warm nakedness against her own, the exciting length of his legs, the hard power of bare arms easing her carefully towards him, then the soft kiss not meant to wake her too suddenly from dream to reality. In her half-sleep, something reminded her to resist, then just as quickly faded as the sensations began to flood her body, floating her mind towards an even better experience than before, skin coming alive against skin.

Urgently, his fingers unplaited her thick hair and tousled it wildly upon the pillow while his own hair, now freed from the usual plait, fell in a soft silky sheet over her face as they kissed under its deliciously sensuous canopy. The softness of it draped her breasts as his hand held the fullness to his mouth, making her arch and moan at the blissful pulling of his lips and teeth, creating a sensation of exquisite tenderness instead of the pain inflicted by a brutish mate. There were other first times in store for her, too, made possible by the perfect conditions as well as by her hazy willingness. Now, in the dark warm peace of her chamber, she found a new freedom to explore him as she herself was being explored with no words of instruction, her delight in having his fine muscular body beneath her fingers drawing from him sounds that said more than words about his enjoyment.

More confident than before about her abilities, she allowed her hands to wander over him and to bring new sensations to her fingertips, the soft silken crevices, the harder undulations, the smooth expanses of chest and shoulder, and the tiny buds of his nipples that had no other purpose than to give pleasure. This time, their loving moved into phase after phase of ecstasy until, when his explorations took him close to the source of her aching desire, disturbing her beyond bearing, she wrapped his slender hips within her legs to feel his hardness throbbing with the want of her. She held her breath, savouring the moment of dilation that once she had dreaded, letting out a long sigh of delight at his slow plunge that sent ripples of undiluted pleasure through her body.

He had no need to fear hurting her this time, for her sighs told him how much this pleasured her and her whispered words, 'Don't stop…', were her only spoken instructions. Then time waited upon them in a rapturous anticipation of an ending both of them tried, and failed, to delay. It came upon them in a blaze of sensation, engulfing them, suspending their breathing, whirling them into a void of perfect bliss before sliding them back down to earth, dizzy and overwhelmed. And although Fearn was no surer than before why this was happening when revenge had already been exacted, except that its pleasures were too great to ignore, she was too tired and filled with wonder to make any bitter remarks about the event, especially when Aric had already exposed her defensive untruthfulness. So she snuggled easily into his arms, accepting that what had just happened was even better than the first time and that this peaceful conclusion was more satisfactory in every way than the snarling she had initiated.

* * *

Next morning, she was realistic enough not to expect anything more from Aric in the way of tenderness than in previous days. It was as if, she thought, their coming together in silence was merely intended to satisfy a powerful urge that both knew could not be disregarded. And although she did not, and would not, speak of love to him, she knew that what she felt was more than a physical desire, but something unique and all-consuming, and that what *he* felt was an ordinary male lust and a reasonably good excuse to indulge himself without the effort of a lasting relationship. It was only for a year, she told herself. For that time, she would have to bear the pain and keep herself occupied, as Mother Bridget had advised.

Chapter Eight

Having discovered not only her roots but also the kind of community where her healing skills would be appreciated, it proved to be relatively easy for Fearn to keep herself occupied almost every day and to concentrate on the plight of others rather than her own.

Through Hrolf, Aric knew and approved of her involvement with the elderly English couple. He had known of them for some time but, because of his frequent long absences, had not understood the full extent of the work they were doing, only that they were Christians whose main interest was to convert the pagans of Lindholm. Aric had no problem with that. People were free to believe in whatever gods suited them best. His own half-hearted belief in Odin's powers had stood him in good stead, so far, in getting him safely back home from each voyage. But when

Hrolf informed him of the English couple's be-
nevolence towards those who suffered, he found
this strangely moving and more useful by far
than the eternal pursuit of vengeance that gave
no one any long-lasting happiness comparable
to a slave's freedom, for instance.

'They're not trying to stop the trade in slaves,'
Hrolf told him.

'So I understand. But you say they buy them
all up? What then?'

'They heal them and feed them. This is how
the Lady Fearn helps. She gives them the kindness they need and she tends the women who
give birth. The old couple find good homes for
them, usually with other Christians. The men,
particularly. The women are good with cloth.
Marvellous stuff, it is. And the merchants buy
everything they make. They've a very lucrative
trade going there, but you should see how they
care for one another. No beatings. No abuse. I've
never seen such a happy crowd. They have a
small church there, too, but no one is obliged to
go. They seem to want to.'

'So what do they do with the infants?' Aric
said.

'The mothers are allowed to keep them and
when they're ready to go back to work, the infants are looked after by the others. There's a

lovely little blonde girl there with a twisted foot who fetches and carries all day long. You'd think they'd have thrown her to the wolves when she was born, but there she is, happy as a lark. Everybody loves her, and—'

'Wait! How old is she?'

Hrolf levelled his hand. 'About so high. Five winters, perhaps. Why?'

Aric did not answer except with a frown. Could it be? About five years ago? Few would have known about the events of that night except the family. Neighbours would have been told that the child had died naturally. The women never condoned such drastic action. He left Hrolf and headed for the stream where he stripped off his clothes and plunged into the deepest coldest pool, dunking his head below the surface to clear his mind of the terrible wailing and howling of his sister, five years ago. As for the English couple, would it be too great a coincidence to connect them with Fearn's banished parents? A long way from home, certainly, but stranger things had happened. By now, Fearn would know the truth, yet it disturbed him to think that she did not trust him enough to share it with him, nor had she told him anything about the help she was giving there, or about the child with the twisted foot. But then, when had he ever given her the chance?

For once, the icy water of the stream did nothing to clear his head of the growing resentment he felt at being kept out of Fearn's thoughts, for the more he knew of her activities, the more certain he was that the English couple must be her long-lost parents, the ones for whom she had grieved so long. He recalled that night on the longship when she had told him of her abandonment and the scar it had left on her heart. Yet now, if indeed she had found them, she was content to let him believe she still suffered. Why? Could it be that this was her way of keeping things even between them? He refusing to discuss her future? She refusing to discuss her past? Or was she afraid of revealing how it came about that she was Thored's daughter and her mother banished along with her husband? What had happened there? Was it too shameful for her to share with him? Perhaps he ought to go and find out for himself who exactly this couple were and the child with the twisted foot, also, with whom Fearn must have been in close contact. Was that another instance of her determined effort to limit his knowledge of her heart's pain at another child's abandonment? Did he deserve such exclusion from her thoughts?

He stood up, grabbing his dry clothes and walking home half-naked, too preoccupied and angry with himself and his woman to care about the stares that followed him to the door.

Asked that same question, Fearn would have given a similar answer, that their night meetings were filled with a frenzy of desperate lovemaking in which the darkness seemed to conceal all other thoughts concerning the present and the future. If she found it beneficial to put her skills to work on most days, she found it far from comfortable to feel that she was being used by Aric, accepting it only because she could not accept the alternative. How much she needed the relief of making love was borne out when she kept her sharp tongue in check on these occasions, yet their daytime relationship was clouded by resentment when Aric did nothing to relieve her of the fears of uncertainty. When she went so far, once, to mention Loki's poorly concealed liking to be near Freya whenever and wherever he could, wondering if Aric had noticed, it appeared that he had. 'I don't see him as much of a threat,' he said, with his usual arrogance. 'She can have her fling now, if that's what she wants. Plenty of time for her to settle down, after she's married.'

'And that's all you care?' Fearn said, discon-

certed by his attitude. 'You would not want to
warn Loki off?'

'Warn him off? No, why should I? They both
know the position.'

'How very understanding you are. That
means, I take it, that I can—'

Quick as lightning, his hand shot out to grasp
her arm as she moved away, hauling her back
to him with a snarling reply that left her in no
doubt of his seriousness. 'You can do nothing of
the sort!' he growled, glaring at her with eyes of
cold steel from beneath a heavy frown. 'You are
my woman until I release you.'

'And isn't Freya your woman, too? You certainly give that impression.'

'I choose to share *your* bed, not hers. That's
the difference.'

She glared back at him, knowing how unset-
tling that could be. 'Not for long, Dane. You cannot delay your marriage for ever, you know. A
woman likes to know where she stands on that
kind of thing. You surely don't expect her to wait
for ever, do you?'

'That's *my* business!' he replied sharply. Then,
because she was so close and the scent of her
skin disturbed him, he took her white veil and a
fistful of her hair and pulled her face to his, sharing with her the kind of fierce, passionate kiss

with which his night-time visits usually began before the rhythm of their loving found a more sustainable tempo.

She found that she was trembling as he walked away, her heart beating to a different pace at the anger welling up around it. On the few occasions when they talked, it was as if their mutual frustration found an outlet in harsh words when she would much rather have taken part in a rational discussion. The only person to whom she had expressed her deepest thoughts, and then only briefly, was her half-sister Elf, Queen Aelfgyfu, in the letter. Fearn had shown it, then read it, to Clodagh, who had shaken her head sadly at the contents, remarking that she wished it had been otherwise for her dearest daughter. 'Have courage,' she had whispered, holding her in a much-needed embrace. 'One thing at a time. God is listening. Trust in Him, Fearn.'

The letter had been sent to Lundenburh on one of the trusted merchants' ships, giving Fearn cause to gloat that Aric was not being allowed to share in this delicious independence. She would like to have sent a letter to Earl Thored in Jorvik, too, to say that she had found Clodagh and Oslac, and that now at last she was able to comprehend the reasons behind her abandonment. But these were not the kind of sentiments one could write in a letter to a man whose reading skills were basic. And there was a limit to the words that Fearn knew to express exactly what she felt about him. It had been difficult to say to Elf how and why she was beginning to love Aric. How much more difficult would it be to tell a man of Thored's status how she forgave him for the pain he had caused? She would like to have known if Aric's sister Tove had fallen in love with him all those years ago. Since her own recent experiences, she now knew that this was entirely possible, despite how it must look from a Danish perspective. Clodagh had admitted it and yet, even as a Christian, had been unable to combat the trouble it had caused to her marriage. Now, more and more, the need to see her natural father occupied her thoughts without being able to see a way forward.

Although Fearn had put Freya's case for a decision about her wedding to Aric, she had never sought Freya's company, thinking that she herself might be seen as a threat to her happiness. She was therefore glad to find that this was not so, but rather as a woman as much at the mercy of men's decisions as she was and therefore to be looked on as a source of mutual sympathy. So it was on a warm day when Fearn was weary with standing at the big upright loom and dropping with a clatter the flat wooden beating sword that Freya arrived to offer a reason to take a rest.

'The time will come,' Freya said, smiling as she handed the sword back to Fearn, 'when some clever person will invent a way for us to sit down while we weave.'

Fearn took the sword with thanks. 'And when that happens,' she said, sliding it between the warps, 'it will be the men who begin to weave. You watch.'

Relaxing against cushions on the fur-covered platform, neither of them found it necessary to say in words what both were thinking, that this meeting had not come a moment too soon and that their similarities numbered more than their differences. With an infusion of elderflowers in one hand and a hot cloud-berry dumpling in the other, they nibbled and sipped and licked sticky fingers as they watched Haesel and Eve skeining wool straight from the spindle. 'That's another thing just waiting for an invention,' Freya said, nodding towards the delicate wooden spindle. 'A thing that spins wool while you sit at it.'

'Men have their uses,' said Fearn, 'but making women's work easier is not one of them. They can invent better weapons and ships, of course.'

'*Do* they?'

'Do they what?'

'Have their uses. I only know of one. Well, two at most.'

All four of them smiled. 'You're being too generous, lady,' Haesel said.

Looking back on this episode, both Fearn and Freya thought how remarkable it was that friendship had come to them with so little effort and how easily they had slipped into the uncomplicated talk that usually took months or weeks to achieve. Inevitably, the conversation turned to their ambiguous relationship with Aric, which Fearn took to be the underlying reason behind Freya's visit. 'I don't want you to see me as a threat,' she said. 'I am here against my will. It's always been my wish to control my life, but so far I've failed miserably and, what's more, I can't see it happening any time soon, either. I got the impression that that's what's happening to you, too, with pressure from all sides. Am I right, Freya?'

In spite of her angled question, Fearn was quite prepared for some opposition to it, for even in so short an acquaintance, and knowing what she knew of Freya's independence of spirit, she had formed an impression of a character quite at odds with her delicate appearance.

'I don't see you as a threat at all, Fearn. I

know you're in an impossible situation and that there isn't much you can do about it. But I'm still free, although everyone in my family seems to think my future with Aric is a foregone conclusion.'

'I thought so, too. Isn't it?'

'Not to me, it isn't. Aric has never consulted my wishes and that makes me angry. We're cousins. We grew up together. He assumes that, because I am part of my father's farm, all he has to do to get it is to marry me.' She waved her hands to show the ease of it. 'That I'll fall into his hands, just like that! He knows he can take concubines if he wishes and I suppose he assumes I shall not grumble too loudly.'

'But, Freya, you could divorce him if he did. Couldn't you? He would never risk it. Besides, if you're thinking I might be given that role, it won't happen. You know I must be returned to Jorvik next year and exchanged for Kean. Aric's long-term plans don't include me.'

'I don't particularly want them to include me either, Fearn,' Freya said with a faraway look that reached beyond the bright light from the doorway. 'I can't discuss anything with my father or Aunt Astrid because they won't admit there's anything to discuss. Father is not well and he wants us to get on with it before Aric goes away again, and neither of them thinks a woman is capable of managing a stud farm without at least one of them.'

'Could you, Freya?'

Freya's fine fair eyebrows rose, showing eyes of a startling blue. 'I wonder who Aric thinks has been managing the place while he's been away. It certainly was not my father. He spends most mornings in bed nowadays. I know as much as either of them about the breeding and rearing and breaking in of horses. I've foaled eight mares this year without help from my father, only from the men on the farm and the slaves who work there. He hasn't told Aric that.'

'Aric offered to give one of them to me,' Fearn said, 'but I refused it.'

'Really? Well, I'm glad you refused, because it was not his to give.'

'I'm sorry. I should have known that.'

Freya put out a hand to rest it on Fearn's, giving it a squeeze before removing it. 'Don't be apologising for him,' she said. 'It just highlights what I've been saying, that Aric assumes the farm is already his. I'm very fond of him, as his cousin, but like most men he's so intent on what *he* wants that he tends to forget that others have their own ideas.'

'Could you not tell him, Freya?'

'Yes,' Freya whispered. 'Yes, it looks as if I might have to.'

It was significant, Fearn thought later, that Freya had not trusted her quite enough to share with her the friendship of Loki, which made her wonder if Loki did indeed have a place in Freya's future or whether her silence on the matter was because she feared that she, Fearn, might let Aric know of it. It did not matter, she told herself. Everyone has their secrets. She had still not told Wenda that her child lived happily on the other side of Lindholm, for she knew from experience how it would break Clodagh's heart to part with her now and probably little Meld's, too. How to resolve the problem in a way that would do least damage would take more co-operation than she could be sure of at this time. Perhaps time itself would provide its own solution. Her talk with Freya had, however, given her some comfort to know that she was not entirely alone in being dissatisfied with Aric's attitude and also that Freya did not see her as a rival or an enemy. They were both in a similarly difficult position, having their futures interfered with so seriously.

As for Meld's future, that was precarious, too. Fearn had played with her and given her little tasks to perform, and thought what a bright and happy child she was, brimming with life and intelligence. But like her own peculiarity of odd-coloured eyes, easily recognisable by a parent, Meld's twisted foot would only have to be spotted by any of Wenda's family for them to know who she was. And that could so easily happen in a place the size of Lindholm. Hrolf had seen her, but would not know anything of Wenda's loss five years ago, and Fearn had been careful not to call her parents anything other than by their Christian names, as did everyone else. Hrolf would have no reason to speak of Meld to Aric, or to know that she had found her parents.

Fearn's extraordinary gift of healing was soon recognised by Clodagh and Oslac as being something beyond the usual knowledge of herbal remedies relied on by all good households. Even in her earliest days of working with them, she had only to lay her hands upon painful knees for the aged patient to walk away without pain for the first time in years and, as on the voyage where a wound had refused to heal for months, Fearn's hands could close a wound with a healthy scar in the space of a day. Although Aric had remembered her remarkable skills, he was far from optimistic about her offer to help his uncle, however. 'He would not allow it,' he said, lifting his new gerfalcon up on his gloved wrist and feeding it a morsel of meat.

'Why?' Fearn persisted. 'Doesn't he want to recover?'

'He won't even admit there's a problem,' Aric said. 'He thinks it's just the tiredness of old age.'

'It is. But he has chest pains, too. Everyone can see that.'

'Anyway, he would never accept the help of a woman. Especially not you.'

'Why not me?' Fearn asked. 'He doesn't trust me?'

'Because you're different. What did Freya want?'

'To talk. Is that so strange?'

'About me?'

'Oh, for pity's sake!' Fearn said, making the falcon flap in alarm. 'You men have such inflated ideas about your importance to women, don't you? No, we didn't' talk about you, we talked about ourselves. That's *much* more interesting.' Stomping away from him and the agitated bird, she did not see Aric's laughing face.

They had discussed him, of course, although Fearn knew he would not have been so cocksure of his place in their hearts if he'd heard their criticisms of his manner, taking them both for granted, refusing to discuss their futures with them, and his own involvement. How far this reflected his own uncertainties they could not know.

Only a few days later it began to look as if matters might be debated at last when Uther sent for Aric for a family discussion.

'You will come with me,' Aric told Fearn. 'For as long as you are in Lindholm, you are involved.'

'But he doesn't like me,' she protested. 'I don't want to be the cause of his ill humour. If things don't go the way he wants, he'll blame me for being there.'

In a surprising gesture of tenderness, he took her into his arms, smoothing his large hand over the curves of her back while pressing his lips to her brow. 'You will come with me as my woman,' he said. 'If he wants me there, he'll have to have you there, too. I want you to hear what's said at first hand.'

'About our future?' she whispered, hoping he might elaborate.

'You know what your future is,' he replied. 'He'll want to know about mine.'

'And Freya's?' she persisted, still hoping.

'She'll be there,' was all he said.

Fearn removed herself from his arms, refusing to beg for more detail.

* * *

It was the first time she had entered the house where Freya lived with her father and aunt. Being 'too different' for Uther Borgsen, she had never been invited, but now at last she was able to see for herself the kind of home Astrid and Freya had made in spite of the owner's insistence on thrift at all costs. His own garments were little different from those of his workers, a simple homespun tunic and baggy woollen trousers tucked into old leather knee boots that looked as if they were rarely parted from his feet. His leather belt, having lost its buckle, was tied around his waist and, on this particular morning, he clutched a matted old fox fur around his shoulders with several white-tipped tails dangling round the edges. As usual, he held a straw between his teeth, seldom removing it to speak, and Fearn noticed that his hair had not been washed for some time, contrary to the Danish custom of bathing every Saturday. Aric was meticulous about such things, but now Fearn noticed other differences, too, for in spite of Uther's wealth, the women's efforts to create a home that reflected his success were spoiled by his personal slovenly habits, unlike Aric's spotless dwelling. It was as if he'd tried to bring the stables into his home, with piles of worn-out harness and old blankets, stacks of buckets containing fodder and a pile of rusty swords waiting for his attention.

She and Aric sat at the long beechwood table opposite Uther, Astrid and Freya, between them a tension not lessened by Uther's frown of displeasure at Fearn's appearance. 'No need to have brought your woman,' he grumbled to Aric. 'This doesn't concern her.'

'Do my aunt and cousin have any objections?' Aric said, looking at them with a twinkle and sure of their agreement.

'None at all,' they said. 'Fearn is welcome.'

'Then tell us what's on your mind, Uncle, if you please.'

'There's a lot on my mind just now, young man, that has to be settled before it's too late. You'll be off a-Viking again next year, most like, and I want the stud farm to be in safe hands before then. I need to know what your plans are, first.'

'Plans about what, Uncle?'

'You *know* what plans, man,' the old man snapped.

'I think he means Freya,' said Astrid, patiently. 'I think it's only fair to her, and us, if you could give us some warn…er…*notice* when you intend to marry her.'

'To my knowledge,' Aric said, softly, 'I have not asked Freya to marry me. Have I, Freya? Can you recall?'

'No,' she said. 'Not as I remember.'

Uther's hand slapped the table, his usual way of making a point. 'Then *ask* her, man, and get it over with. It's the only way you're going to get this business when I'm gone. You can't have it without her and that's final.'

'Uncle,' Aric said, wearily, 'you've made that point so many times we're all sick of hearing it. Has it never occurred to you that the reason I've not asked Freya to marry me is that she doesn't want me to?'

Uther's colour was rising, along with his voice which squeaked with annoyance. 'Of *course* she wants you to, you great oaf! Who else is going to, if you don't? She's not exactly the best-looking wench you'll ever see, but she has the farm and the money, and that's—'

Astrid cut across her brother in mid-flow. 'That's enough!' she said, loudly.

'That's what I was about to say, woman. That's enough for any man—'

'No! That's enough from you, Uther, about Freya. She has feelings, you know.'

'No she doesn't, Astrid. This is business. Feelings don't come into it.'

With a grateful glance from Freya, Aric contradicted him. 'I think you may be wrong there, Uncle. Freya's feelings *do* come into it. Would you be prepared to tell your father why, Cousin? I think it's time he knew. Don't you?'

'Knew what?' Astrid said, looking intently at her niece on the other side of Uther. 'What have you been up to, young lady? If it's—'

'Aunt! I beg of you to let her *speak*. She's perfectly capable, if only you'll give her the chance,' Aric said. 'Tell them, Freya.'

'Thank you. You've all got my future wrapped up, but not once has one of you asked me about my plans until now. I don't know how Aric knows it, but he's right. I don't want to marry him. I'm going to marry someone else.'

Jumping to his feet so fast that his stool fell over behind him, Uther roared like a bull, redfaced and furious. *'What?'* he bellowed. 'Don't be ridiculous, girl. You'll marry your cousin if it's the last thing you ever *do*. If you think the stud I've built up over the last thirty years is going to some lad who's been sneaking round you like a randy—'

'*Uther!* Stop this, *immediately*!' Astrid yelled at him. 'Keep your farm talk for the stables. Sit down and let Freya tell us herself without you making up things to suit your argument, such as it is. Carry on, child.'

'Thank you, Aunt,' Freya said, watching her father fumble with his stool. 'You may have noticed that I'm not a child, but a woman, and I am perfectly capable, as my cousin says, of making my own mind up about who I marry. Whether it suits you or not, Father.'

'Ungrateful little minx!' Uther shouted, sitting down hard. 'Nobody's asked *my* permission yet, so who *is* this mysterious idiot?'

'Not mysterious and no idiot, either, Father. It's Loki. We've been in love for years. He wants to marry me and I've accepted him.'

No sooner had Uther's behind touched the stool than it was knocked over again, but this time not to the sound of a bellow but a choking attempt to say her lover's name, cut off by a strangled cough and a fist pummelling hard at his chest. Turning away from the table, he doubled up in pain, then pitched forward headlong across the stone floor, spattering it with bright red blood. The crash shook the table, throwing him into the edge of the platform where he lay sprawled in a crumpled heap of fox furs with his lifeblood gushing away before any of them could stop it.

Astrid caught Freya and pulled her away,

sobbing and screaming, sure that this was entirely her fault. Aric and Fearn reached him but could do nothing to help, for Uther had left them in a frenzy of powerlessness, having relied on his power to control the lives of others. Stunned, shocked beyond words to have actually witnessed what each of them had privately predicted, they said nothing as, one by one, the servants and slaves gathered round in silence until Aric signalled them to remove his uncle's body with all the respect due to the master of the house. So while Freya sobbed, full of guilt, in the comforting arms of her aunt, Aric held Fearn close to him, which she knew he would not have done had Uther been there to see. Already the small shift in relationships had begun, especially now that Freya's secret was out in the open at last. Indeed, it was only a matter of a few moments before Loki himself came to see what had happened and to offer Freya the support of his presence, soothing her weeping in a gentle manner far removed from that teasing episode on the banks of the River Humber when he had snatched at Fearn's circlet.

'You knew about Loki?' said Fearn as Aric's chin rested on her forehead.

'They were growing careless,' he whispered.

'Come, I think you should return home. I'll come later. These two need my help.'

'Yes, of course. You must stay as long as they need you.' She went to embrace Freya and Astrid and to ask if there was anything she could do to help, but aware that their preparations would now centre around their gods and all that must be done to invoke a safe passage for Uther into the next world.

For the next few days, Fearn saw very little of Aric while he was so deeply involved with the organisation of the funeral to which most of Lindholm would be expected. Each night Aric would come to her to seek the comfort of her arms before falling into an exhausted sleep that came before any questions about her day or any information about his. Lovemaking was suspended and Fearn knew not to expect anything from him at this difficult time, not even the briefest discussion about whether his uncle's sudden death made any difference to his personal plans, or not. Nevertheless, she could not help but assume that, with Freya's intention of marrying Loki and her father no longer able to bully anyone into doing his will, Aric might at last consider including her, Fearn, in his future. That, however, would depend on the depth of his feelings for her. So far, he had given her very little indication that she meant anything more to him than a rather spectacular and unique prize who was apparently willing, after some persuasion, to share his nights. Uther's death had not yet prompted him into divulging any of his thoughts on the new situation for which there could be several reasons, one of which was, as Freya had agreed, that he habitually wore blinkers so as to keep his mind focused on his goal. In his case, revenge.

The day of the funeral was more like a storm at sea with lashing rain, high winds, thunder and every other indication that Thor was very much present. The massive grave dug out of the sandy soil had been shored up on all sides with timber staves with the chamber creating a space for a wooden pyre upon which Uther's richly clad and ornamented corpse was laid, surrounded by many of his favourite personal belongings. Whatever they thought he would need for his next life was consumed by the fire. As expected, most of Lindholm's population were there to watch the great event, huddled under soaking hoods, but kept warm by the blaze and relieved to see that Uther's slaves had been spared making the journey with him. Aric had forbidden that, too.

* * *

So, it was in the early hours of the next morning when the mountain of ashes was covered by the displaced soil, hissing as the wetness fell on to the heat and sending up clouds of steam into the dark sky. Every available man and boy joined in, finally patting the mound into a boat shape with their spades, after which came the herculean task of outlining the shape with boulders, for this would be Uther's ship to take him into the next world. Then they knelt round the edges while their priest chanted invocations and threw sacred herbs upon the mound. Uther was on his way.

At the longhouse, Fearn had stayed up all night with food at the ready, should it be needed, now and then going to the door to see the brilliant blaze up on the hillside before returning to her own fire. She heated huge cauldrons of water, ready for Aric's return, sure that, after the cremation and burial, he would need to bathe. Towels were warming by the hearth when he returned at dawn, too tired and emotional to speak, his face and clothing spattered with ash, soot and mud, his hair dulled by rain and flying debris. Without a word, she removed his clothes and put them aside to be washed, then undid his plait and led him to the large half-barrel with a stool set inside, where he sat with eyes closed, already half-asleep, head in hands.

He murmured as each ladle of water was poured over his head and shoulders where red weals had appeared beneath the friction of wet clothes. The tub filled up to his waist before Fearn took handfuls of soapwort flower heads and rubbed them over him to make a lather, gently washing and caressing the grime away and bringing back the pale shine to his hair. He held up his face to her like a child, keeping his eyes closed as she wiped it clean and patted it dry, thinking as she did so how different this was from the rowdy and boisterous bathing in the river when the men tried to outdo each other in boyish bravado. She thought he would not respond when her lips touched the nubs at the back of his neck as he bent forward, but she was held back by his wet hand on her arm, drawn down to him and kissed with an energy that surprised her.

Climbing out to stand beside the warm hearth, he indicated that he wished to be dried by her and, when she reached the most intimate parts, he did not relieve her of the task to spare her any embarrassment. Nor did he realise that this was actually the first time she had seen him at close quarters, naked, in the light.

As she paused, he opened his eyes. 'What is it?' he said.

'You know what it is,' she replied, pushing the damp linen cloth at him to conceal his obvious excitement. 'I think you should dry those parts.'

'I'm sorry, sweetheart. I did not mean to distress you.' Holding the linen between them, he eased her forward into his arms. 'Is it...bad memories?'

She nodded. 'You have a right to know,' she whispered, 'that my...late husband...obliged me to bathe him...and dry him...but then...he would go too far.' A sob rose in her throat as she recalled the pain and humiliation of those times. 'And I thought it would be all right with you because I...' The words almost slipped out, but she stopped them just in time. 'Because you do not abuse me as he did. Forgive me. I think I'm tired.'

'It was thoughtless of me and there is nothing to forgive. Come, over here.' Blowing out the two lamps, he led her to the bed and, lifting her legs, helped her to snuggle between the blankets and furs, wrapping her closely in his embrace, still moist and sweet-smelling and damp-haired. 'That was the most memorable bath I've ever had,' he said, stifling a yawn. 'Thank you, sweetheart.'

Within minutes, they were both sound asleep.

* * *

Dawn had broken some time ago as the servants and slaves tiptoed through the longhouse to begin their duties. Fearn stirred as the sounds reached her through the walls, her hands smoothing over Aric's clean skin, reminding her that he was still wrapped round her. As if by some hidden signal, their lips found each other, fusing them still closer until the heat began to course through their veins, bringing them to an awareness of their needs after so many nights of abstinence. With a growing urgency, Fearn helped him to remove the kirtle she had slept in, sharpening the tingling senses in her skin as warm tender surfaces slid over her limbs to waken them. His hands touched and fondled, finding again those hidden parts that had ached for his attention, melting her, springing her apart with a gasp of pure yearning for him to make a new life inside her, before she could think rationally of reasons not to.

'Now!' she whispered. 'Quickly!'

Responding to her plea and sensing that, this time, a long and leisurely wooing was not what she needed, he joined her with the vigour he usually reserved for the end, jubilant that he need not exercise his usual restraint, for she was already near the point of ecstasy. Moaning with desire, Fearn was unaware of her nails digging into his back or of the tangled blond strands of his hair that teased her skin, and when the blaze of passion consumed them both in a simultaneous white heat of sensation, she cried out at the intensity, hearing him groan into the thick black mass of her hair.

On every previous occasion, sleep had overtaken them immediately, leaving no chance for any endearments which, she thought, was not entirely unintentional. Aric had always disappeared before she was awake, removing any chance of discussion. On this particular morning, however, they lay together for some time, sated and euphoric, as if moving might disturb whatever it was they had made between them. Fearn's head nestled into the crook of his shoulder, her cheek against his breast. 'I shall go and speak to my Christian friends,' she said. 'I expect they'll have heard, but they'll want to know if it affects my position here.' It was a prompt. The best she could do.

'In what way?' he said.

'Well, now the pressure is off for you to marry Freya. Doesn't that change anything?'

'It certainly changes things for her. She's surprised me. I had no idea she had developed such courage, speaking out to her father like that. Of course, she blames herself for his death, but Astrid and I don't believe that's the case. Nor does Loki.'

'So she really intends to marry him?'

'Loki? Yes, that's the way it looks,' he said, peeling the covers down, already bringing the discussion to an end before it had properly begun, 'but how much help he'll be to her on the farm I cannot imagine. She'll need a manager.'

'You mean, you?'

'Yes, of course me,' he said, rolling off the bed. 'Who else?'

Fearn had it in mind to warn him of what Freya had said to her about being able to manage without him, but a disturbing wave of irritation prevented her as she clambered on to the floor and pulled a blanket around her shoulders. The discussion, if one could call it that, had inevitably swung towards Aric himself as, once again, he preferred not to see what was behind her line of enquiry.

She could have insisted.

Grabbed his face and made him listen.

Pleaded for a sign of his love, or whatever he used as a substitute.

Could he love? Was he capable of it? Was he still determined to keep it out of their relationship?

Was it still all about revenge? Even now?

So she let it go and hoped that, once the farewell feast was out of the way and Uther Borgsen's last wishes known, Aric might at last acknowledge how much, if anything, she meant to him and where she fitted into his future. One thing was certain: life without him was too painful to think about. The only crumb of comfort she took from last night was that, twice, he had called her 'sweetheart'.

She took her concerns to Clodagh and Oslac who, although sympathetic, were unable to offer much comfort except to say that all would come right in the end and that God's will would be done. If the all-seeing all-knowing God could have given her some indication about His will beforehand, Fearn would have liked it better, but Clodagh felt it might be best if she were distracted from her heartaches by showing her the workshops of the skilled gold-workers who made their gold thread for embroidery. They used a strand of horsehair to wrap with finely beaten narrow strips of pure gold which had first been pulled through tiny holes, a very painstaking and slow method that required years of practice. They lingered in the workshops where women couched the gold threads over the silken surfaces, working by lamplight that shone across a rainbow of coloured silks stretched over frames. And although this was captivating and wonderful, Fearn felt that her mother was not quite as helpful with her problems as she would have liked and that the work with the patients came before everything else, even her daughter. Naturally, there was a limit to the help she and Oslac could offer and, being elderly, their answer to most things of a personal nature seemed to be patience. But it was not what Fearn preferred to hear.

On many occasions, Hrolf went along with Haesel, joining in with the tasks, helping children to feed, thoroughly enjoying the feeling of being needed. Haesel teased him about this new fatherly side to his character as they walked along the water's edge, now perfectly at ease together and unobtrusively in love, as if they'd slipped into it without quite knowing how. Sitting together on a boulder, Hrolf slipped an arm around her and pulled her close to him, kissing her long and tenderly, sure of her compliance. Like Fearn, Haesel kept her hair covered with a fine white linen veil which helped to conceal the disfiguring scars on her neck and chest. So when Hrolf slipped his hand under her hair to bare her neck to his wandering lips, she pulled back, holding the veil over it. 'No,' she said, looking down. 'You should not see that.'

'Why ever not, my little love?' he said. 'You are beautiful, Haesel.'

'No, I'm not, Hrolf. Not there. You'll be revolted. I prefer to hide it.'

'Listen. You know I love you. There is no part of you that will revolt me. Let me into your secret and I will show you. Come, love. There's no one to see us.'

Reluctantly letting go of the veil, she pulled down the neck of her kirtle to show him the tightly puckered skin and mass of scars, livid and still tender across her throat where the blast had caught her. Her anxious eyes searched his face for signs of shock, but found nothing there except a tenderness in his expression as he bent his head to kiss every part of the terrible wound, soft as a butterfly's wings.

'This is part of my lovely girl,' he whispered. 'Cover it from the stares of others, if you wish, but you need never cover it from me, beloved, and you can tell me about it when you are ready to. I adore you. I want you to be my wife and, yes, before you ask, I will learn about your religion and become one of the Community. They're wonderful people, like you and the Lady Fearn. We could make our home with them one day.'

'But you forget, Hrolf, I shall have to return to Jorvik with my lady next year.'

'Then I shall come with you.'

'Would the Jarl allow it? You are sworn to be his man. He'll need you.'

'Then we shall find a way round the problem. It can be done.'

If Haesel could not imagine how, at that moment, such an obstacle could be overcome, she had faith that this remarkably positive young man would find a way.

Later in the day, however, when she and Fearn were together preparing to attend Uther's feast, she told her lady of what she had seen that day when she had been with Hrolf. It had been far out down the fjord, apparently too far away for Hrolf to see, until she realised that the distant ship had been for her eyes only. One of her 'seeings'.

'Was it coming, or going?' Fearn said. 'Danish or English?'

'I couldn't tell. It was not one I recognised from that distance.'

'Not Aric's, then?'

'I think not. But it was hazy. Then it disappeared.'

'What does it mean, Haesel?'

The blonde curls shook. 'That's the trouble,'

she whispered. 'I never know what my seeings mean, do I? Coming, going, Danish, English. Just a ship with the wind in its sails.'

'Then it's a sign of hope,' Fearn said, shaking out her green lichen-dyed kirtle. 'I shall wear green, the colour of hope.'

'Which reminds me, lady. According to my tally-stick, your courses are due any day now. Do you want to wear some protection for this evening?'

'Yes. What a good thing you reminded me. Now, the green glass and amber beads, I think.'

Neither of them questioned that what Haesel had seen might have been one of the many ships coming and going along the fjord every day, nor how she could tell it from them except that, in her mind, it was somehow different and it had to do with them alone.

The day after Uther's farewell feast, Aric and Fearn returned to where Freya and Astrid now lived in a house already cleared of the clutter that had made the hall look more like a storeroom than a wealthy man's residence. Gone were the piles of worn-out saddles, rusty tools and moth-eaten furs. The walls were now covered with co-lourful textiles, the shields polished, the floor covered with new rush matting, new candles in all the holders and the sweet smell of fresh herbs instead of the stink of horse sweat. Freya and Astrid had not lost a moment of their newfound freedom but, although the welcome was cordial, it soon became obvious to Aric that his cousin was about to take her father's will literally when it was confirmed that the house and estate was entirely hers, including the much-prized stud farm, and that she was not about to share any part of it with him.

'But you need a manager, Freya,' Aric said, glancing at Loki for his agreement. 'Won't she, Loki? Don't tell me you're as good at horse breeding as you are at navigating a longship, for I'll not believe you. And anyway, you'll be going with me on our next voyage.'

Before Loki could reply, Freya took the words out of his mouth. 'No, he won't, Aric. He'll be here, learning the business.'

Aric frowned. 'What are you saying, Cousin? That he's going to be the new manager? What about me? I've been doing the job since I was a lad. Ten years, in between Viking raids. I know the business inside out. You can't do it without me.'

'Then who do you think managed the place while you were away for well over a year, Aric, and while my father was unwell? I did. With the men and the slaves, I organised the breeding, the foaling, the selling and buying of new stock, and the training, too. Me, Aric. On my own.'

'I thought your father...'

'No, not Father. Me. I know as much about it as you do. Aunt Astrid will tell you so. Perhaps you've been assuming too much. You, my aunt and my father, without once thinking that I deserve a say in things. If you're disappointed, blame yourself. I can run this place as I did while you and Loki were away, but now I shall have *him* to help me.'

'But do you really *want* to, Cousin? What if I bought the farm from you? That would leave you free to do other things.'

'I don't want to do other things, thank you. My plans are for this place.'

'Sell it to me, Freya? I'll give you a fair price.'

'No. Loki has never taken me for granted the way you have, Aric. He actually *wants* to marry me, not the farm. No woman likes to be used.' Stretching out her hand, she smiled prettily as Loki took it and drew her to his side, and Aric knew she had never looked at him like that, not in all the years they'd known each other.

So far, Astrid had said nothing, but now she had seen a facet of Freya's character of which she clearly approved. 'She's right, Aric,' she said.

'We have all assumed too much for too long and Freya is extremely capable. She doesn't need another manager. Perhaps you've been getting your priorities wrong, too.'

To Fearn's surprise, Aric's only response to this onslaught was to stare long and hard at his aunt's unsympathetic expression as if he was trying to read what else she might have meant behind the words. 'I think we should leave now,' Fearn said.

Without another word, Aric took Fearn's arm and left the hall, walking in subdued silence down towards the quay where a large ship was coming in to tie up at one of the jetties. 'That's not one I recognise,' he said, shading his eyes against the sunlight. 'It's English. One of yours, Fearn, and not a merchant ship, either.'

'I've been hoping for a message from my sister in Lundenburh, but she would not have sent… not unless…'

He looked at her, sharply, still frustrated by the recent meeting. 'Not unless what?'

Instead of replying, Fearn walked along the timber gangway to the ship where men were tying ropes to the posts. One man wearing a fur-edged cloak stepped over the side of the ship on to the jetty and then, seeing Fearn with Aric some way behind her, unbuckled his leather pouch, drew out a piece of folded parchment and, with a courteous bow, handed it to her, speaking in English. 'The Lady Fearn of Jorvik? I am sent by Queen Aelfgyfu to give you this.'

Smiling with relief, Fearn took it, the first communication she had received since coming to Lindholm. Delight shone from her eyes as she turned to Aric. 'Look, a message from Elf. May I invite the men to stay with us until their return?'

'You are more than welcome to our hospitality for as long as you wish,' Aric said. 'Bring your baggage up to the great hall when you've made the ship safe. So,' he said to Fearn, 'what's the news? Go on, read it. I can see you're itching to know.'

Breaking the royal seal along the overlap, she prised open the stiff folds, holding it before him so that he could watch her finger move along the words as she read, her voice excited over the first lines of greeting until she slowed and stopped, her finger hovering over the name.

'Isn't that Earl Thored's name?' Aric said. 'Surely I've seen it before.'

'It is. My sister says, "Dear Sister, I write this as soon as the news reaches me of our father, Earl Thored, who died peacefully soon after you left. He was…surrounded…by his…"'

The letter trembled, and the words stuck in her throat as the terrible news made her gasp, instantly bringing to mind the way she had refused to say farewell or to accept his blessing.

'Oh…oh, no! How cruel! Now it's too late,' she whispered. 'Too late.'

'Too late for what?'

'For me…to tell him…that I understand…oh, how very *cruel*!'

His arm came across her shoulders to feel the shaking of her body against him. 'Fearn,' he said, 'it was bound to happen one day and then it's *always* too late to tell them something. And if you had been there with him, who is to say you'd have known what you know now that has helped you to understand him? We cannot always be in the right place at the right time. What else does your Queen say?'

'That she hears he was surrounded by his loved ones and that his funeral was a very grand affair in the cathedral at Jorvik, and he was buried there. And me,' she added, 'his daughter, not with him. Oh!' Shaking her head in sorrow, she looked out across the fjord towards the west and the wild North Sea that divided them. 'I ought to have *been* there.'

'So neither of his daughters were with him, then.'

'No, neither of us. But you see what this means, don't you? The situation is quite different now, isn't it?'

His arm slid off her shoulder as he began to walk slowly back along the jetty towards the houses and already Fearn sensed that the conversation was in its final phase. 'No,' he said. 'Thored's death has not changed anything here.'

Fearn knew that this was not the right time for her to pursue an argument when his mind was still reeling from Freya's decision and while she was stunned by the news of Thored. She ought to have waited, but felt compelled to argue the point there and then, despite the men rolling barrels and loading packhorses around them. 'Well, of *course* it does, Aric. How can you say otherwise?' she said, skipping over a coil of ropes. 'Now my father is no longer alive, your quarrel with him is at an end, isn't it? You can send me home and I will see that Kean is returned to you straight away. Earlier than expected. Isn't that good? *Please* will you stand still and hear me out?'

'I don't want to hear you,' he said, walking on ahead. 'I've told you, nothing has changed here. My sister was held by Thored for a year and I intend to do the same with you, lady.'

'To what purpose?' she almost screamed behind him. 'For *revenge*?'

'Yes!' he bawled. 'For my family's honour.'

'I don't *believe* you!' she yelled at his back. 'I will not *believe* that!'

'Then think of another reason. Or is your imagination not up to it?'

'What?' Stopping in her tracks, she watched him stride away. And for all her fertile imagination, she could think of no credible reason why he should wish to keep her here.

Chapter Nine

The square of parchment, creased and crumpled from weeks in the pouch of the English messenger, trembled in Fearn's hands as she scanned the words yet again for the last grain of meaning in the Queen's news.

...surrounded by his loved ones and loyal friends...

'Kean would have been with him,' she said to Haesel, 'but not me and not Elf, either. There will be a new earl there already, I expect. She doesn't say.'

'There'll be some changes, then,' Haesel said.

'Which will give Hilda even more to moan about,' Fearn muttered, adding hurriedly, 'I must not be uncharitable.'

'It would be charitable,' Haesel said, folding

her lady's linen shift, 'for you to go and tell Clodagh and Oslac. Tomorrow?'

'Yes, of course. Tomorrow. And I shall send
a message back to the Queen.'

'Shall you tell her your courses have not appeared this month?'

'Not until I'm more certain.'

'It's never happened before.'

Fearn lay back upon the furs that covered her
bed, placing a hand over her womb, protectively.
What if it were true? What if she was expecting
his child? How many more reasons would Aric
need to keep her here?

His intransigence angered and puzzled her.
Why did the death of Thored not cancel out the
need for revenge? How could he revenge himself
on a dead man? She had given him countless opportunities to say if she had a part to play in his
future and now not even Freya could be used as
an excuse when she had taken matters into her
own hands, after all Aric's expectations. Perhaps
she, Fearn, should do the same. If he would not
let her go, nor would he invite her to stay here as
his legal and beloved wife, then there was only
one course of action, for the prospect of staying
with a man who did not love her and did not want
her to love *him* was unthinkable. If she were indeed carrying his child, she would prefer to give

birth in the safety of her sister's royal care, not here where nothing was certain, not even the life of a newborn child.

'Hang my clothes on the line as you usually do, Haesel, will you?' she said as a wave of nausea swept over her. 'I shall not be telling Clodagh, either. Not yet.'

Aric had not come to her the previous evening, having parted on a sour note. He had offered her no more words of comfort nor, she suspected, did he feel the need to explain his unreasonableness. In the morning, after recovering from an unusual bout of sickness, she learnt from Haesel that he had departed for Aggersborg with Hrolf to attend to the building of a new ship designed to his own specifications. It was to be a fast seagoing vessel for which Deena, the deaf slave, had been weaving the sails for many months. Naturally, Fearn's first assumption was that this was a ship being made ready to take her home next year, since Hrolf had mentioned that it was to have a permanent shelter erected on the deck for the use of passengers. Feeling out of sorts and cynical about his mission, Fearn also wondered if he would be seeing anything of the woman who had threaded blossom in his hair on their one-night stay at Aggersborg.

In desperation, she took her troubles to the elderly priest of the small church where her parents worked close by, finding him sympathetic, but of no real help except to offer her some vague advice to have faith that all would be well, in the end. As 'the end' was precisely what she would like to have known more about, now, she came away even more determined to create it for herself and not to wait on faith alone. Had the ship that Haesel visualised been the one carrying news of Thored's death? Or had it been Aric's new one? These sightings were all very well, she thought, but could Haesel not be a little more exact?

'You're looking rather pale, my dear,' Clodagh remarked as they entered the sweet-smelling infirmary. 'Are you not well?'

'Perfectly well,' Fearn said. 'Just the time of the month.'

'Ah, then I have a nice little task for you. There's a young lassie over here who's having problems suckling her new bairn. It's her first. D'ye think you could sit with her and help? She gets so upset… Fearn…what..?'

Fearn had turned away, hurrying to the door, reaching the ditch just in time. Haesel held her as she doubled up. Clodagh followed. 'What's this about?' she said. 'Time of the month? Or something else?'

'Something else,' said Fearn, 'if you must know.'

'Of course I must know, child. I'm your mother. Come, I'll give you something for the sickness. It always works. Then you'd better tell me about it.'

Telling her mother about it, repeating what she had told the priest, made her wish she had gone to her first, for here she received the physical contact of motherly arms and the practical advice she needed to hear, even when she had heard it given to others on numerous occasions. Nevertheless, Fearn did not go as far as to discuss any plans to leave Lindholm before the allotted time, knowing that Clodagh would insist on her being delivered right there, with her, when the time came. She did not care to get into an argument of that kind, or to make promises she could not keep.

Her own concerns had taken first place, so far, though Fearn had not forgotten the news she had come to convey about the death of Thored, Clodagh's one-time lover and father of her only child. She expected Clodagh to take the news badly, but time had mellowed her love and death had been a constant guest at the infirmary. Grief came more quietly, these days. They sat together on a bench in the sun, Clodagh being comforted in her daughter's arms the way she had been doing only moments before at the possibility of a new life, rather than a death, as if one made up for the other. Both events were neither expected nor unexpected.

There were no tears as Clodagh spoke of it. 'A pity we could never communicate,' she said. 'There are always things to be said that come too late and one wonders if they needed to be said at all when we thought each other's thoughts. Perhaps he knew how I felt, the way I knew *his* mind. Time softens the sharp edges of pain, though I think there has not been a day when he was far from my thoughts.'

'I regret,' said Fearn, 'that I left without his blessing, without being able to tell him I understood.'

Clodagh's hand squeezed hers. 'I regret that he will never know that you and I found each other. That would have made him as happy as it has made me.'

Later, walking towards home, Fearn compared her mother's reflections with those of Aric, who had said much the same thing—that it was not always too late to tell them something, that we cannot always be in the right place at the right time. She saw now that Aric, like Clodagh, was probably speaking from experience and that, if he had opened his heart to her, he might have shared those regrets with her. She thought it unlikely now that she would ever truly know the man behind the façade. They had agreed, she and her mother, that it would serve no good purpose to tell Oslac of Thored's death, for he might then feel obliged to show a sorrow he could not feel for the man who had stolen his wife's heart.

As it happened, the timing of Fearn's revelations to her mother, one of them unintended, coincided only three days later with a surprise visit from the Jarl Aric and the young man named Hrolf who was known to them. Having just stepped on to the jetty, Aric agreed with his companion that now would be a good time to introduce himself to the elderly Christian couple whose work with slaves and other unfortunates was of such benefit to Lindholm. The visit had another purpose. Aric had intended for some time to discover for himself if these two were in fact the parents who had deserted Fearn and, if they were, why she had not told him so.

Both Clodagh and Oslac had known that there would be a time when they and the Jarl would meet face to face although, now that it was happening, and despite a kind of mental preparation, they were rather unsure about how to greet him. He was, after all, the most important man in Lindholm and yet he was their daughter's lover, too. And how did one greet the man responsible for bringing her back to them in this unorthodox fashion? Ought they to thank him while condoning their daughter's reluctance to inform him of his good deed, such as it was? In the end, these issues mattered less when his manner was so courteous and not at all the picture Fearn had painted of him as arrogant and self-obsessed, as any *jarl* had a right to be. Leading Aric into their large and comfortable hall, they poured mead and allowed him to lead with his questions.

'You are, I believe, the Lady Fearn's parents? She has not confided in me, you see, so this is why I am here without her knowledge. I'm not even sure she wants me to know, though I don't know why.'

Clodagh was the first to sympathise. The situation was delicate and without precedence. 'We are,' she said, 'but Fearn knew we would have to meet, one day. One cannot govern a place the size of Lindholm without knowing exactly who is who, can one?' She smiled, putting Aric's mind at ease. 'And I dare say she kept us apart because…well…the situation is fluid, isn't it?

She tells us she'll be obliged to leave us again and what point would there be in you knowing you were responsible for another sad parting? She was probably trying to spare you, my lord. Could it be that, do you think?'

Clodagh's kind and charitable explanation struck a chord in him, deep within his consciousness where, many years ago, a young man had returned from his first Viking expedition to find that his mother had left home, gone for good, with not a single word of farewell to ease his breaking heart. He felt the pain of it still, placing his hand there to comfort it. 'Yes,' he whispered. 'Yes, that could be it.'

Clodagh saw the gesture, but Oslac was keen to impress their guest with his own credentials. 'Yes,' he said, with a trace of elderly pride, 'we are indeed the Lady Fearn's parents. My wife and I were in Jorvik for many years, when I was eventually honoured with the Earldom of Northumbria. Of course, it's not the kind of position one can hold for ever, you understand.'

Aric understood nothing of the sort. He knew of men, like Thored, for instance, holding earldoms until they died in harness. 'Indeed not,' he said, sipping his mead.

'No, my wife and I decided the time had come to leave it to a younger man.'

'We didn't come straight to Lindholm,' said Clodagh. 'Oslac wished to visit some of the Irish monasteries, thinking that he might become one of their community, but when we saw how the young people were being stolen and sold from the port of Dublin, we knew we had to do something to help them. We were obliged to leave our daughter behind, you see, so we understood the pain. So we came to Denmark and set up this little community and we've had a very good reception. It was a good move.'

And at that time I was about fourteen years old and my sister Tove left Lindholm with her new husband to seek a better life and to escape my father's tyranny. Aric smiled and nodded in agreement. 'I had just started my career as a Viking then,' he said, 'which must be why our paths have not crossed until now. It's a demanding occupation,' he added. 'It leaves little time for relationships.'

Clodagh was about to ask him if he might ever reconsider the exchange between their daughter and his nephew, when Meld skipped lopsidedly into the room, hopped across to hold Clodagh's knee, then smiled at Hrolf. *'Hej!'* she said.

'*Hej*, Meld,' he replied.

'Where is Haesel?' She twirled a bluebell in her tiny fingers.

'She and the Lady Fearn are probably sewing,' he guessed. 'What do you have there?'

But halfway through her reply, Meld's attention had been caught by the good-looking man at Clodagh's side whose grey eyes held an admiration worth exploring, even for a young lady of only five winters. 'I am Meld,' she told him, 'short for Raegenmeld. You may have this, if you wish.' She held out the bluebell, daintily.

Time held its breath for Aric as his eyes swept over the enchanting child, finding no visual link with the bawling infant who had been wrenched from her mother's arms five years ago. If ever he felt shame, guilt, wretchedness and pity for a woman with the sins visited on her by others then it was now, as he struggled with the ragged sobs and the sudden rush of scalding tears that, somehow, he must blink away and convert to a smile for her. It took all his efforts to control himself, to whisper, 'Thank you, Meld. I have never received a bluebell before.'

My niece. My sister's beautiful child. How she would love her. How could this happen? Who had found her and saved her life?

'Do you not have a wife?' the child asked, with all the innocence of her years.

'Not yet,' he said, stealthily swiping at a tear with one finger. 'I've been away, you see. I haven't had the chance to find one.' A hard ball of pain stuck in his throat as he remembered Wenda, crooning over this child as a babe, almost losing her mind when the men came for her and he had stood by, appalled by the tussling, the screams and shouts, then by the weeks of tears until Olof came to her rescue. Brave Olof. Cowardly Aric.

'I know someone,' Meld said, brightly turning to Clodagh for affirmation. At any other time, he would have laughed at the child's pertness, but this time he was glad when Clodagh came to his rescue with, 'Not now, sweetheart. This is not the best time. Our guests need to go home now.'

'Will you come back?' Meld asked him.

'If you will be here to talk with me, I shall certainly come back. Would you and Oslac allow that?' he said to Clodagh. He was shaking.

'You are welcome here at any time, Jarl. Our country has suffered much at Danish hands over the years, but we try to set an example of peace and love and the healing of wounds here in our little community. Anyone is welcome if they come in peace. And none of us can afford to reject love when it is offered, can we?'

Clodagh's words echoed in Aric's mind as he and Hrolf walked through the tidy garden and past the green plots surrounding each cluster of houses and workshops. 'What an amazing couple they are,' he remarked to Hrolf. 'At their age, making a new life for themselves in a country they have every reason to fear.'

'I've come to admire them,' Hrolf said. 'I shall accept their religion before I marry Haesel. It makes far better sense than anything our gods have to offer.'

'So does that mean an end to viking and the wealth it brings?'

'Not necessarily. But the appeal of it lessens. One can get tired of burning people's houses down and robbing countries of their wealth. I'd rather be with Haesel and a few kids round my feet. And a ship to sail.'

'So. You *and* Loki. Who next, I wonder?'

Aric's concerns, however, were not for the loss of his two men, but for his sister Wenda's loss five years ago of the delightful child he had seen just now. Nothing could have prepared him for the feelings he had experienced as she skipped into the room, her twisted foot partly hidden by her long skirt yet in every other respect a perfect creature with a sunny nature and the face of an angel. Her white-blonde hair curled round her head like a sunburst, her wide blue eyes seeing only the good in people, eyes that might have been closed for ever if his father and Wenda's overbearing lover had not been cheated by her rescue from death that night.

The terrible deed had sat heavily on his conscience since then, for he had done nothing to plead Wenda's cause, believing that his father and tradition could not be wrong about such things. As an ambitious Viking, he had opted to show the hardening side of his heart even towards his own sister. The gods willed it, he had said. Well, apparently there was another more powerful god with other ideas who did not condone the pointless waste of a life, a god he had a mind to find out more about before it was too late.

But one thing about which he felt profoundly uncertain was whether Wenda should be told that little Meld with the twisted foot was now living with the old couple, risking a demand for her return and yet another breakage of hearts. Meanwhile, he himself could only satisfy his conscience and make amends for his cowardliness in the affair by bringing Kean back, so that Wenda could bring up her sister Tove's child in place of the one she had lost. That was a promise he could not go back on, but nor would he advance the timing of it and deny himself his year with the Lady Fearn. His loins ached with the need of her as he and Hrolf strode up the path to the door of the longhouse from where the sound of women's laughter reached them.

They were, as Hrolf had guessed, making new clothes for all four women from the yards of cloth Fearn's sister the Queen had given her. The laughter was for Deena who, being deaf, had not understood instructions about which were the armholes. Consequently, until she could emerge giggling from the tangle, she neither saw nor heard the reunion of the four lovers, two of whom headed, hand in hand, to the Lady Fearn's private chamber at the end of the hall. Closing the door with his foot, Aric drew her into his arms, delving one hand through the thick waving mass of her unveiled hair while holding her head for a kiss, hard and urgent, until she pleaded for a space to breathe. Placing a hand on each side of his face, she prised him away, scolding him with her brilliant eyes, a look totally at odds with the enthusiasm she had just shown. 'So now,' she said, 'perhaps you'll tell me where you've been these last few days?'

His eyes were dark now, warm and mischievous. 'Do you care?' he said.

'No. But nor do I want to be informed of your whereabouts by my women.' His pale hair was loose, tangling through her fingers and falling between them, contributing to the impression of roguishness. She raked it back, roughly, keeping hold of it on top of his head. 'You are not supposed to be laughing.' She scowled.

His white teeth shone. 'I've been to Aggersborg,' he said, 'to see how my ship is coming along. It will soon be ready to sail.'

'To England? With me?' Desperately, she willed him to say no, that he would never return her, that he could not live without her, that he loved her.

'Sail back here, to Lindholm,' he said, gently. 'We shall not be sailing to England this year. You know that. It will need sea trials first, then the days will shorten and no one with a grain of sense sails far at that time of the year. You know that, too.'

She released his hair and watched how it slid silkily down on to his forehead, twisting at her heart with love for him. She must not spoil the moment. If he had indeed been with a woman at Aggersborg, her own shrewishness would drive him straight back there. She knew his talk about sea trials was a poor excuse. There were plenty of ships he could use whenever he needed one. Her hand cupped his bearded chin. 'You need a shave,' she whispered, 'but come lie with me first. Just to lie. Nothing more.'

'I understand,' he said. 'Just here in my arms.

That will do for me.' Lifting her as if she weighed nothing, he carried her to the bed and lay against her, nuzzling and lapping at her skin, nibbling her lips and searching her lovely body for the soft curves and mounds, thoughts of which had kept him awake at night in Aggersborg, alone. Fearn lay a gentle hand upon his crotch to comfort him until it softened and stilled, and slept like its master. This was the first time they had been apart since her arrival at Lindholm and she was sure now that she would never hear him speak of love.

An hour later, as they lay in delicious half-sleep, Aric told her who he had visited before returning to her. 'Why did you not tell me you had found your mother and stepfather?' he said, smoothing his hand over the soft wool of her gown. 'Did you want it to stay a secret between us?'

For a moment, she was silent, not wanting to disturb their tranquillity with the harsh truth. 'At the time,' she said, 'it seemed best to keep it to myself. We had…still have…secrets from each other. There was no good reason why you ought to know when I shall never be a part of your life, or theirs. It can hardly make any difference whether you know or not. The one who ought to have known is my father, Earl Thored, and now it's too late.'

'I would like to have known, too,' he said, sadly.

'But you have ever been careful to tell me nothing of your family, and I have never asked you. All I know of you has been told me by your brother-in-law, your aunt and cousin, and that's very little.'

'Did your mother explain to you why Thored fathered you instead of Oslac, her husband?'

'She did. It's a very sad and personal story. And now I understand why I was left behind in Jorvik. It was not by Thored's demand, but Oslac's.'

Aric raised himself on one elbow to look deeply into her eyes. 'Is that so?' he said. 'Because he…?'

'Because I was not his. Male shame at being unable to father his own child. My late husband also, I think, unless the fault was mine. His shame took a different form and I have been the one to suffer for it. Oh, don't offer me your sympathy. Both problems are resolved now, at last.'

'Then perhaps I should tell you what Clodagh revealed to me, about Oslac. Apparently his guilt was such that, in Ireland, he was minded to enter a monastery.'

Fearn shook her head upon the pillow. 'As if that would have solved anything,' she whispered. 'Leaving his wife alone. Thinking of his own troubles. How like a man. Did my mother talk him out of it?'

'I think she simply redirected his pity from himself to the plight of slaves.'

'Our God works in mysterious ways,' she said.

'I think he probably does, sweetheart. I saw little Meld with the twisted foot.'

'Your niece.'

'Yes, I truly believe she is. And adorable, too. She gave me a bluebell.'

Fearn smiled. She had seen it drop out of his hair.

'I have brought something for you, from Aggersborg.'

So far, Fearn had refused to accept any gift from him, but now it was not in her heart to refuse again. She rolled to the edge of the bed to watch him draw something out of his leather pouch, wrapped in linen. 'Here,' he said. 'Take a look at this.' Sitting beside her, he heard her gasp of surprise and wonder at the pile of scintillating beads strung on to a fine leather cord. Pieces of black jet from her own country, chunks of polished translucent amber from the Baltic shores, tiny gold and silver discs between orbs of pure rock crystal and glass of every hue, many of them embellished with fine threads, dots and chequers of molten-glass strands. There were beads of precious carnelian, garnet, carved ivory and amethyst, which she knew must have come from the ends of the earth and cost a fortune. She would not ask, nor would she refuse it, for it showed that she had been in his mind. She let him take it from her and, lifting her hair out of the way, bent her head for him to slip it over. 'Thank you,' she said. 'It's the most beautiful thing I've ever seen.'

'And you'll keep it?'

'Always.'

'At last,' he said, smiling. 'I have found something to give you.'

Placing her arms around his neck, she could so easily have told him that she believed he had already done that, except that she could not be sure he would be pleased to father a bastard on the woman he was determined not to keep for more than a year.

'You're trembling,' he whispered into her hair. 'What is it?'

'Nothing. Just a chill. Let's go and disturb Haesel and Hrolf, shall we?'

As the summer heat rose over the flat landscape, warm rain turned the fields into a green-

and-yellow patchwork scattered with red poppies, while the men used the weeks to erect more houses, to repair ships and to pile the warehouses with merchandise ready for the last of the foreign buyers. Graciously, Aric helped his cousin with the horses, secretly admiring Freya's determination and independence, and Fearn would have been at a loose end had it not been for the gentle tasks her mother gave her in the infirmary. Now was the time for gathering the medicinal herbs and preparing them, an occupation she would have enjoyed more if she had been able to rid herself of the nagging doubts about her future and that of the child she was now certain she carried. Thanks to her mother's recipe, the sickness was under control, making it easier for her to conceal her condition from Aric and his relatives.

If Aric had had more experience of pregnant lovers, Fearn thought, he might have suspected the reason for her swollen breasts and a certain lethargy in the daytime. Their loving, if one could call it that, had entered a different phase in which she preferred a gentler approach, just as satisfying, but less desperate than earlier encounters. She felt badly about maintaining a pretence of her monthly courses, but this happened only three times before a significant event made it imperative for Fearn to decide on some action after weeks during which it looked as if everyone except herself was in control of her situation.

That day, the quayside was crowded with merchants and their wares, with dejected groups of slaves, buyers and hagglers, and what looked like the total population of Lindholm, including children and animals. Aric and Loki had spent the last hour loading three mares and their excitable foals into the hold of a ship and now stood with Fearn and Freya to watch the ship and its cargo move out into the fjord, the backs of the men's tunics dark with sweat. Berths along the quayside were occupied by an assortment of vessels, except for a space left by the one that had just departed, towards which a large seagoing ship with a mightily curving prow and a complement of twenty or more rowers approached with expert precision.

The Danes watched in admiration as the crew, well drilled and wearing matching blue-and-red livery, brought the ship alongside the jetty and tied it up, stowing the long oars on to the brackets under the neatly tied up sail. 'That livery... that ship...is exactly like...no, it cannot be,' Fearn said.

'Who? Who can't it be?' said Aric. 'You recognise it?'

'That's Earl Thored's livery and that's his ship. And there…look…a boy is waving to us.' Holding on to the curve of the prow as it sprung upwards, a slender young boy waved to them excitedly, his flaxen hair shining in the bright light, his face a picture of glee at recognising familiar figures. 'It *is* him,' Fearn cried, shaking Aric's arm. 'It *is*. It's Kean and there behind him…his parents, Arlen and Kamma, too. Oh, they've *come*! In the Earl's own ship!'

'The *new* Earl,' Aric said. 'He's sent Thored's son away. Back to his family. Well, well! He doesn't want the lad under his feet, by the look of things.'

Ignoring the negative tone of Aric's voice, Fearn ran along the jetty to the ship from which Kean was leaping. 'Freya!' she called over her shoulder. 'Come and see! Aric's nephew, at last.' Opening her arms wide, she waited for the soft slam of Kean's light young body and his skinny arms around her as they had never been before, still hardly able to believe this was not a dream. Totally unexpected and even un-hoped-for, it seemed to be the answer to all her worries and to Aric's insistence on revenge and retribution. Here was the final phase to his absurd saga.

'Lady Fearn!' Kean grinned up at her. 'See, I'm here! What a voyage! I'm going to be a sailor and have ships of my own. The men say I'm one already, but I'm so glad to see you again, lady.'

'And I you, Kean. You'll never know how much. Here comes your uncle and this lady is Freya, another relative of yours. Shall you greet them with respect?' She need not have been concerned about any latent animosity towards his uncle for creating a rift in their family that day in Jorvik, for Kean had been well schooled in good manners and needed no prompting. His parents came along the jetty with a noticeable roll to their walk, Kamma clutching at her husband's arm for support and Arlen proudly watching his foster son's dignified bow to their surprised host and his avuncular hug in return.

'You certainly have a knack of taking people by surprise, young Kean. Eh? But you are more than welcome. Have you come to stay?' he said to Arlen, rather unnecessarily, Fearn thought.

'I can only apologise, my lord,' Arlen said. 'We were given no say in the matter. Our new Earl, a man known as Alfhelm, was none too keen on having Thored's bas…er….*son* around. Thinking, I suppose, that he might one day be a threat to his position. You know how these things can happen, I'm sure. Quite without foundation, I might add.'

Arlen might have added quite a bit more had

Aric not put up a hand to stop him, perhaps remembering how once he had offered information
out of turn. 'Quite so, these things do happen,
but you have been sent to friends. Our family has
been eager for the day when we could have Kean
to live with us, but to have his parents also will
make the transition so much easier. Have you
brought your entire property, too?' He looked
towards the ship where the liveried men stood
around a huge pile of canvas-covered luggage
stacked in the centre.

'All our goods and chattels, my lord,' said
Kamma, 'though my husband has now been replaced as Moneyer, so has had to leave behind
all the tools of his trade. A great loss to us, it is.'

If Aric detected a hint of self-pity here, he
chose to ignore it and the slight suggestion that
he might offer Arlen a similar employment,
though the position of Moneyer was in the
King's gift, not his. Instead, he offered them
his hospitality and immediate attention to their
needs. Placing an arm around Kean's shoulders,
he shook the hand of the English shipmaster,
and gave orders to Loki to attend to the crew
and bring them up to the longhouse. Glancing
at Fearn, he could not have missed the expression of undiluted delight in her eyes as she took
Kamma by the hand to lead her through the cu-

rious crowds who parted, gawping at the Jarl's English guests. He could hardly have guessed, however, at the level of hope in her heart at the implications of Kean's arrival. It was a perfectly logical act for Thored's successor to rid himself of any potential opposition, however young, but how could he have known that this now removed Aric's last objection to Fearn's return home? In her mind, at least.

'Was that ship the one you saw?' she asked Haesel at supper that evening. 'Is that what your seeing meant? That Kean would be returned to his mother's family?'

Yet again, Haesel searched her mind for the vision but could not be sure. It could have been, she told Fearn, but one ship was very like another to her.

The supper tables were packed with Aric's family and friends, invited to welcome the English guests and the hearty hungry crew who had brought them. Chief amongst the relatives was Wenda, Kean's aunt, still rather a fragile creature, but overjoyed to make contact with the good-looking English son of her sister. She lost no time in telling him and his weary parents how well she and Olof would care for him and how he would spend his days with his cousins. When her husband reminded her that his parents would probably do that, the question of exactly where Kean would be living was referred to Aric. 'With his parents, of course,' he said, smiling at his nephew. 'There's an empty plot at the side of yours, Olof, isn't there? We'll clear that and put a house there. We can start on it tomorrow while we've got all these extra hands to help.'

The burly English shipmaster was not quite so eager. 'I have orders, my lord, to return to Jorvik immediately, once we have restocked with provisions. Your hospitality is of the finest, but we must not trespass on it one day more than we need to.'

Aric laughed. 'What? Come, man. You would dump your precious cargo here without making sure they have a roof over their heads? Your new Earl would not reward you for that, would he? One day will make no difference to a fine ship like yours carrying a lighter load. Another few meals and warm dry beds will do your men good. What do you say?'

'We shall be happy to help, my lord,' said the shipmaster with as good a grace as he could muster.

'A house, so soon,' Arlen said. 'We are truly grateful, my lord.'

To Fearn, this seemed like the ideal oppor-

tunity for Aric to announce, in public, that the
promise he had made to his family to reunite
Kean with his relatives was now fulfilled, even
though events had been brought forward by the
death of Thored. But though she waited, nothing
was said to give her any hope that Aric might
arrange for her and Haesel to sail with the English shipmaster and his experienced crew back
to Jorvik, or even to Lundenburh. She did not
dare suggest it yet, to risk spoiling the celebra-
tion, to risk a disappointing refusal, or an argument. This was Kean's occasion, not hers. She
must be patient and choose her moment with
care. And if the opportunity was ignored by him,
then she would have to resolve matters in her
own way, for she could not allow this chance to
slip through her fingers. She spent the rest of the
meal talking to Kamma about events in Jorvik,
asking for news of Mother Bridget and the nuns,
and anything else that would ease her curiosity.

Bedding down so many guests in the great
hall called for some good-natured organisation,
so it was very late when Fearn retired to her
chamber and settled down to rest, tired by the
excitement of the day, but by no means ready for
sleep with so many facets to the problems in her
mind. Ought she try to speak to the shipmaster

in private? Would he be willing to risk Aric's wrath? Would it be fair to ask him to help? She had but one day to make up her mind before the chance was lost for good.

The door opened quietly, and one decision was resolved as Aric came to her, as naked as she was and as hungry for the bliss of warm arms. Pressing herself along his length, she wondered how she would live without this, a question closely followed by thoughts of the year ahead, watching her infant develop and him turning to another woman for the kind of comfort men craved when their women were pregnant. Not being able to discuss the issue with him, all she had to feed her concerns were assumptions.

Almost angrily, her lips sought his as her arms cradled his head in a grip he could hardly escape until, sensing her rising passion, he rolled her until she was beneath him, her face half-covered by her hair. Holding her hands away, he moved his lips downwards, following a teasing path along throat and shoulders, coming at last to the tender swell of her breasts where the nipples, had he been able to see, were noticeably darker and more pronounced. A cry escaped her, part-desire and part-fear for the energies she herself had unleashed which, although recently diminished, now surged into a torrent of emotion that paid no heed to the delicate thing that lay between them. For weeks, her thoughts had revolved around this new life, alternating between joy and fulfilment, inconvenience and physical discomfort, yet now these thoughts were overtaken by a need to experience the full flood of his virility before she was forced to renounce it altogether, as she knew she would have to.

Taking full responsibility for the pace, she teased him in turn, sending him mixed messages of willingness and reluctance, opening herself to him, then fighting him off until, taking pity on his groans of frustration, she took him into her hand and guided him to the place that ached and throbbed with desire. He had refused her demands of a different sort over the past few months. She did not know, at that moment, a better way to revenge herself. Bracing herself for the inevitable fierceness of his pent-up craving, she gave herself up to him generously while savouring each and every moment, writing it into her memory against those years of self-imposed abstinence, urging him on towards an experience neither of them would forget.

There was very little of gentleness, this time, he having no reason to suspect that it might have been more appropriate in the circumstances of which he knew nothing. For Fearn, it was what

she wanted to experience, this being the essence
of Aric, his potency and power, his strength and
skill in bringing her, every time, to a place of
unchartered ecstasy by whatever route he chose.
It was a risk and she chose to take it, for their
time together was running out. When the mind-
numbing spasm had passed, Aric spooned her
into him and placed a hand over her breast. 'That
was rough, sweetheart. Did I hurt you? I didn't
want to,' he whispered.

'It's all right,' she replied. 'Really. That was
wonderful.' How much more, she thought, would
she rather have discussed the state of her heart
and the pain she would have to prepare it for.
Why did *he* not have a heart that she might break
instead? Why was it always the woman to suffer?

Fearn rose early the next morning, but her
chances of speaking to the English shipmaster
disappeared when she saw that the men had all
been out since daybreak working on the plot
for Arlen's new house. The family had stayed
overnight with Wenda and Olof's family, ready
to lend a hand with the constant refreshments,
so Fearn took the opportunity to visit Clodagh
and Oslac, hoping for their approval of her ru-
dimentary plan. She had not been prepared for

the strength of their opposition, however, when she told them how she hoped to make use of the English ship and its crew. 'Of course you cannot leave, Fearn,' said Oslac, putting forward reasons that only a man would think of. 'Supposing the new Earl doesn't want you to return to Jorvik? If he doesn't want Kean there, he certainly won't want you, will he?'

'I have a half-sister in Lundenburh,' Fearn reminded him. 'She will.'

'But we've only just found each other,' he urged, 'after all these years and I was just beginning to get used to having you around.'

Clodagh rolled her eyes, dismissing his argument. 'Fearn, love,' she said, 'you're not thinking of what's best for the babe, are you?'

'I *am*, Mother, but I'm also thinking of how much pain my heart will endure if I have the babe here in Lindholm and Aric doesn't want it, for some reason. He can put me aside as soon as he discovers I'm expecting his child, if he wishes. Besides, he has no love for me. He said right from the start that there was no room for sentiment and I truly believe he doesn't know how to love a woman. He told me I'd have to find my own way of dealing with it, if I thought I loved him, because that's not what he wants. He wants to eke out his revenge for a whole year, no more, no less. I dare not ask him to reconsider letting me go now that Kean is here, when he was so adamant before. Better to let him think I've accepted the situation. I don't want him to suspect I might try to escape on the English ship. That would ruin all my chances.'

'But if it's Aric's acceptance of the babe that concerns you, you know you could come here to be with me. You'd both be quite safe here and Aric respects what we do.'

'It would be safer to be with Elf, out of Aric's reach. In England. She and Ethelred are Christians, too, remember, and there'd be no exposing of girls or weaklings there. The plight of poor Wenda haunts me, Mother.'

'It probably haunts Aric, too, my dear. He was very taken with little Meld. I cannot believe seeing her has not made him think differently about such things.'

'He's determined to keep me here for a year, though. So what if I had a strong healthy boy? A son of Aric the Ruthless. You think he'd let the child go to England with me? Think again. He wouldn't. He'd keep it here.'

'But, Fearn, dearest, you cannot travel so far in your condition. It would not be wise, would it? Think of the discomforts and dangers. For all you know, the English shipmaster may take less

care of you than Aric did. You cannot leave now,
Fearn. We'd be losing each other again, wouldn't
we? After such a short time, too.'

'Mother! *Please...stop it!* Can you not see how
hard this is for me, too? I thought of all people,
you would be the first to understand.'

'I do understand, love...'

'No, you don't!' Despairing, Fearn went to the
doorway, but halted by the large loom against the
wall, resting her forehead upon the upright, trying to force back the tears, her shoulders trembling with the effort.

Clodagh went to lay a gentle hand upon her
back. 'Then tell me what it is I don't understand
and I will try. I know that you are deeply in love
with him.'

Fearn nodded, croaking an affirmative. 'More
than I can say,' she whispered. 'But there is no
love in his heart, Mother, and I cannot let him
see me growing big with a child he doesn't want,
growing clumsy and so unlike the woman he
stole because he desired her. I cannot live with
him like that, in spite of loving him. Seeing him
turn to another woman would kill me. And yet I
want his child so very much.'

Her mother's voice was soft and sad. 'I lost my
lover, Fearn. I almost lost my husband, too. And
I lost you for all the years I should have been

there for you. I had to hand you over to Hilda, knowing she did not want you. And I survived. You and I are strong. As women, we have to be.'

Fearn did not want to be convinced. 'No, I'm not strong enough to wait and see what happens, nor am I strong enough to bear the pain when it *does* happen. I'm due early next year. I dare not leave it any longer. Soon it will start to show. I have to leave.' She felt Clodagh's arms encircle her waist and the weight of her head rest upon her back, and for some time no more was said as the two came to the end of their arguments. They clung, weeping, agreeing to say nothing to Oslac when he could not be trusted to keep the information from Aric, though Fearn still had no idea how her plan might be carried out. Their goodbye was over hands drenched with tears.

Heavy-hearted, she and Haesel walked up past the houses towards the plot now crowded with men and materials, women and children, dogs and foraging hens. Apart from the crew of the English ship, the whole of Aric's family were there helping to fetch and carry, to dig and carry stones for the foundations, Olof and Wenda's two boys already treating Kean as a brother while his parents gossiped between bouts of usefulness. The infant whom Fearn had helped to heal was now a sturdy child, shrieking with excitement, running to meet Haesel and to haul her away. Fearn approached Aric, who was speaking to a stranger as she reached him, turning to her with a boyish excitement.

'My ship at Aggersborg is ready for collection,' he told her. 'Good news, eh?'

'Indeed yes,' Fearn said, keeping her voice level. 'But surely you cannot go yet, with all this happening?'

Like the other men, he was revelling in the physical effort involved on the site, sleeves and tunics tucked up to free their limbs, faces streaked with grime, hair stuck down with sweat. Aric's hair was tied up with twine, his fingers sticky with mud as he accepted a beaker of ale from Freya and passed it to the man, then took another for himself. Looking across at the progress of the house-building, he seemed to be deliberating as the messenger reminded him, 'I have my ship waiting to take you there, Jarl, if you wish to take advantage of it. You would not then have to bring back one of your own. I must return before dark.'

'Wait,' Aric said, giving Fearn his beaker to hold. Striding off through the piles of timber, he went to speak to the English shipmaster who had expected to be well out of the fjord by now. Fearn could see how the man frowned, Aric's spreading hands, his persuading posture, the man's quick tip of the head, the reluctant expression, then his turn away to speak to one of his crew while Aric returned to them. 'Yes, I'll come with you,' he said to the messenger. 'He's agreed to stay here until I return.'

Fearn felt her hopes plunge like a pebble in the sea, so quickly raised, so soon dashed. The English ship would not be leaving until Aric returned. 'How long will it take you to bring it back?' she asked, meaning, how long will you be away?

'Might be two days. Might be three, depending on last-minute adjustments. We shall have to try it out. Shouldn't take long. Now, I'll take Loki and Hrolf with me. Where are they? Hey!' he yelled. 'Loki! Find Hrolf! Fast!'

Whether he had asked the shipmaster to remain here ostensibly to help on the new building or whether it was to safeguard Fearn while he was away, she could not help but believe it was more likely to be the latter. His farewell kiss had been hard and preoccupied, snatched at the last minute before she waved him off, chattering to Hrolf and Loki like children with a new toy.

That night, after work had ceased on the building, everyone came to Aric's longhouse where a generous meal had been prepared. The men had all jumped into the stream's deepest pool to wash off the grime, coming to the trestle tables with hair still damp and arms stinging from the water. The women acted as joint hostesses, passing round huge platters of roasted meats and waterfowl, warm breads, new peas and succulent tops of nettles dripping with butter. There was fish, shellfish and eels, with mead to drink, ale and elderflower 'wine' for the children. On purpose, Fearn placed herself next to the English shipmaster, whose name, she discovered, was Calder, a well-built serious man who took his position with a grim determination, giving Fearn the impression that he had not enjoyed having his plans changed at his host's convenience.

To Fearn, he was exceptionally courteous, being in possession of the facts surrounding her abduction. By now, he also knew that she was probably the natural daughter of the late Earl and that young Kean was his son, though there were some anomalies that had not been explained. 'The Jarl Aric tells me you are a hostage here,' he said as the harpist tuned his strings and the din began to subside.

'Then perhaps you have misunderstood the situation,' Fearn said, keeping her voice low. 'As a hostage, I would be required to make a promise not to try to escape. I have never given that promise. Indeed, I intend to do all I can to return to England as soon as possible. As any other prisoner would.'

Calder's heavy eyebrows twitched as he guessed what might come next. 'I see,' he said, 'that you and I have the same problem. I did not make any promises, either, although if I had refused to stay here while the Jarl is away, he would somehow have prevented me from leaving by some other means. I am in the enemy camp, you see, and my loyalties are to our own Earl of Northumbria, and your Jarl should have known better than to forget that.'

'Are you saying that you do not intend to stay?'

'My orders were to return to Jorvik immediately and that is what I shall do.'

'Then…do you think…you could find a corner of your ship…for me and my lady? I need to get to Lundenburh rather urgently. I would pay you well for the favour.' She had put on her rare beads over her new kirtle of pale yellow silk and saw by the man's appraising glance that he had noticed every detail, including the circlet over her veil, the bracelets, the rings. Expecting a positive response, she waited.

'But we shall be sailing to the mouth of the River Humber to reach Jorvik,' he said. 'A much shorter voyage than to the mouth of the Thames to reach Lundenburh.'

Fearn inclined her head towards him, careful to keep her voice softer than that of the minstrel. 'The Queen is my half-sister,' she whispered. 'She will reward you handsomely.'

The suspense was almost unbearable, but at last she saw his slight nod and his mouth framing the words, 'Tomorrow, at first light. Bring nothing but your valuables.'

'Thank you. We shall be there.' Guilt stalked her heart like a dark shadow, knowing how her plans would affect her loyal maid's future with Hrolf. Was she asking too much of her?

'No,' Haesel said, emphatically. 'Where you go, I go too. I shall never leave you, not even if you command it.'

They embraced and clung, needing no more words.

Chapter Ten

The remainder of that evening dragged on at a snail's pace, dividing Fearn's thoughts between apprehension, relief and sadness at leaving those she had come to love, including those for whom the discovery had come too late. Goodbyes were out of the question. Alone at last, she and Haesel packed only her valuables into a canvas bag that they could carry between them. Only the warmest clothes were taken, worn one on top of the other and, to top them all, the beautiful beaver cloak she had made for Barda that had been so useful on their voyage to Denmark. Their belts dangled with pouches and small tools, including Fearn's knife, but even these comforting accessories did nothing to ease the queasiness in Fearn's stomach as they crept through the hall in semi-darkness, now cleared of the English crew who would have gone to prepare the ship for its stealthy voyage.

Outside, the sky showed only the faintest glow of light on the eastern horizon. Fearn tried to identify the tallest mast until Haesel reminded her otherwise. 'They won't erect their mast until they're out in the fjord,' she said. 'They must row until they can catch the wind.'

Fearn frowned into the dimness. 'But they were tied up here yesterday,' she said. 'Have they moved already?' The quayside was eerily quiet. They stood on the jetty, scanning the berths for the largest ship and for any shadowy movement of the crew, but all was silent except for the gentle slapping of the water on the timbers. 'I can't understand it,' she said. 'They cannot have gone without us, surely?'

'They have,' Haesel replied, looking out across the water to the west where faint silver ripples shone upon the blackness. 'Look out there. See it? Right out there in the distance, against the sky. That's them.'

Fearn's voice squeaked with incredulity. 'They've hoisted the sail. They've left us! They had no intention of taking us, did they? This must be what you saw in your sighting, Haesel. That was it!'

Haesel didn't think it mattered now. Placing her arm around Fearn's shoulders, she felt the slump of sheer despair and heard the repeating, 'No...no...no! Oh, no!'

Immobilised by disappointment and uncertainty, they waited on the quay as if at any moment the English ship might return to collect them, hardly noticing that the place was already coming to life with the growing light and that men were preparing for a day's work. Some leapt into boats, slamming gangplanks into place for the use of well-dressed merchants and last-minute provisions, crates of hens and an unwilling goat. 'We're not going back,' Fearn said. 'Not now. We have to find someone to take us.'

Although Haesel understood her lady's motives, she did not entirely share her burning need to leave Lindholm when the man she wanted to marry lived there. Torn by conflicting emotions of love and loyalty, she made the half-hearted observation that several of the merchant ships were preparing to leave, but how would one know where they were bound? East, or west? The fjord was open to the sea at both ends. She was about to suggest that they should return home when a man who had been watching them from a distance came to ask courteously if they were waiting for someone. Looking at their canvas bag and travelling clothes, he also noticed the English headdress and the jewelled circlet worn last night by Fearn, an indication of certain wealth.

The man's apparent respectability made Fearn less cautious than she might otherwise have been, for although he had a foreign accent, as she did, he was clean and handsomely dressed, and clearly a man of some authority. 'We were hoping to find a ship bound for England,' she told him, 'but other than asking each one, it's difficult to know, isn't it?'

'Without knowing all the owners, lady, almost impossible, I'd say. However,' he said, glancing across at a sturdy high-sided cargo ship making ready to depart, 'my own ship will be setting out for Lundenburh any moment now. If you care to take the risk of travelling with strangers, I can assure you and your maid of a safe passage and whatever comforts we can arrange for you. We stow our cargo in the hold below the deck, you see. My name is Boris.'

He smiled at them reassuringly and, in the dim light, they could see the glint of gold on his fingers as he offered to take their luggage.

'May I?' he said. 'My crew are indicating that they're ready to cast off.'

There was no time to think of any reason not to accept such a convenient offer, so without hesitation they followed Boris across the gangplank on to the deck where a canvas tent supported on wooden cross pieces made an inviting place to hide until they were well clear of the increasingly busy quay. Pulling the beaver cloak tightly around her shoulders, Fearn settled herself upon the furs with Haesel next to her, then felt the deck rock as the last man came aboard, at which moment the flaps of the tent were pulled down from the outside and tied. The noisy rake of the gangplank, the rattle of oars being fitted, a quiet word of farewell and a man's laugh made them realise how different this experience was from Aric's bustling longship, for here the silence was broken only by the squeak of the oars, the bleat of the goat and some subdued conversation in a language they did not understand. The water whooshed past them, rhythmically.

Holding Fearn's hand, Haesel voiced her concern. 'Are you sure we've done the right thing, lady? We have only this man's word that he's bound for England, but can we trust him? And there are not many crew. Did you notice?'

'They don't need many,' Fearn whispered. 'Two fore, and two aft. And a helmsman. They're still rowing, though, so they must be staying close to the shoreline. It's just as well we're hidden from view, because we'll be passing Aggersborg before too long.'

Visualising how the flat fields were slowly sliding past them in the dawn, they sat huddled together with nothing for them to observe except how the light grew and cast a greenish hue over their skin. 'Are you all right?' Haesel said.

Fearn hugged her arms across herself. 'Not very. I was not seasick before.'

'I'll go and ask for some water for you. Hold on.'

Her fingers untying the flaps were seen from the outside. 'What is it?' said the man called Boris. 'Best to stay where you are for a while, until...'

'My lady needs water,' Haesel said. 'Quickly, if you please.'

'Certainly. Stay there. I'll get some for you.'

The triangular gap in the canvas gave them a view of the ship's stern, the great wooden mast block and, more puzzling, the lower half of a man's long gown, a rich green brocade with a sable fur edge, which they immediately recognised as having been last seen in Lindholm's marketplace. Ducking their heads lower to see his upper half, they saw the large sable fur hat of the man who had shown an interest in them at Aggersborg, too, when Fearn had slashed his hand. They had hardly needed Eve's warning of this man's reputation, but now they were on his ship, with no doubts at all that he was the owner.

Fearn's face reflected her horror. 'It's *him*!' she whispered. 'Isn't it? What a *fool* I am, walking right into their trap. Oh, Haesel, I should have waited.'

'What are we going to do?' Haesel said. 'We must *do* something!'

'We have to get off this ship. We must attract attention to ourselves. Come on, before he ties the flaps again, we must get out on deck to wave something. And scream!'

'Yes, give me your cloak, lady,' Haesel said, hurriedly unpinning the large circular pin that Aric had left on it. Beneath this, Fearn's newest necklace of beads rested upon her kirtle. She had intended to keep it hidden. 'I'll wave your cloak when someone comes near enough to help us,' Haesel said. 'Let's see where we are, first.'

The sable fur hat turned as they emerged to the sound of Boris's protests. He was holding out a wooden beaker of water towards Fearn. 'No… no, ladies! Not yet! You must stay—'

But he was interrupted by Fur Hat's welcome that flapped his black beard upon his gold-hung chest, his shifty beetle-browed eyes laughing at the discovery. 'Ah,' he said with a deep Russian growl, 'here is the lady with the gemstone eyes and her pretty maid. So was not the Jarl Aric much to your liking, then? Cast you off already, has he? Dah?'

Facing the direction from which they had come, they saw how the sky had brightened considerably and how close they still were to the land instead of moving out into the fjord. 'No, he has not!' Fearn retorted, hating his leery grin. His greedy eyes skimmed over her figure with the wind pressing the fabric layers into its curves. 'But neither do we intend to stay here with you. Look,' she said, touching her necklace, 'this can be yours if you will pull in to the shore. It's very valuable.' The offer twisted at her heart, for its worth to her was more than anything this man owned.

'Hah!' he bellowed, showing a row of discoloured teeth. 'But you and your baubles are already mine, are you not? You *and* the girl. You'll make me a very rich man, lady. Few men will have seen eyes like yours. And as for *her*, what does she have to offer except that hair? Shall we take a closer look, Boris?'

Boris knew what was expected. Dropping the beaker of water, he reached out and grabbed at the white veil swathed around Haesel's head and neck, pulling it away so quickly that the wind snatched it from him and flung it over the head of the nearest oarsman into the sea, where it lay like a line of white foam. 'No…*no!*' Haesel screamed, clutching at the beaver cloak in her arms to hide herself from the men's stares. 'No, you must *not!*' But it was too late to dodge his grasping hands and, before Fearn could come to her rescue, the neck of Haesel's kirtle was torn down to reveal the mass of scar tissue that was hideous to everyone except Fearn and Hrolf.

'Argh! What's this?' the man yelled, reeling back in horror. 'This one we cannot keep. She will bring us bad luck. She is cursed!'

'Throw her overboard!' Fur Hat shouted back. 'Get rid of her!'

Haesel was not going to make it easy for him. Nimbly, she side-stepped and dodged just as Fearn, who was lurching to her aid, was yanked backwards by Fur Hat and held in a grip so brutally tight that the breath was knocked out of her lungs. A spasm of pain made her cry out and the sickness she had managed so far to hold back was now released in a torrent that spewed over the dreadful man's arms. Taking advantage of his rage, Fearn writhed out of his grip in a frenzy of fury and pain while willing herself to find the haft of her knife and to pull it from its scabbard. Then, half-stumbling, she lunged, plunging the point into Boris's ribs as he raised his arms to lift Haesel above his head.

Struggling and screaming, Haesel was about to be thrown into the sea in the space between fore and aft oarsmen, but now both she and her captor fell in a heap on the deck, uttering screams that carried across the calm waters of the fjord, making even the seagulls scatter in alarm. In the distance, a sleek ship with a full striped sail sped towards them, towards the crazily rocking cargo ship where a young woman with pale hair was waving a beaver cloak, holding it into the wind like a banner. Her screams of, 'Hrolf! *Hrolf!* Save us!' could be heard from that distance just as they had been months before in the marketplace of Aggersborg.

Struggling to remove his stinking brocade gown, and seeing what was happening ahead of them, Fur Hat bellowed at the helmsman to come about and then at the oarsmen to turn the ship with their oars. None of them responded to his command but, despite being tired by their long row, pulled even harder to close the gap between them and the approaching ship where three furious men stood at the bow. Fearn was in no state to see that rescue was at hand, for she was doubled up with sickness while trying to stay beyond Fur Hat's reach and to protect her maid.

But Fur Hat was determined to get rid of the ill luck that was Haesel and, striding across the deck, he picked her up like a toy and would have thrown her directly into the path of the sailing ship had not the nearest oarsman seen what he was about to do and, leaping over his oar, threw himself bodily at Fur Hat, knocking Haesel over in the process. 'You not paid us, you filthy *pig*!' he yelled, landing on top of him. 'We work for nothing! Now *you* get something!' His fists pummelled but would have made little difference to the man had it not been for the others who left their oars to help, glad of the chance, at last, to wreak some revenge.

It was Haesel who, clambering out of their way, saw the expressions on the faces of Hrolf, Aric and Loki as their skilful crew manoeuvred the new ship alongside, leaping like goats over the sides and on to the deck. She thought this was how they must look when they went raiding and pitied the poor souls who got in the way of their fury. But if Aric had it in mind to throw the battered Russian overboard, he was beaten to it by Fur Hat's own crew who, unpaid, underfed and overworked, took him by the arms and legs and, with a roar of triumph, heaved him over the side with a splash that rocked the ship. Grabbing their oars, they maliciously prodded him until he disappeared from sight to the sound of their hooting cheers. The unconscious Boris was the next to go, but this noisy scene was hardly registered by Fearn who lay on the other side of the deck, overtaken by her sickness and by more waves of pain that made her cry out like a child.

Lifting her carefully into his arms, Aric assumed she had been injured. 'Sweetheart... where are you hurt?' he said. 'Haesel? Tell me where she's been hit.'

'I think she may be losing it, my lord. The child. I'm so sorry. She didn't want you to know.' She saw Aric's face contorted with astonishment and grief, and her heart melted for him. There were, she thought, many things that both of them ought to have been told before now. 'Her mother will know what to do,' she said. 'We must take her there.'

Grim-faced, and with hands to help him, he carried her to his own ship, cradling her on his lap as preparations were made to leave the cargo vessel, to retrieve Fearn's baggage from the tent and to send the jubilant crew on its way, with thanks and a bag of silver. Floating away on a journey of its own, the beaver cloak spread itself wide upon the waters of the fjord and was soon lost to sight. Aric's eyes rarely left Fearn's pale face, soft with concern, bewilderment, guilt and overwhelming love. How had he allowed it to come to this? Remembering Clodagh's words, he knew now that she had meant them for him. *None of us can afford to reject love when it is offered.* And he had rejected it, every single day since he'd known of it, hardening his heart against a force stronger than any other, even revenge. 'Fearn, my own love, my darling woman,' he whispered. 'Don't leave me. I love you. I want you. For ever. Beloved, stay with me.'

Through the haze of pain, Fearn heard the voice she adored, with the words she had never thought to hear. He loved her…his darling woman…he wanted her, for ever. Was it really true? Or was she dreaming? She felt the comforting strength of his arms holding her safe against the painful lurch and bump of the ship as the following wind billowed in the sail. Vaguely, she recalled that this was why the crew had been rowing, because the west wind was against them. And now it sped them back home, which she should never have left. 'Forgive me,' she murmured. 'I should not have left you. I would have given you more time, if I'd had it. But…ah!' Her eyes squeezed shut against the powerful ache.

'Don't try to talk, my love. We'll be there soon.'

He was right. The new ship flew like a bird. Lindholm was already in sight.

In the curtained, sweet-smelling chamber reserved for birthing mothers, Aric stayed beside her all that day throughout Clodagh's assistance to hold back the threat to her pregnancy that had begun before Fearn realised it and, although it was not usual, he was allowed to stay and hold the warm herbal infusions to her lips and administer a soothing draught, remaining with her well into the evening. Fearn had scarcely been aware of the crowd that had gathered on the quay to see them arrive, for the news of the two women's disappearance had been received with an alarm and a concern far deeper than either of them had been prepared for. The women, even Aunt Astrid, had wept openly as Aric had carried Fearn to Clodagh's place, giving the badly bruised Haesel messages for her, along with cries of praise for the maid herself and not the slightest recoil from the sight of her exposed neck. Haesel, however, kept her other secret to herself, being quite certain now that what she had seen in her sighting had been Aric's new ship with its full sail against the sky, bearing her loved one, bringing safety and her future.

* * *

Towards evening, candles were lit in the little chamber where Fearn's recovery was well under way, inevitably with tears that she was unable to stop, racking her with sobs for all that had happened, the misunderstandings, the pain and longings, for wasted time, for the despair. Were they to go back to that? Had she really heard him say, for the first time, that he loved her?

Kneeling beside the bed, he eased her into his embrace. 'You were not dreaming,' he said. 'Don't weep, my darling. What's done is done, but I owe you an explanation, even so. What happened today has made me see more clearly and it shames me to say that I should have told you long before this how much I adore you. It would have saved you so much unhappiness, which you have done nothing to deserve, my dearest love. Your unhappiness breaks my heart. How can I ever make it up to you?' His voice broke with emotion as he asked her the question she could not answer when he had never allowed her to know him well enough, except in bed.

Keeping hold of his hands, keeping contact, Fearn sat back against the pillows. 'I don't think,' she whispered, her voice husky with spent tears, 'that you need to make it up to me, Aric. My love for you grew so slowly. I was not prepared for it, either. I could not stop it, though I knew it would only give me pain.'

'And I tried so hard to hold my love away. It was not part of my plan. Ever.'

'You held it away? Why? I thought you were not capable of love.'

He bowed his head, resting his forehead on her hands, spilling his windswept hair over them before raising his face to hers, clearly affected by her image of him. 'Just the opposite, beloved. I resisted love and rejected yours because, for me, that meant pain. I didn't want it to happen again that the one I love would be taken from me, so I rejected love, knowing that I must take you home. Yes, I know what you will say, that the reason for my revenge was no longer in place after Thored's death and Kean's coming, but you were so determined to leave, asking me to take you before the year was up. And I could *not* let you go sooner, my darling. Not one day before I had to. I wanted my full year of you while denying my love to ease the pain that would come. It had nothing to do with revenge, by that time.'

'I pestered you to return me,' she said, feeling again the ache of emptiness, 'because I could not live with a man who did not want my love. That was what you said to me, remember? That broke my heart, Aric.' Tears ran down her cheeks at the memory of that day and the bitterness she had used to combat it. 'When a woman loves, it's useless for her to pretend that she doesn't. Few people are deceived by that pretence and I don't suppose you were either, were you? But you told me I'd have to learn to deal with it, that it was not love you wanted.'

Aric shook his head at the cruelty of it. 'Forgive me,' he said. 'That day was no less remarkable for me than it was for you, my darling. I knew even then that you were my heart's desire. Everything a man could hope for. But I had given my word to take you back and I thought that if I denied love, the pain of parting would be less.'

'What is this pain you suffered? Are you talking about your family?'

He nodded. 'My mother. My sisters. My father. I should not have allowed it to affect me so, but it did. I couldn't bear the thought of it happening again.'

'Can you tell me about it? Your mother left you?'

His fingers caressed her hands as he brought back the powerful painful memories. 'She refused to stay with my father any longer. She had a right to divorce him for violence. She had only to say the words. I was away learning to be a Viking warrior at the time. She left me no farewell. I never saw her again.'

'She went to Iceland?'

'That's what Astrid told me. I suppose there was another man. I've had no word. I was supposed to be hardened to loss. After all, that's the kind of loss I was taught to inflict on the victims of our raids. But it hurts. I loved my mother.'

'And your sisters?'

'Both wanted to leave my father, but he needed them to look after the house. He did his best to prevent them from leaving. So Tove, who was a few years older than me, found a man who wanted to leave Lindholm altogether and set up in Jorvik. There were bad words between us. She'd be leaving Wenda alone with Father and me away every summer. She went off. No loving farewell. My lovely sister. You know what happened to her in Jorvik. I vowed to revenge her death.'

'Did you never think she might have loved Thored? As my mother did?'

'I was about fifteen. I didn't know how or why people love as they do.'

'So Wenda was left at home. But she's happy now, dearest.'

'Poor Wenda. She believed that, if she got pregnant, Father would have to let her marry and leave. But he threatened to turn her out instead, wouldn't give her a dowry and told her to go and live with the father of her child. But he was a bastard. Didn't want her and certainly didn't want a girl child with a deformity. I was no use to her because I was not there when she needed me and when I returned, they'd decided to expose it. And I did nothing to help her. I failed her when she needed me most. It was partly to get Kean for her that I asked permission to go up to Jorvik. I felt that having her sister's child might ease her pain.'

'What more could you have done?'

'Confronted my father, or found somewhere for Wenda and the child to stay together. I should have asserted myself, but I was no help at all to her. If it had not been for Olof, I think she might have taken her own life. And now I've seen little Meld for myself and the guilt of it hits me all over again. We might have lost her for ever and Wenda, too.'

'So your father was left alone, after all.'

'He drank himself to death. As a child, I adored him and looked up to him. But he changed and I hated what he did to our family. I shall make sure that such things never happen to ours.' He saw the lift of her eyebrows and realised what he'd said. 'Am I going too fast for you, my wonderful woman? Did I tell you that I want you to stay and be my wife? I shall never let you go, Fearn. You're far too precious. I missed so many opportunities to tell my mother and sisters how I loved them, but I was a warrior and warriors are trained to be hard. I nearly made the same mistake with you, didn't I? But I love you, Lady Fearn of Jorvik, and I have used you badly. Forgive me and I will do anything to win your hand.'

Placing a hand over his hair, she stroked it in place as tears of happiness followed the despair of lives torn apart by circumstances. 'Anything?' she said. 'Does that include having a family of our own?'

'As many as you wish, dear heart.'

'But…what if…what if one is…?'

'I know what you're going to say. Is that a reason why you fled? Because you thought I might not want a physically deformed child?'

'You told me it was the custom. And although you've seen Meld, that's not like having one of your own, is it?'

'Christians don't do that. And I shall become one, because I want to be like those I know. It was Clodagh, your mother, who showed me a better way of living.'

'Oh, my darling, we've wasted so much time.'

Taking his head in her hands, she laid her own upon it to nuzzle into his hair, breathing in the sea scent of a sailor. She would not ask him to stop adventuring in his fast new ship, for that would have been like asking a fish not to swim. The sea was in his blood. She would have to accept periods when he would be away from her, as other women did.

'Will you stay with me, Fearn? Will you be my beloved wife, the mother of my children? I promise to be kind, and loving, and faithful, and all those things my father was not. Will you, Fearn?'

'If only I had known,' she whispered. 'If only you had opened up your heart to me, showed me those terrible scars you've carried and the heartache. I could have helped to heal them before this. You have suffered, my love.'

'And I made you suffer, because you were mine for only one year.'

'I shall never leave you,' she said, touching his bearded cheek. 'Never.'

Turning his face, he placed a kiss upon her palm. 'My beautiful English wife,' he said.

Aric had stayed by Fearn's bedside all that night, ministering to her just as her mother would have done, had she been allowed. The next day, while Aric went home to change, the small chamber was seldom empty of visitors bringing little delicacies for her to nibble and gossip to make her smile. The visit of Eve and Ivar made her weep a little, however, when they told her of Aric's plans to free them from their slavery, though they had both decided not to leave their service. Deena, the deaf weaving lady, was also promised freedom, the news of which had been conveyed by mime rather than words, which Aric had been obliged to perform himself, so Freya and Astrid told her, laughing.

In two more days, Fearn was carried home in Aric's arms to sit outside in the sun while Haesel, directed by Freya, Astrid and Eve, dressed her hair in the Danish style with coils and plaits behind her head and a long ponytail hanging down behind. Astrid gave her two bronze egg-shaped brooches with which to hold up her Danish-style pinafore dress, worn over a pleated linen shift, and the transformation from English to Danish was so effective that Aric could hardly speak the words of pride that filled his heart. 'My...my beautiful Anglo-Danish woman,' he said at last. 'Marry me?' The applause and laughter almost drowned out her acceptance.

* * *

Neither of them saw any reason to delay the simple marriage ceremony that was to set a seal upon their love and, because in the weeks that followed, Aric and Hrolf had been baptised into the new faith, the four lovers took their vows on the same day in the small church packed with relatives and friends, and many more outside, both Christian and pagan. While a second marriage for Fearn was in itself a remarkable event, to have both parents there beside her was something she could never have dreamed of.

The feasting on this occasion was different in every way from anything they could remember, held out of doors on the newly mown hayfield next to the longhouse to which the whole of Lindholm was invited. An ox, two pigs and several hundred assorted birds were roasted and tables were piled high with warm loaves of bread, biscuits and honey cakes, fruit from the hedgerows and last year's nuts and apples, plums and pears, cheeses, baked fish, ale and beer, mead and fruit drinks. It was the first feast that Fearn had ever really enjoyed, for here she was loved by everyone not only for her healing skills, but for her kindness, too. Here, she was not ogled by lusting warriors, but admired and respected by friends. The good-natured rowdy celebrations

went on well into the summer's night when bon-
fires were lit, danced round to the wail of reed
pipes and drums. Haesel and Hrolf's exit from
the event went unnoticed, but when Aric and
Fearn made a bid for freedom, they were spotted and serenaded to the door of the longhouse,
carried on the shoulders of Loki, Einar, Oskar
and Olof.

Alone at last in their dimly lit chamber, Aric
removed the wreath of wild white flowers from
Fearn's brow. 'Do you remember when I came
to you here?' he said, pulling her gently into his
arms. 'Late at night. You were asleep. Or pretending.'

'I was *not* pretending,' she protested. 'You
woke me. I did not want you.'

'Your body told me otherwise, lady. After...'

She placed a finger over his lips. 'No, don't
remind me of that first time. The memory of it
still pains me. Let's go forward now, not backwards. We've both done and said things we regret, but now we can love each other without all
those stifling reservations.'

'You're right, sweetheart. We've allowed other
people and events to shape our lives until now,
haven't we?'

'No. I didn't *allow* it. As a woman, I had no
choice.'

'Are you arguing? Already?'

'Yes,' she said, knowing where this was leading.

'After promising to obey me?'

'I didn't *promise*. I said I *might*.'

The twinkle in Aric's candlelit grey eyes was at odds with his dramatic sigh of despair. 'Ah, I knew there was something that priest ought to have explained to you. Now I'm stuck with a wife who has a mind of her own. How did *that* happen?'

Laying her arms across his shoulders, she pressed herself against him in a manner she had not used before, abandoned and overtly seductive, wriggling her hips beneath his questing hands and lowering her black-lashed eyelids to show him the merest glint of the jewels that were green and blue, holding him spellbound with their message. 'Like this,' she whispered. 'It happened without either of us knowing it. It just happened, beloved.'

His answer was to begin a slow undressing of the bride while she hindered him, showering him with her kisses. When it became impossible for him to continue, their laughter broke them apart as Fearn was lifted and dumped unceremoniously upon the bed, already halfway through divesting her new husband of his best embroidered tunic. The resulting tangle both hampered and excited them, having slept apart since declaring their love for each other, and this had been on both their minds, wondering in what way it would be different, once their secrets were revealed. But now, although they had spoken of their love, they were at last able to use those words in a new context; words that had been missing before and carefully withheld, now freed in a poem of praise and adoration, of desire, pleasure and fulfilment. There was joy, too, in the new carefree element that came with laughter, as if their cares and constraints had never affected their previous loving or caused a certain desperation, at times.

Naturally, the period of abstinence would have affected Aric's performance if he had not been an experienced lover, but he wanted Fearn to remember this time more than she had the first, taking her slowly through each phase while keeping in mind what she had been through to come as far as this. Her sighs and cries of ecstasy, now embellished by words of love, were to him the sweetest sounds, urging him towards a climax that came together with hers, sending them both soaring into a new kind of happiness where dark thoughts of time and separation had no place. 'Dearest love,' Fearn said softly into his ear, 'is this what marriage does? Is this how it is when we can tell of our love instead of keeping it hidden? I do not believe I could be happier than I am now.' With a squeak of sheer contentment, she snuggled in to his side, breathing in the male odour of his powerful body, his exertions and the heady scent of success.

'From now on, sweetheart, this is how it will be for us,' Aric told her. Then, after a long pause, he said, 'Talking of families…'

'Were we?'

'Well, in a way. Did you see where Meld went after she'd finished pelting us with flowers? Did Clodagh manage to prise her away from Wenda?'

Fearn smiled, smoothing her hand over his chest. 'So much for our plans to keep mother and daughter apart. We should have known they'd have to meet. It was wonderful to see how Meld and the boys played together. They were so caring of her, while Wenda and Clodagh looked on like two mother hens. The last I saw of them was my mother holding little Meld in her arms, fast asleep, while Wenda kissed her forehead and said goodnight.'

'No hysterics?'

'Not at all. Wenda kissed my mother, too, before they parted. Then she and Olof went off with their arms around each other, perfectly content.'

'It's Sunday tomorrow.'

'Today, actually.'

'And isn't there some rule about not making love on a holy day? Whoever made that one up didn't have a wife like mine.'

'So that means you won't be observing it?'

'Certainly not, Lady Fearn of Lindholm. That would be expecting too much.'

Fearn's hand slid further down on to his stomach, and beyond. 'Good,' she murmured. 'We must not ask too much of an expectant father, must we?'

One of Fearn's first tasks on the next day was to write to her half-sister the Queen to tell her the exciting news and to ask her to send a message to Mother Bridget in Jorvik. She had always kept her quills and ink in the precious golden reliquary casket of Irish origin, but when Haesel opened the lid, she hesitated. 'Lady,' she said, 'I think perhaps you should come and see this for yourself.'

Aric, who was pulling on his leather boots, raised his head to watch.

'What is it?' said Fearn, looking inside. 'Carry it over to the light.'

A flash of gold scintillated as Fearn lifted out the magnificent object and held it lovingly in her hand, turning it this way and that to see the details. It was a tiny model of a sleek Viking ship made of pure deep yellow gold complete with sail, ropes, oars and a dragon-headed prow, and recognisably Aric's new ship that had brought her and Haesel back to Lindholm. He stood beside her, basking in her delight. 'Do you remember what you once said to me about gifts, sweetheart? You said that the only gift I could give you would be a ship to take you home. Will this one do instead?'

'Yes, beloved. Thank you. Indeed it will. I *am* home now.'

Haesel tiptoed away as husband and wife came together as if, she thought, they had been meant for each other from the start.

Epilogue

Within days of their marriage, a new house had been built for Haesel and Hrolf near enough to the longhouse for them to be on hand at all times. The maid, however, did not follow her mistress's lead in adopting the Danish dress, preferring to wear her veil swathed around her neck as before. When Haesel's child was born in the spring of the following year, Eve took on her responsibilities until Haesel felt able to resume them, after which they worked in tandem, for by that time the mistress herself was a new mother. The strong, lusty and quite noisy infant was named Finn in acknowledgement of his Irish ancestry, with eyes as blue as the fjord on a summer's day and hair like a silver halo. After the two marriages, Haesel no longer received any 'seeings' because, she assumed, neither she nor Fearn needed to know what the future held for them. Fearn's gift of healing, however, remained as strong as ever.

With Loki's help, Freya managed the stud farm and expanded it, selling stock far and wide and gaining a reputation for excellence that made her much wealthier than her father had been. When Aunt Astrid died quite suddenly one night without any kind of warning, she was buried with great honour and affection up on the cemetery field next to her relatives, where her ashes were marked with a triangular outline of stones, as some women's were.

Fearn and Aric went on to raise a family of five healthy children, but Aric did not take part in any more raids on England, having been easily persuaded to take a hand, as he had once done, in the breeding and training of Freya's horses. Which pleased everyone, particularly Fearn.

* * * * *

If you enjoyed this story, you won't want to miss these other great reads from Juliet Landon

TAMING THE TEMPESTUOUS TUDOR
BETRAYED, BETROTHED AND BEDDED
MISTRESS MASQUERADE
SCANDALOUS INNOCENT

Author Afterword

Although Lindholm is situated on the Limfjord in northern Jutland, I hope my Danish friends will forgive me for moving the early settlement a little closer to the water's edge than it actually was. The shoreline in the Viking era was likely to have been marshland, with the famed cemetery of boat-shaped graves on a rise of land known as Lindholm Hoje—heights—positioned inland. The settlement was regularly covered by sand and had to be moved more than once. The cemetery was completely buried, to be excavated as recently as 1952-58. The Lindholm Hoje Museum is devoted entirely to Viking artefacts discovered in Jutland and is impressive in every way. It is a must for all Viking enthusiasts.

The characters of Earl Thored, Earl Oslac, King Ethelred—the 'Unready'—and Aelfgyfu, his Queen, are all based on fact. However, although Jorvik—now known as York—received many demanding visits from the Danish Vikings, the one I have described in the story took place one year later in 994, when a demand for sixteen thousand pounds was paid to persuade them to leave. This kind of thing continued for several more years, each time costing more than the last, until the Danish Cnut became King of England.

Only a few miles north-west of Lindholm is the Borglum Kloster—priory—now an arts and exhibition centre, which houses, amongst other things, an exact replica of the Bayeux Tapestry made by a group of embroiderers known as the Vikingegruppen of Lindholm Hoje. www.bayeuxtapetet.dk. It is to these ladies I dedicate this story as thanks for their hospitality while guiding me round Lindholm and its Viking past.

MILLS & BOON®
HISTORICAL

AWAKEN THE ROMANCE OF THE PAST

MILLS & BOON®

EXCLUSIVE EXTRACT

When aristocrat's daughter May Worth's life
is endangered, only one man can protect her:
government agent Liam Casek…the man whose
sinfully seductive touch she's never forgotten!

Read on for a sneak preview of
CLAIMING HIS DEFIANT MISS

Liam wasn't willing to chance it by letting May roam
free and unprotected. It infuriated him she was willing
to take that chance. She had blatantly chosen to ignore
him and vanish this morning just for spite. He knew
very well why she'd done it; to prove to him she didn't
need him, had never needed him, that he hadn't hurt
her, that indeed, he had been nothing more than a speck
of dust on her noble sleeve, easily brushed off and
forgotten. But that wasn't quite the truth. He had hurt
her, just as she had hurt him. They were both realising
the past wasn't buried as deeply as either of them hoped.

To get through the next few weeks or months they
would have to confront that past and find a way to truly
put it behind them if they had any chance of having an
objective association. The task would not be an easy
one. Their minds might wish it, but their bodies had
other ideas. He'd seen the stunned response in her eyes
yesterday when she'd recognised him, the leap of her
pulse at her neck even as she demanded he take his hand

off her. Not, perhaps, because he repulsed her, but because he didn't.

Goodness knew his body had reacted, too. His body hadn't forgotten what it was to touch her, to feel her. Standing behind her in the yard had been enlightening in that regard. He wasn't immune. He hadn't thought he was. He had known how difficult this assignment would be. His anger this morning at finding her gone proved it.

Anger. Lust. Want. These emotions couldn't last. A bodyguard, a man who did dirty things for the Crown, couldn't afford feelings. Emotions would ruin him. Once he started to care, deeply and personally, it would all be over.

Don't miss
CLAIMING HIS DEFIANT MISS
By Bronwyn Scott

Available May 2017
www.millsandboon.co.uk